D1328678

SARAH HOGLE is a mom of three who enjoys trashy TV and provoking her husband for attention. Her dream is to live in a falling-apart castle in a forest that is probably cursed. She is also the author of *You Deserve Each Other*.

🐦 witchofthewords

ALSO BY SARAH HOGLE

·······

You Deserve Each Other

SARAH HOGLE

PIATKUS

PIATKUS

First published in the US in 2021 by G. P. Putnam's Sons,
an imprint of Penguin Random House LLC
First published in Great Britain in 2021 by Piatkus
This edition published in Great Britain in 2022 by Piatkus

1 3 5 7 9 10 8 6 4 2

A CIP catalogue record for this book
is available from the British Library.

ISBN 978-0-349-42438-5

Printed and bound in Great Britain by Clays Ltd, Elcograf S.p.A.

Papers used by Piatkus are from well-managed forests
and other responsible sources.

Piatkus
An imprint of
Little, Brown Book Group
Carmelite House
50 Victoria Embankment
London EC4Y 0DZ

An Hachette UK Company
www.hachette.co.uk

www.littlebrown.co.uk

I dedicate this book to myself

Twice Shy

Chapter 1

I AM UP IN THE clouds now, drumming my fingernails on a countertop. Outside the window, in an ever-swirling fog, there's a pink neon sign that spins at an all-the-time-in-the-world tilt, which reads: MAYBELL'S COFFEE SHOP AU. Beneath, with one of the letters blinking out: *Open 24 hours.*

My AU (alternate universe) café has taken years to build, the past three months being its busiest season yet. I've put up fairy lights and aqua tiles, floppy houseplants and red vinyl booths. A jukebox comes to life whenever I glance its way, spontaneously playing one of my favorite songs. Maybell's Coffee Shop AU is the most beautiful place I can imagine, and I've imagined lots of places.

The fog breaks on cue. I glance up, on high alert, knowing what happens next because it's happened before a hundred times. A story with a scripted beginning and boundless possibilities for how it might end.

The man who throws open the door is tall, broad shouldered,

strong jawed, in a suit of blackest black. Dark blond hair falls in tousled wet waves that make me think of a fallen angel who almost drowned, thrust out of the sea by Poseidon and made alive again with a lightning strike. If he were in color, his eyes would be topaz—a glass of root beer held up to the light.

He's all edges and shadow, black and white. Raindrops sheeting off the windowpane behind him project onto the right half of his face like a monochrome film reel, and his gaze sweeps the café before settling on me. I suck in a deep breath, gripping the counter to stay tethered. This is the moment I've been waiting for all my life.

"I've been looking everywhere for you," he tells me. "Why haven't you returned my calls?"

My having seen all of this before does nothing to dull the elation of seeing it again. Joy bursts in my chest, no room for air. "Jack! What if someone sees you here?"

"I don't care anymore." He leaps over the counter to gather me up in a passionate embrace. "I'm not hiding us. Yes, you're a coffee shop girl and I'm the prince of Effluvia. What does it matter? I love you. That's all there is to it."

"You love me?"

This is my favorite part, the love-declaring. I rewind so that I can hear it again, and make some small adjustments for dramatic flair.

"Yes, you're a coffee shop girl and I'm the prince of Effluvia," he repeats, a bouquet of stargazer lilies materializing in his left hand. And in his right, a glittering engagement ring. I silently mouth the rest of his lines along with him. "What does it matter? I love you. That's all there is to it."

"But . . . the monarchy," I whisper against his shoulder. "They don't want us to be together."

"They can't stop us. Our love is a force too powerful to be defied."

"Maybell," I hear a faraway voice chirrup. I rearrange the sound into background noise, letters becoming rustling leaves.

Jack lowers to one knee. The stargazer lilies triple in size. A string quartet appears.

"My beloved . . . light of my life . . ." Jack clears his throat, but my gaze flits uneasily to reflections that don't belong here. They stir in the silver napkin dispenser, the coffeepot, the gleaming backsplash, like they're two-way mirrors. A tiny knob on the vintage rotary landline, boxy and beige, lights up red a half second before the phone's metallic ring interrupts Jack's proposal.

"You are the most special person I've ever met," Jack begins, totally oblivious, tears in his eyes. "Intelligent. Beautiful. Capable. Unparalleled. There's nobody else like Maybell Parrish." According to my schedule, we're going to kiss in thirteen seconds. The passionate kiss that follows the declaration of love is another very favorite part. It's the essential ingredient to every romance that ensures it bakes properly.

The red light is impossible to ignore now. A piece of masking tape at the knob's base glows with each flash, bringing my handwriting into sharp focus. *IRL Calling.*

I wave impatiently for Jack to speed it up, but before we can get to the *Will you marry me* and the inevitable *Yes, a thousand times, yes*, mainlining serotonin directly into my brain to get me through the next two hours of my shift, a disembodied hand touches my shoulder.

The proposal hits pause. I smile wistfully at this perfect man and his perfectly love-struck, adoring expression. He would move mountains for me. He would walk the earth for me. He would avenge and protect and come back from the dead for me. Really, the only bad thing about Jack McBride is that he doesn't exist.

A sidewinder of white light blows across the café, shattering windows. My ears are ringing, my vision patchy as it adjusts. I drop out of the clouds of my dissolving happy place and back into the here and now, which is the last place I want to be. And standing before me, with her unwelcome hand on my shoulder, is the last person I want to see.

Gemma Peterson doesn't realize that, of course. She thinks we're BFFs.

"Hello! Earth to Maybell!" She snaps her fingers in front of my face. "Someone threw up all over the second-floor ice machine. Projectile vomit."

I groan. The *here and now* is Around the Mountain Resort & Spa, a Southern charm–infused hotel and indoor water park in Pigeon Forge, Tennessee. All the appeal of an old-fashioned timber lodge, but with souvenir shops, HBO, and a lazy river.

When I'm not zoning out into imaginary worlds, I'm planning fun guest activities as the newly promoted event coordinator, and then getting my ideas shot down by my co-coordinator, Christine. Up until New Year's Day, I worked here as a housekeeper, so getting flagged down with reports of vomit on ice machines was par for the course. Unfortunately, it's now April first and people are still running to me with these issues. It's as if the promotion never happened.

"That's for housekeeping," I remind Gemma.

"Oh, you're right! I'm just used to . . ." She bestows a huge smile on me, hooking her arm in mine as I pick up my pace down the hallway. I check the time on my phone and internally despair. My detour into the coffee shop in the sky only burned through ten minutes? I just want to go home, throw all the memories of this place into an incinerator, and sleep facedown on the couch for twelve hours. "Wanna play hooky in the arcade?" Gemma asks. "The claw machine's actually grabbing prizes today."

"We'll get in trouble with Paul."

Paul's the Big Boss, and while it's true that I'd probably get chewed out for losing to rigged Skee-Ball on the clock, Gemma's his daughter and can do whatever she wants. She gets paid five dollars an hour more than I do to stand in the lobby wearing a cutesy train conductor's costume, informing guests in an exaggerated twang that *RainForest Adventures Zoo is only five miles down the road, visit the customer service desk for coupons!* Then she disappears to the pool for the rest of the afternoon.

It's hard to hate Gemma—she's fun and bubbly. What's not to like? After she was fired from a string of jobs, Paul got rid of seventy-four-year-old Dennis, a veteran, to make room for her at Around the Mountain. She latched on to me on day one. Gemma brings me banana nut bread samples from our resort's breakfast bar, Sunrise in the Smokies, and is enthusiastic about everything I say even if it's just chatting about needing to get groceries. Whenever I wear new jewelry, she zeroes right in on it with an ego-inflating compliment. The only bad thing about Gemma is tangled up in the only bad thing about Jack McBride.

For a period of two wonderful months, I thought he was real. I look at Gemma now, radiant with friendliness, and I want to adore her to bits. But I can't.

"Did I tell you that Eric and I are moving in together?" she asks, steering me away from the direction in which I was heading. We turn left at the end of a corridor, fading out the constant loop of "Welcome to Around the Mountain Resort and Spa!" that blares from a big screen in the lobby, cartoon bear cub in a straw hat pointing at a map of entertainment options.

"I don't have time for the arcade right now." I strain to present myself as nice, harmless, nonthreatening, even though I wish I could be direct and assertive. Slipping up for even a moment and forgetting that Gemma has Paul's ear is dangerous. "I've gotta talk to Christine."

Gemma makes a face. "Christine's the worst. You don't want to talk to her."

"I don't *want* to, no, but I have some new ideas about—"

"Honey." She laughs. "I love you, but you know it's never happening. Christine's too obsessed with weddings. I heard her discussing your Halloween dinner theater idea with Dad and basically she thinks that sort of stuff degrades the resort and makes it less appealing as a venue. We get so much money for weddings, you know, so that's got star priority."

"When did she say that? She told me she was considering—"

"Anyway," she interrupts, "Eric and I are moving in together next week! Can you believe it? We're gonna throw a huge housewarming party. You're at the top of the list, so you'd better come, no excuses. And bring those amazing cinnamon twist donuts of yours! Everybody's gonna love them."

I'm still pissed about Christine's disregarding my contributions yet again, but a new irritation sidetracks me. My donuts *are* amazing, but when Gemma compliments them, I second-guess what the truth is because she lies all the time for no reason. Maybe she's lying about how much she loves the cinnamon twists, too.

"We need to get you a man, Maybell," she's saying now, dragging me over to Whack-a-Mole. She bangs her mallet with a scary degree of violence for someone so petite. "Then we can double-date! It'll be *so* fun, having both of my favorite people together with me." She beats the crap out of the plastic rodents as she talks, silky brown hair tumbling from her ponytail.

Gemma has such an abundance of nerve that it makes me question my own sanity. I know I didn't imagine the last few months because Gemma apologizes for them incessantly, bringing it up at least once a week. Her apologies are reality-warping mysteries that somehow end with me comforting *her*, and reassuring *her*, about everything that happened. "Everything That Happened" is how Gemma, Paul, and my other coworkers phrase what she did: a thick coat of sugar slathered over one of the most depressing experiences of my adult life.

"Your turn." She hands me the mallet, which means I'm the one who looks bad when Christine happens to walk by. Fantastic.

"Are you on break?" Christine barks at me. No attitude for Gemma, naturally. Gemma could be holding a chain saw dangling human innards and Christine would find a way to praise her for it.

"I stole her away for a second," Gemma replies, fixing on an angel's smile. "Blame me, not Maybell."

Christine holds my stare. "If you have time to waste, you have time to work. There's vomit on the ice machine and all over the walls on floor two."

It's on the walls, too? Good lord. "But—"

As she turns away, I gather up the courage to call out, "Have you finished reading my proposal for the scavenger hunt?"

"We tried a scavenger hunt in 2018," she says without turning. "Nobody was into it."

"I think the pirate theme would be fun for kids."

She claps her hands three times. "Get! To! Work!"

Gemma waits until she's out of earshot and pats my shoulder. "Ugh, I hate her, too. I think she's having an affair with my dad."

"I don't hate her," I'm quick to say, simultaneously imagining pushing Christine into the lazy river. Gemma probably waits until I'm out of earshot to whisper, *Ugh, I hate her, too*, about me to other people. At least now I have an excuse to leave. "Gotta go clean up, I guess." Two hours. Two more hours and then I can go home.

She slides away to a game called Ticket Jackpot. "Wish me luck!"

Padding down the dark green hall, I replay Christine's words and am strongly tempted to rip off my "Event Coordinator" badge. After changing trash bags, making beds, and bleaching Jacuzzis from the time I turned eighteen, I'd moved out of house-keeping just before hitting thirty and into an arena where I could finally flex my creative skills. Now I'm told the events I want to produce are too big, too niche, or too much. No matter what I do, I'm perpetually ending up alone in a room with a roll of paper towels under my arm and cleaning supplies to take care of some-body else's mess.

"I'm going to quit," I grumble. It's my personal anthem, which I sing every day. "Job is in title only. This is stupid. It's stupid!"

Caleb Ramirez nods in greeting as he walks by, likely on his way to Sunrise in the Smokies, where he works. Seeing him is like being stabbed with a very small pin, because he was the unwitting catalyst for Everything That Happened. Unfortunate, because Caleb's such a great guy. The only bad thing about him is that once, several months ago, we shared a bag of popcorn together in the break room and he mentioned he liked my sneakers. I'm bad at receiving compliments, habitually reciprocating with a compliment of my own to erase the one given to me, and I said I liked his car. He grinned. *I'll take you for a ride sometime.*

Gemma, who falls in love about a dozen times a year and falls *hard*, had a huge crush on Caleb. As I came to find out, on a deceptively ordinary Wednesday evening two months afterward, with Gemma snotting all over my shirt as she wrapped her arms around me and wouldn't let me squirm away, she'd simply done what she thought she had to do. She was *sorry*. She was insecure and desperately in love. People who are in love can't think straight, don't act normally. *Please don't hate me. I couldn't keep it going any longer, my hair's starting to fall out and I'm losing sleep.*

Gemma had catfished me with a fake Tinder profile.

I'm nursing some conflicted feelings over this because I wasn't the victim of a personal vendetta; I was collateral damage in Gemma's quest to keep the object of her affections single and available. Now that it's over, I'm less surprised—a couple months before it happened, a guy loafing about the lobby asked me where the ATM was. While leading him there, we got to talking a little bit, just innocent chitchat, which culminated in his asking for my number. I was doing my job. Being friendly. I did *not* flirt with him.

But it definitely looked like flirting to Gemma, who, as it transpired, was casually dating him at the time. He claimed that she'd misheard him, that when he asked for my number he meant "what number of the month it was, like, on a calendar." I told her I never gave him any of my contact information, and she said that she believed me, but if Caleb's offering me a ride in his car was enough to make her pull some pictures of a random hot guy off the Internet and trick me into a long-distance relationship, maybe she still had some trust issues.

In Gemma's defense (literally, she used this as a defense), she tried really hard to be a considerate fake boyfriend. Jack would "just know" when I was having a bad day and could benefit from a surprise delivery from my favorite takeout place. He played the ukulele, which I thought was so cute, and he was drop. Dead. Gorgeous. A giant who could probably crush pebbles between his fingers if he wanted, but he wore the sweetest smile and softest expression. My favorite picture "Jack" sent was a black-and-white one of him in formal wear, and when I envision my imaginary ex-boyfriend I still see him without color sometimes, like he belongs to a different era.

The longer our relationship went on, the more I wanted from Jack, and the harder it became for Gemma to keep the ruse up. I wanted to meet in person. I wanted more selfies of him. I wanted concrete plans. After a while it didn't matter how gorgeous or supernaturally insightful he was (Gemma's advantage of knowing me as well as she does was an awful, lovely, double-edged blade); I didn't like that he wasn't putting in as much effort as me. Didn't he want to meet up, too?

Then Gemma met someone else, lost all interest in Caleb, and was tired of expending energy on this. She had to come clean. *I feel terrible. I'm the worst person ever. Can you forgive me? I'm sorry I did it, but in a way it wasn't all that bad because you were happy, weren't you? You've been so happy these past few months! If you think about it, I gave you a gift.*

She begged me not to tell her dad, but another housekeeper overheard the whole confession and told a pool attendant, who told everyone, and before I knew it I was shaking Paul's hand and accepting a promotion. It was coded into Paul's upbeat congratulations that the promotion hinged on my not making any waves. I'd keep to myself, and be sad in private, and it meant no more scrubbing wine stains out of carpets. Which was fine. Maybell Parrish doesn't make waves. She doesn't even make ripples.

As I wipe down the ice machine, I listen to the distant chime of a door opening up in the clouds. *What's your daily special?* a patron asks. Mentally, I follow the sound.

A different Maybell smiles back at her customer from behind a glass case of pastries on display. Like me, she has round glasses with rose-gold frames and honey-brown hair growing out in a *Rumours*-era Stevie Nicks shag. She sports the same constellation of freckles on her upper arm that I do, and we both wear a dainty heart-shaped ring on our right index finger that our mother got us for our sixteenth birthday.

But this Maybell is smooth and confident. She has a devoted boyfriend, Jack, and an honest, authentic best friend called Gemma. No indentations on her lower lip from nervous nibbling; her fingernails are manicured, not the kind you'd hide in your pockets. Her fresh-from-the-oven donuts are famous in five counties. *This* Maybell Parrish knows how to stand up for herself and gets what she wants on the first try, her little corner of the universe protected by magic. She controls the weather, the conversation, the emotional mood, who stays in the café and who goes. Here, she is *somebody*.

Slipping away into the dream version of my life is sometimes a conscious decision. But frequently, I don't realize I've been daydreaming until a loud noise jars me, and when I check the clock,

I'll find I've lost an hour. A whole hour, just gone. The more anxious or stressed or lonely I am in reality, the less time I'm inclined to spend in it.

It requires effort to resist spiriting away to my coffee shop. I choose to focus on a topic that will keep me grounded: Gemma. Enough time has passed that she isn't embarrassed about the catfishing anymore. Now she thinks it makes for a good anecdote, spreading it around, adding embellishments as she goes. I've heard her tell Javier that Jack and I had even gotten engaged, which isn't true.

I blink and center myself, ice machine drifting back into focus. I've moved past it and now I'm smearing Clorox circles onto the soda machine. The paper towel in my hand is soggy shreds.

"Excuse me?"

I turn wearily, knowing in my gut that I'm seconds away from being asked to fish a wedding ring out of a bathroom drain. It happens once a month.

It's a woman in a pink tweed coat. She eyes my name tag and her face lights up. "Well, hello there!"

I offer her the most customer service-y smile I can muster. *Please, please don't tell me someone's done something unspeakable in the elevator again.* The restroom is *right there* across from it, for crying out loud. I'll quit. I'll legitimately quit, right now. "Hi. Can I get you anything?"

"Actually, I'm here to give *you* something," she replies, stepping forward. A thick folder is tucked under her arm. "I hate to be the bearer of bad news, but your great-aunt Violet is dead."

Chapter 2

CONTACTING VIOLET'S RELATIVES HASN'T been easy. So many of you aren't on speaking terms with each other!" The woman chuckles uncomfortably. "I tried a number listed as Julie Parrish's, but it's out of service."

"Yeah, she has a new . . ." My throat is suddenly dry. I don't know why I feel like I might break down—I haven't seen my great-aunt Violet since I was ten. I swallow. "A new number. I'll pass the news along."

Not that Mom will care that Violet's dead. She was mad at Violet while she was alive, and she'll stay mad at her now that she's dead.

"Maybe we should sit down," she suggests.

I lead the way to a table situated outside a Tim Hortons on the first floor. The seats are riddled with puddles of pool water. No one ever pays attention to the sign on the water park's exit to towel off before leaving.

The woman is probably in her late fifties, Afro-Latina, with silver threads in her curly black hair, which is pulled tight into a bun. "My name's Ruth Campos. I was your aunt's home health aide for four years, and she gave me power of attorney ten months ago. Right now I'm here as the executor of her estate."

Ruth Campos. I've heard that name before. I'm pretty sure she got into it with my mother over the phone one time, not too long ago, when Mom tried to pass herself off as the person who had Violet's power of attorney in hopes of getting a little bit of money. It didn't go so well.

Ruth lays out the details both kindly and matter-of-factly: Violet passed away in her sleep on Sunday morning. She was ninety years old. She remained sharp as a tack until the very end, and while her mobility had declined, she'd gotten highly invested in local outreach concerning the preservation of forests. Per her wishes, there was no service, no public fuss. Her cremated remains have been scattered all over her land, to be with her husband Victor's ashes. He died right after I turned eleven. I heard about it but wasn't allowed to attend the funeral.

The whites of her eyes are a bit pink, mascara smudging as she blinks rapidly. "I'm gonna miss that lady."

"I can't believe she's gone." I can't imagine her not being in that big house anymore, watering her pretty garden, humming as she dusts the spindlework around her living room doorway. All this time, even though I've certainly been a blurry speck in her past, she's been a bright, stabilizing presence in the back of my mind, and my emotions are being crushed under that rock as it rolls away.

I haven't seen her in twenty years. My summer at Falling Stars, Violet Hannobar's late-1800s estate resting on two hundred and ninety-four acres of land an hour southwest of here, is my happiest memory. For a little girl who was passed from relative to relative and then cast out when Julie Parrish burned bridges, Violet's friendly pink house was nearly as big as a castle and pure fairy tale. I never wanted to leave.

And according to Ruth, now it's all mine.

She shows me a few papers from the envelope, but my mind is reeling and I can't make sense of any of it. The splash of a water slide and shrieking children press in around my ears; a kazoo blasts from the loudspeaker whenever kids fire the water cannons in Rocky Top Tree House and my concentration fractures, life as I knew it this morning and life as it's going to be slamming into each other like oncoming trains.

My gaze wanders over the lobby that's functioned as my second home from the time I turned eighteen and joined Mom as a housekeeper. We weren't the kind of family who could afford vacations, so being employed at a water park hotel was the next best thing. I remember walking beneath the giant statue of a bear strumming a banjo in the parking lot, which you can see from Dollywood, and feeling very *adult*.

Like being on vacation every day, my mother said. *Living the dream.* Now she's in Atlanta, living a new dream. I've been stuck here, not remotely feeling like every day is a vacation.

"She said she was going to leave me everything," I murmured, "but that was forever ago. I was a kid."

"She loved you."

"She didn't love anybody else better than me, in the twenty years since we saw each other?"

"Those twenty years didn't stop you from being her niece." Ruth lays her hand over mine. "She understood why you didn't return. Time away can make coming back awkward. And your mother held a fierce grudge." She draws back, straightening the contents of the envelope. "You were the only apple on the family tree she liked, if you don't mind my saying. Who better to inherit the estate?"

I'm struggling to process this information, but it won't sink in. If this means what I think it means, I can leave my living situation: a tiny apartment I'm being crowded out of now that my roommate's boyfriend moved in and his friends are always sleeping over. I don't know what I'll do for a job, but with a house already paid for, it isn't such a big risk to leave Pigeon Forge.

I can leave Around the Mountain Resort & Spa. I can leave Gemma.

"I can move in now?" I ask suddenly. I nearly pounce on her, I lean forward so fast. "Like, *today*?"

Ruth nods, eyes cutting to a herd of people decked out in their bathing suits, heading to the water park. The doors blast open and the roar and gurgle of water rides rushes out before the doors muzzle it again. "All ready to go. There are some dying wishes of Violet's to run over with you, but the fine details can wait until after your arrival."

A blue mist sweeps across hoods and trunks in the parking lot, swirling up in capricious spring winds. My heart lifts with new hopes, new plans taking shape, pumping ferociously.

"The property is mine," I say quietly. My voice sounds strange, not like myself.

"The property is yours," Ruth affirms. Minutes slip away as I sort through this reality, but Ruth shows no signs of impatience. She merely excuses herself to buy a coffee and croissant, then returns and eats in companionable silence.

"What's the catch?" I ask. "There has to be a catch."

She chokes on her croissant and gulps the coffee, wincing.

"Went down the wrong pipe. Don't worry yourself, it's all in order. No debts, no mortgage. Violet thought of *everything*."

I flatten my hands on the table. That's all there is to it, then. "Okay." *Deep breath, Maybell.* "I guess that means that . . . I quit." It comes out sounding like a question. *I quit? Can I do that? Is this really happening?*

Christine is at the checkout desk, berating a temp for parking in her spot. I could stroll up to her right now and make a big, dramatic scene. A satisfying "I quit!" story for the ages.

I could throw my name tag in the pool.

Confidently lay out all my grievances and how she'll be sorry when I'm gone. How many hours I've given to this company, only for them to stick me with a health insurance policy that's riddled with holes, no paid overtime, and none of the bonuses I was led to believe I'd receive. I could point at the wet seats and say *Clean. That. Up.* Punctuating each word with an obnoxious clap of my hands.

Dark spots speckle the edges of my vision as I stare at Christine, who senses being watched and turns to give me a *Why are you sitting down on the clock?* look. God, how gratifying it would be to utter the magic words.

But when Christine taps her watch and frowns pointedly, old habits die hard. I'm a meek little mouse, rising to my feet as if I'm going to head straight back to the dorm-room desk behind a folding wall that is supposed to be my office, which I am never at because they've eternally got me shampooing gum out of the carpet.

No one's around to bear witness when I carefully leave my name tag, key card, and lanyard in the break room. No one looks twice when I retrieve my purse from my locker. I almost take my stash of Mountaineer Tickets with me, good-behavior rewards

I've been saving up to cash out for a large lemonade slushee. They're useless in the real world, so I shove them into the temp's locker. It's surreal to be leaving, and just as surreal to be leaving so quietly. After more than a decade of dreaming I might be the type of person who goes out with a bang, I'm not even giving a fizzle.

My hand's on the front door, ready to push, when Gemma shouts my name from up on the giant novelty rocking chair that families like to sit on and pose for a single picture that costs them $29.99. She's taking a selfie. I quit even harder.

"Hey, Maybell! Are you going on break?"

This is it.

You suck astronomically and I will miss you the least. You screwed with my head, abused my trust, and had the audacity to be so nice that it will never not confuse me. You're a rock in my shoe. An out-of-order bathroom stall. A traffic jam. A loose handful of gumballs in a trick-or-treat bucket.

Anybody else would say that—and worse. But unfortunately I'm me, a passive doormat who probably *will* miss her, so I wave back with a tight smile.

"Yeah. See you in a bit."

And then I'm out the door, my back turned to her. My last words to Gemma Peterson weren't brave, but it lifts a weight off my shoulders to know they're the last. A new smile, one that is small but one that is *real*, tugs at my lips. The last time I wore a real smile . . . it's been long enough that I can't remember it.

There's a superstition about luck, and it goes like this: a run of bad luck is followed by a run of good luck. This is the silver lining, the softening edges. I spent my teenage years in dingy motels or on sofas belonging to whoever my mother was dating at the time, carted behind her all over Tennessee, missing chunks of school.

I've picked all the wrong, cheating boyfriends and should have accumulated a hard shell of trust issues, but my heart's too cowardly and still runs jumping into whoever's arms will open for it. I've scrubbed toilets and been demeaned and ignored and promoted as a consolation prize, only to be shoved aside yet again. My best friend isn't my friend at all. The love of my life doesn't exist.

My heart has been humiliated. Pulverized. And here, right out of the sky, drops my run of good luck.

I'm making my fresh start at Falling Stars.

TOP OF THE WORLD is a blink-and-you'll-miss-it unincorporated community in Blount County with a population too meager to warrant a school or a post office. Growing up, I thought it probably wasn't *really* called Top of the World—probably, it was just a local nickname—but then I found it in a phone book. And I thought that was simply the most enchanting thing ever.

The last time I was here I was wedged in the passenger seat of a blue '91 Toyota Camry, ten years old and crying my eyes out. Mom couldn't focus, she was so mad, lurching horribly in a stop-go-stop-go frenetic escape from town, checking the rearview mirror like a thief on the lam to make sure no relatives were on our tail. Part of me has never recovered from my disappointment that we weren't followed.

Now I'm in the driver's seat of that same car, and it all looks so unreal through rock-bottom Maybell's grown-up eyes. Both different and the same, like the image has been flipped and I'm viewing the scene from the opposite side. A storage tote, three boxes, and a gym bag squished into the trunk and backseat contain all of my worldly possessions. You don't amass too many worldly possessions when you work for minimum wage and you've spent most of your life with someone who helped themselves to whatever you had.

My GPS leads me through twinkling dusk back into nowhereland, trees breaking every now and then to reveal a breathtaking view of mountains. Headlights splash across a fluorescent dead-end warning that someone's repainted to read *Hannobar Lane*, and my blood hums with awareness. *We know this place, we know this place*, my instincts sing, nostalgia too large to fit properly inside the brief time that spawned it, which couldn't have lasted longer than four months. One familiar landmark jump-starts recollection of another, and another, and even though memories of my surroundings were obscured by grainy film fifteen minutes ago, this terrain has become back-of-my-hand in a snap. The Civil War–era smokehouse that leans at forty-five degrees and the cemetery with time-smoothed gravestones are old friends. I know where the dented guardrail's going to be before it enters my field of vision, and I know who dented it.

Around one last bend, beams from a rising moon surge down like stalactites and I automatically slow, squinting to make out a succession of threatening signs. NO TRESPASSING. PRIVATE PROPERTY. BEWARE OF DOG. BEWARE OF BEARS. YOU'RE UNDER SURVEILLANCE. My heart beats in my throat. Tears spring to my eyes, but they won't fall.

You should have come back long before now, I think. *She might have needed you. Now it's too late.*

And then I hold my breath, because:

Falling Stars sprawls grandly before me. The manor's pink masonry is the color of twilight on a hydrangea sea, four chimneys jutting against a cold, black sky carved out of mountainsides. Every tree and flower, every blade of grass and stepping stone, is precise. Intentional. Short, neat hedgerows border an obsessively manicured lawn.

Years one through nine of my life were a blur of "Don't touch that" and "You can have the sofa tonight, but tomorrow you have to find somewhere else to go." I was the burden in guest rooms, top bunks, and at kitchen tables, the kid without a seat belt because the car was already packed with cousins we had to cram into the back of a sedan. From years eleven to seventeen Mom and I couldn't depend on family anymore, having alienated them all by asking for help so many times, so I roughed it with my mother and grew up fast. When I think about the dozens of roofs I've ever had over my head, there is one to rule them all, to which I have compared every other roof. Nothing can live up to it.

For one glorious summer, I was welcomed and wanted. We established our own unique family rituals straightaway: birdwatching in the morning, stories before bed. I helped water the violets that burst along pathways, feeling like the little girl from *The Secret Garden*, learning the names of all sorts of plants I've since forgotten. I wasn't merely being cared for, I was building a life.

The reason my imagination is such a runaway is because no matter what's happened and where I've gone since then, in the back of my mind I've always known a place like this has been allowed to exist. Well maintained and ageless, a world locked inside a snow globe.

Except it isn't.

What used to be rolling hills with an edge of woods is now overrun by them, that once-distant forest so close that it's now in danger of eating up the house as well. Vines have overtaken the manor. They crawl the walls, chipping stonework away. My head-lights pour through ground-floor windows, smashed out, blades winking like shark's teeth.

Strips of black-spotted plaster hang from ceilings. The walls peel. Strange, dark shapes rise all the way up to the chandeliers. Falling Stars has been consumed by disease, more like Sleeping Beauty's castle after the curse took hold. The house isn't even pink anymore: it's silver gossamer.

I exhale a sharp denial. "*No.*" Violet took such amazing care of her house—daily dusting, vacuuming, mopping. Never a burned-out lightbulb left sitting in a fixture, never a book put away crook-edly in the library. Beds were made as soon as you woke up, plates were washed right after you ate off them, and you folded your clothes when they were still warm from the dryer. This estate was her pride and joy. She ran it like a queen.

My attention is drawn to two squares of light tucked into nearby trees. Windows. And attached to them, a triangular cabin. It used to be Uncle Victor's work shed, but when I went exploring as a kid all I found inside was a hot, dark mess of rusted farm equipment and spiderwebs. Now the lights are on and somebody's pickup truck is parked outside.

I make my way over cautiously, the path rough and uneven where tree roots have ripped up asphalt, nature reclaiming its ter-ritory. I mentally skim through everything I know about squatter's rights as I approach, car keys poking from my balled fist like Wol-verine's claws. The pickup truck isn't the only unexpected com-pany here: on its other side sits a yellow Volkswagen Beetle, just like the one Ruth Campos climbed into as we said our goodbyes.

The same Ruth who's swinging the front door open to greet me.

"Maybell! Wonderful, you're right on time."

"Right on time for what?"

She answers my question with a question. "How was the trip?"

Is it me, or does she seem nervous? "I just saw the house. It's bad. It's real bad. I didn't expect to see you here . . ."

I peer around her, grabbing a fleeting glimpse of a rosy, low-lit living room that contains no rusted farm equipment or spiderwebs. Instead, I find a plaid couch and a table lamp with mustangs galloping around the shade. Split-log walls. Bluish light flickers at random intervals, a television glowing somewhere within.

"Who's out there?" a different, deeper voice inquires. I straighten.

A man abruptly fills the frame, blocking my view. I stumble and his hand shoots out on reflex, as though to help me, but I'm already backing up.

A man, and not just any man. *The* man. In my deepest, darkest dreams, still the *only* man.

He is tall, broad shouldered, strong jawed. Dark blond hair falls in short, tousled waves that make me think of a fallen angel who almost drowned, thrust out of the sea by Poseidon and made alive again with a lightning strike. His eyes are brown topaz, a glass of root beer held up to the light, widening as he fixates on my face. Every thought that's ever swept into my head in the thirty years I've been alive blows away. There is dust in my throat, my eyes, my ears.

The windstorm inside me shrieks and pulls and shakes its head no. *Impossible.*

Impossibilities are all coming true today. It's Jack McBride.

Chapter 3

WHO'S THIS?"

The impossible Jack McBride is irritated by my sudden presence as Ruth beckons me inside and, in my haze, I actually obey. No, the impossible Jack McBride is *angered* by my presence. I'm not exactly on an even keel, either. I can't stop gaping at him. If I don't pass out at his feet it'll be a miracle.

"You exist," I croak, too quietly to be overheard. Or at least, I think so—my grasp of volume is rolling down a hill along with my vision, good sense, self-control, everything I thought I knew about life, etc., etc.

"This is Maybell Parrish, Violet's great-niece," Ruth tells him. "Julie's girl." Her voice is sugary, like I'm a used car she's trying to sell. "And she's a sweetheart, so *be nice*." She picks up my limp hand, waving it hello at him. "And this is Wesley Koehler, Violet's groundskeeper."

Wesley Koehler.

Wesley Koehler, Wesley Koehler, Wesley Koehler. It's a foreign language. It's inconceivable. He doesn't look like a Wesley Koehler at all—he looks like a Jack McBride: deeply romantic, musically inclined, with a keen interest in real estate. Charismatic, charming. Avid traveler, surfer, and environmental activist. Has a real way with the ladies.

There's no such thing as a Jack McBride, I remind myself.

But!

I open my mouth, a bag of wind popping inside it to let out a deflated *Eeeeeeeeeeeeehhh.* He frowns, which I can't blame him for. The expression on my face right now must be a trip. I want to do a thing people only do in movies and wipe off my glasses on my shirt, then put them back on to see if I've been looking at an illusion.

"My goodness, you're shocked," Ruth remarks. "I know you weren't expecting anyone. I'm sorry to spring this on both of you."

Jack—no, Wesley—turns sharply to face her. "Spring what?"

Ruth casts around the room for something to distract her. She centers a teacup on a coaster with life-and-death precision. "Hm?"

"Spring *what?*" he repeats, now with an edge. He's even taller than I imagined, so solid and intimidating. I'm struck by the shadow he throws upon the wall, spanning from floor to ceiling, hard jaw in black profile. I'm struck by gentle modifications to the image that appears in my head whenever I pull up his name: His hair's a couple inches longer than it was in his pictures, and messier. There are four tiny acne scars scattered along the right side of his face, and the lamplight traces his features in a way that changes the shape of his mouth, the line of his nose. It's *wrong.* And lovely. And strange. There's a freckle an inch to the left of his Adam's apple. The fact that I am now privy to this knowledge, that he is a real man and I am in a room with him and I know about a freckle I could not have previously fathomed . . .

My brain is so thrown by these deviations from that memorized image that I keep shutting down every other second. It's not him, but it's him, but it isn't, and yet it is. The image is crumbling, being replaced with real-time observations. The Matrix glitches, vertical strands of green code raining down on either side of him. I'm dying, maybe?

"Ruth."

I flinch. His voice is lower, the rumble of gravel crunching under a heavy boot, prickling all the microscopic hairs in my inner ear. I am dying, definitely.

Ruth presses her lips together. Fiddles with her watch until it displays Pacific Standard Time.

"What is going on?" I finally cry. "How are you *here*?" I'm losing it. That *face*. My god, that face, I've visualized it a thousand times. At one point I thought I was maybe falling in love with that face. Now I have a voice to match it. Throughout our brief relationship, we never spoke over the phone. We messaged back and forth on a dating app until I hinted that I was ready to delete it and take the next step with him, at which point we started emailing. Service was spotty in Costa Rica, where he was supposedly volunteering to help rebuild after a hurricane. He said phone calls were impossible right then but that he couldn't wait to get back to the States and meet me in person.

I ate it all up. I thought the emails were so romantic, like old-fashioned love letters with a modern twist, but then I grew frustrated because the emails weren't long enough, frequent enough. Not enough in general. I wanted to hear his voice. I wanted physical touch. Every night when I climb in bed I thank the gods my fake relationship with Jack never advanced to a sexual stage. Whenever I came close to skirting suggestive topics, Jack shied away, which at the time made me worry about a lack of chemistry. In retrospect, I'm glad Gemma couldn't cross that line. I don't know how I would have survived it if I'd unknowingly sent my colleague nudes.

I'm an idiot. It's never quite dawned on me before that even though the persona Gemma created was fiction, the pictures she sourced for Jack were of course real, and it stood to reason that somewhere out there, a facsimile of my fake ex-boyfriend would be walking the earth, up until this very moment oblivious to my existence. Now he knows I exist, but he doesn't know *me*. He doesn't know me like "Jack" did, and he's observing me in a cold, harsh way that makes me cringe right down to my bones. There's no affection, no recognition, in that gaze.

"What do you mean, how am I here?" he replies shortly. "I live here."

"What the hell do *you* mean?" I retort. "*I* live here." This is too much. "Where did you come from?"

He's bewildered. "Excuse me?"

Ruth's hand touches my shoulder, but I barely register it. She asks if I'm all right (obviously, I am not) at the same time Wesley throws his hands up and announces he doesn't know what anybody's talking about. The only thing I can think to do is to pull out my phone. Two texts from Gemma pop up on my screen: Hey you're late followed a couple hours later by Are you okay? One from Christine: You didn't clock out before leaving and didn't receive permission to leave early. Expect to be written up. A missed call and voicemail from Paul, my boss, that I am never going to listen to.

As I scroll through my emails to hunt for the pictures Gemma sent from Jack's fake email (I used to have the pictures saved on my phone but deleted them months ago), I consider that maybe I'm wrong. I've heard about this sort of thing happening: you get hyper-focused on a person and start seeing them everywhere. Wesley might look nothing at all like Jack, but my overworked brain has been wrung out like a sponge after the long day I've had, so now I'm hallucinating him into being. The power lines between my eyes and neural pathways have been sawed in half by feral attic raccoons.

Or not.

"Aha!" I thrust my phone at them, triumphant. There he is, in black and white, my very favorite Jack McBride photo. It's him. It's *him*. He has stubble on his jaw now, and he isn't wearing a black tux like he is in the photo, but I'm right. Oh my absolute god.

Wesley's gaze lifts slowly to pin on me, monochrome flushing into rich Technicolor. I watch the perturbed thoughts flashing across his beautiful brown eyes like I'm leafing through a picture book. His eyes have no equal, truly. They're like stones in a riverbed. They're bronze coins. They're the leather journal of a sad, sensitive empath who writes poetry about lost lovers—

"Why," he utters quietly, slicing off my wandering thoughts, "do you have a picture of me at my brother's wedding?"

"That's . . . a good question."

I pause, as though he's the one who should answer it. "I don't get this. No one's supposed to be here. Plus, the house is a mess! What happened to the house? And you're a *groundskeeper*? The grounds are a mess, too!" He opens his mouth, the furrow between his eyes deepening, but I rattle on: "I want to know who you are, right now. Are you friends with Gemma Peterson? Were you in on it?"

"In on *what*?" He's getting louder, too. "Who's Gemma?"

"Gemma Peterson!" I have *had* it. I am done with people messing with me. I tap at my phone furiously until I find Gemma's Instagram and show it to him.

"Am I supposed to know a Gemma?" Ruth cries in confusion. Wesley shrugs, but then a transformation happens. I watch it click as he recognizes Gemma's picture.

"That's the woman from the golf place."

Ruth and I both say, *"What?"*

"The golf place. In Pigeon Forge." His gaze darts past me to Ruth. "I did landscaping for them a while back, Professor Hacker's Lost Treasure Golf, and *that* woman"—he points at my screen—"worked there, over a year ago. She kept sneaking her friends in after hours to play golf for free, messing up my work, kicking up the new sod. They fired her for it."

Gemma smiles up at me from my phone. I can absolutely picture her doing that and the timeline makes sense. She likely came to Around the Mountain Resort & Spa directly on the heels of losing her job at Professor Hacker's Lost Treasure Golf. I fully get why she'd track down Wesley's Internet footprint and use him as bait to keep me away from Caleb. Who *wouldn't* be lured in by that? He's gorgeous. She took some liberties developing Jack's personality, which, again, makes perfect sense. Jack McBride was my type: incredibly outgoing, sociable, ready and waiting to say the right thing. I don't know Wesley, but so far he doesn't seem very friendly.

My lips and fingers are numb.

"What does that woman have to do with you having my picture?" Wesley asks.

No way am I spilling the truth. It's too mortifying. "Never mind. I thought you were someone else."

"But that doesn't—"

Maybe if I keep interrupting him, he'll forget. "You said that you live here, then?" My voice is numb, too. I want to fold myself into a suitcase. I want to transport myself to the moon. I want to be anywhere but here, unraveling in front of him.

"I've lived here for a few years," he returns grudgingly, speaking to a spot of nothing over my shoulder instead of looking at me. "This cabin is for the estate's groundskeeper. Which, as we've established, is me."

I release a faint, involuntary laugh. "Yes. Which is you."

To think that this past Christmas, when I mailed Violet a holiday card—as I do every year—and when she read the words *Hoping my love life takes a turn for the better in 2021*, as in, hopefully Jack and I would get serious about our relationship and move beyond emailing, the man who wears Jack's face might have been right beside her. The universe is just plain mean sometimes.

My voice is a wheeze. "Small world."

"I guess?" Wesley rakes an aggravated hand through his hair, eyes tracking up the wall. He's the most beautiful human I've ever seen, and I don't think he likes me at all. "Listen, I don't know what's going on. You're Violet's niece? Are you here for something of hers, then?" I didn't miss the face he made when Ruth introduced me as *Julie's girl*. If he knew Violet, then he would've heard about my mother. He assumes I've come begging for handouts.

"I'm here for the house." My speech is almost coherent. It's a proud moment for me.

"You're here for the . . ." His brows slam down. He turns on Ruth, whose smile wobbles.

"You know, I've been preparing for this, and so far it hasn't gone anything like I've practiced," she tells us with faux cheer.

She plunks down on the plaid couch and pats the empty cushion at her right, then the one at her left. "I can explain. Let me first explain that I wasn't *allowed* to explain."

I sit down on her left. "You're losing me already."

Wesley does not sit. He leans against the front door, narrow eyed, arms folded protectively over his chest. I cannot get over the sight of him; it's an out-of-body experience. It's so weird to have to sit here and pretend I'm not freaking out.

"Don't shoot the messenger," Ruth begins, "but I, ah, was instructed to fudge the specifics of the will until *you*, Maybell, arrived at Falling Stars." She turns to Wesley. "Which is why I dropped in on you. She said she was coming today, and I needed to be here when she arrived."

Wesley looks as if his top and bottom molars are trying to crush each other. Aside from a small grunt, he says nothing.

Ruth decides I'm the easier person to focus on. "Violet thought about you every day. She wished she could have done more when you were growing up, but she was getting on in years and didn't think she'd successfully win custody."

It's odd to hear that someone has, without my knowledge, felt concern over my well-being. It's odd to think anyone out there cared enough to remember me, to think about me when I wasn't physically right in front of them.

"Wesley," Ruth continues, "Violet was so grateful for you. You really went above and beyond to take care of her, and I know in my heart she wouldn't have lasted as long if you hadn't come to Falling Stars."

She clears her throat. "She loved you both, and wanted both of you to have the house. She couldn't choose. The estate belongs to both of you."

A thick silence expands. Wesley assesses me with new sharpness, as though before this statement I was inconsequential but now I require a closer look.

"Both of us," I echo woodenly.

"I was ordered to tell each of you separately that you inherited the house, the land, the cabin, all of it. And then, once we were all together, that's when I could come clean that you were equal inheritors." She straightens her shoulders, expecting to be attacked, maybe. "I'm faithfully executing *Violet's* directions, so please don't hold this against me too much."

Wesley stares past both of us and into a different dimension.

I'm stuck on a loop. "*Both* of us."

Ruth nods. "The estate is fully paid for, but unfortunately there isn't much left as far as financial inheritance. She left her vinyl record collection and ten thousand dollars to me, two thousand dollars to each of my three kids, and five thousand dollars plus her car to her nurse. Oh, and she left a few savings bonds to her mail carrier. After cremation costs and very, very generous donations to charities that were stipulated in the will, Violet has . . ." She squints, recollecting. "Thirty-one dollars and change left in her bank account."

Victor Hannobar started off with a local flagship store (for wallets and handbags, mainly) that expanded into multiple stores throughout Tennessee and gradually built himself a luxury goods empire (by this point, Hannobar was best known for their watches), which he sold later in life for *loads* of money. Enough to keep the next several generations comfortable, if they'd had children, which they didn't. "What happened?"

Ruth draws a breath before responding, but I have too many

questions filling my head and have to interrupt. "How does being equal inheritors work? It's not like we can"—I shoot a glance at Wesley—"*both* live in the house. Can we see the documents? Maybe she put down how to divide the assets, like . . . I get the manor and Ja—uh—Wesley gets the cabin."

At this, Wesley's soul returns to its human vessel. "Come again?"

"You'll have to decide for yourselves how you want to divide the assets," Ruth replies. "Violet didn't dictate." She retrieves the papers from her oversized handbag and shows us. At the bottom of each page, in tiny eight-point-font footnotes, my aunt has gone to purposeful lengths to make this inheritance as thorny and inconvenient as possible.

"I will say," Ruth says to her stunned audience, "that you don't have any existing debts, but from now on you're responsible for insuring the property and for paying taxes on it."

My jaw drops. I've never owned my own home before, so this didn't even occur to me. "How much is that going to cost?"

"It all depends. If you sell the property—"

"No," Wesley and I say at the same time. Then we narrow our eyes at each other.

"—you're going to run into some high costs in taxes. That's how it works with inherited homes. It's cheaper for beneficiaries to keep them than to sell." She loses me when she starts talking about capital gains tax, but I enter the chat again when I hear, "Making Falling Stars your primary residence is the best decision, tax-wise. But I wouldn't dream of telling you what to do. Now, Violet, on the other hand . . ." She unfolds a sheet of lilac stationery and walks over to the wall. As she tears off a few pieces of Scotch tape and fusses with the paper, Wesley pivots and blasts me with his powers of intimidation until all that remains of me is my ghost.

"I'll buy you out." Brusque. Factual.

"What? No way."

"Ruth told me I was the only inheritor, so I've already made plans. There's so much I want to do with this place, improvements I've always wanted to make, but Violet wouldn't listen to my suggestions. Let me take it off your hands. I'll fix up the estate, get it appraised after renovations are finished, and you can have half of whatever the house is worth." He's thinking quickly but isn't adept at persuasion. Instead of soft, careful coaxing, his words fire out of a machine gun. "We'll draw up a contract for a payment plan."

Is he out of his mind?

"I'm not giving up ownership," I sputter. "This is my aunt's property, so I think it should stay in the family."

His head falls back a fraction, unintentionally distracting me with the column of his throat, Adam's apple pronounced. "Your definition of *family* is a little strange. I've lived here for four and a half years, but I have *never* seen you before. What kind of niece visits her aunt only after she's died, and only then because she's getting presents?"

My face heats. "You don't know what you're talking about."

"Do with this what you will," Ruth announces tiredly in the background. In my peripheral vision I notice she's taped the lilac stationery to the wall. "You aren't legally obligated to honor it. But speaking as Violet's friend and not as the executor of her estate, I believe it would be wrong not to."

I'm about to ask her for clarification when Wesley takes a step closer to me and the words in my throat evaporate. He's at least six three or six four, but that dark, burning demeanor adds an extra ten feet. The longer our gazes hold, the lower the ceilings drop, walls shrinking to box us in. "The manor's in horrible condition," he says with quiet but fierce intensity. "A fire hazard. You can't even turn the heat on until it's undergone an inspection by the fire department. You don't want this mountain of problems, I promise you. Give me a few months. After the appraisal—"

"I can't wait a few months," I snap. "I don't have anything else. I already told my roommate I was moving out. All my stuff's outside in my car. I literally . . . this is all I have! I thought it was all mine."

"Then how do you suggest we proceed?"

"I don't know." I rub my eyes, a migraine beginning to bloom behind them. "I don't know! I'm tired. It's been a long day." I glance at Ruth, hoping maybe she'll have the crystal-clear solution, but I don't see her anywhere. Her purse isn't on the couch, either.

She's given us the slip.

With her gone, now I'm alone in this cabin I sort of own but am clearly not welcome in, which sits on property I have to share with a darkly burning man who looks like *that*. The manor's unlivable, and yet it appears I'm going to have to live in it.

My run of good luck has already run its course.

Chapter 4

OPTIONS ARE THIN ON the ground. Is there a motel around here? Actually, the answer to that doesn't matter: I can't afford to waste my savings on a months-long hotel stay, which is the duration of time I'm looking at while I somehow get the estate up to code. I might have to sleep in my car, but it wouldn't be the first time.

I've walked right out of the cabin and am back in my car. This is . . . I resist even thinking the sentiment, because my mom's voice filters into my conscience. *Life's not fair. Get used to it.*

I attempt to harden myself. It's too cold for wallowing.

Really cold, now that I'm sitting still and my nerves are fading. My phone's home screen tells me it's thirty-nine degrees, and I can't keep the heat blasting or my car battery will die.

I let my forehead slap the steering wheel. *All right, Maybell. You can wallow just a little.* At this point I thought I'd be lounging on Violet's living room couch, fire blazing, evening news on a low drone to take the edge off the silence, utilizing her supersized pantry of baking ingredients to whip up something sweet.

I don't remember making the decision to get out of the car. I go *poof* and reappear on the steps of the manor, twisting the handle. The key Ruth gave me earlier today is unnecessary, because while the knob is locked, the door hangs loose on its frame and gives way at the lightest touch.

My phone's flashlight function illuminates the foyer, grand curving staircase blocked with overstuffed trash bags, some of them ripped open. I expect to be greeted by a familiar wicker bench with a blue floral cushion. The eighties lampshades in Southwest pinks and sands—out of fashion even then, but to my ten-year-old self, the incontrovertible ideal. It was like living on the set of an early-nineties sitcom, but whatever size scale you're thinking—think bigger. And with more secret doors.

There's so much stuff packed in here that the sound of my footsteps absorbs instantly, no trace of an echo. Aunt Violet has ordered every *As Seen on TV!* product to hit one a.m. programming, whole walls of it, towers and battlements of it, weighing down so heavily that it curves the floorboards. My dumbfounded eyes wander over purchases that look like they've never been taken out of their boxes: waffle makers, miniature Christmas village sets, snow cone machines. A waist-high stack of children's coloring books. Enough Hasbro inventory to play a different board game every day of the year. Wigs, tackle boxes, sequined cowgirl hats, aprons. Hundreds of books and DVDs. My jaw's come unhinged, and my eyes burn for all the staring, and the dust, and something else that's never going to leave me alone now.

Your fault, it whispers.

Two narrow paths fork off, left and right, ignoring the staircase altogether since it's impossible to access. The paths are just barely wide enough to allow an elderly woman to squeeze through. I angle my phone upward to see how high it all goes, dust glimmering in the streaks of light hanging so thickly that I could almost trick myself into believing it's snowing in here.

Thirty-nine degrees has dropped to subzero. Cold seeps all the way through my skin, into my temporal lobes, moving torpid old memories down the pipeline for forced replay. I can't believe the same Violet Hannobar who wouldn't let anyone walk through the house with their shoes on became the Violet who lived in this mess.

I make the questionable decision to keep going, because surely it can't be like this everywhere. The kitchen was her favorite room in the house: upscale and shiny, decked out with all the best appliances and double ovens (*"for double the desserts"*). I maneuver over and under packaged cookware like I'm in a game of life-sized Jenga, batting away cobwebs, foot delicately crunching the small bones of something dead.

A dark shape flies at me from out of nowhere and I scream, ducking, dislodging the wall. An Easy-Bake Oven falls onto a birthday-paper-wrapped package that spins and lights up. A voice screams, *"Bop it!"* in the demon-possessed snarl that could only be produced by dying batteries, and I scream right back.

When the path widens at last, I'm in the living room.

Which means I've bypassed the kitchen completely. The shining apple of Aunt Violet's eye, with fancy double ovens for double the desserts, has fallen victim to the hoard monster.

I find my shell-shocked reflection in the blank, grubby television set, and if I close my eyes, everything is as it was. I hear the soft whir of Uncle Victor's oxygen machine in the next room. Violet and I are on the burgundy sofa—I'm insisting that I'm mature enough to watch *Unsolved Mysteries*, but Violet doesn't like it. I tell her I've seen worse at my cousin's house—he used to watch R-rated horror films while I slept (or tried to) in the armchair. Violet purses her lips. *Looks like I'll be giving Brandon a phone call, then.*

I feel like a glamorous movie star in my tinted lip balm and glittery nail polish, smelling of Love's Baby Soft perfume. Violet wears Elizabeth Taylor's White Diamonds and curlers in her hair, flaming red with pale roots. Her earrings were gifted to her by Marlon Brando when she was younger, *but don't tell Uncle Victor that.* Six fingers are adorned in heavy jewels that, she tells me, out the side of her mouth like she doesn't want anybody to overhear, her siblings would gladly kill her to get their hands on.

I hiss out a long, unsteady breath. The little girl on the burgundy sofa has grown up, but being a grown-up isn't at all the way she thought it'd be. She's so lost now that it's scary. The only one who's ever looked out for her is gone.

The Violet in my mind's eye winks conspiratorially at my childhood self, then dissolves. No one's been looking out for her, either. At my feet, there's a grimy blanket and a cup with a moldy toothbrush in it. A hot plate's switched off but still plugged in, ceramic bowl on top, instant noodles glued to the rim. A dead rat's tail peeks out from under a pillow.

My aunt's house is eleven thousand square feet in total: elegant and sparkling, with a wine cellar, a butler's pantry, and a surplus of unnecessary, beautiful extras. She has special rooms bigger than some people's houses that were, in my time here, used only one day a year, doors kept closed for three hundred sixty-four days. Yet at the end of her life she was confined to a nest that roughly spans four by three feet.

"I convinced her to move into the cabin not long after I was hired."

At the sound of another voice I emit a scream so powerful that it could probably carry a paper airplane on its wave. I jump and turn at once, ankle twisting, toppling right onto the dead rat, which turns out to be a live possum. Which rends another terrible shriek out of me.

Wesley doesn't offer a helping hand, watching with a closed expression.

My knees knock together as I scramble to my feet, heart thumping something dreadful. It's like I've swallowed a bomb. "Jesus Christ! Where did you come from?"

He points wordlessly behind him.

"Well, yeah, no shit. But how did you sneak in so quietly?" He's huge. I should have heard him hacking through this jungle long before I saw him. Maybe he used a secret entrance. I try to summon a mental blueprint for this house, but all my Falling Stars knowledge has been turned upside down and shaken for loose change. With it looking the way it does now, I can't even remember which direction my old bedroom is in. Somewhere upstairs. That's all I know.

He scrutinizes me as though I'm the one who's acting suspect. "What are you doing? It's not safe in here."

"Looking for somewhere to sleep." I bend to unplug the hot plate, paranoid it'll turn on even though the electricity's shut off. This place would go up like a Fourth of July sparkler.

"Somewhere to sleep," he repeats flatly.

"Yes. I moved out of my apartment because I was under the impression I had a new home with a nice warm bed waiting for me. Living it up like royalty." I prop my hands on my hips, surveying our less-than-impressive environs. "I did not have 'colossal hoard' on my bingo card."

"There aren't any nice beds here."

"I got that, thanks. I'm improvising. Saw a whole pallet of Nintendo 64s back there; maybe I'll build myself a bed out of them."

Wesley doesn't smile at my joke. He's frowning at me again. I think he has a low opinion of my mental competence. "You can't stay in here, it's dangerous."

He's absolutely right. "I'm a big girl. I can take care of myself."

Wesley hesitates. The worry line in his forehead cracks into a full-blown trench, and he's silent for so long that I begin to think he's a robot who's spontaneously shut off, but then he opens his mouth. Slowly, he forces out the words: "You can come stay in the cabin." It's the most reluctantly issued invitation in history. "I suppose." Another eternity passes. "For now."

There is simply no way.

"Why not?"

It transpires that I've said that out loud.

Obviously, I am not going to tell Wesley that he's my most recent ex and doesn't know it, so I say, "There's not enough room. The cabin only has one bedroom, from what I saw, which you're already occupying. If I'm crashing on your couch I'll just be in your way." And I will not be a burden on anyone. "It's fine. I'll burrow into another room here that has fewer possums." I try for a casual lean but accidentally kick over the toothbrush cup. Cockroaches scatter. "Never mind, I'll sleep in my car. How good are you at jumping dead batteries, by the way?"

The disapproving frown deepens, bracketing his mouth. He wields silence like a weapon, letting it hang over us for several moments, before responding, "The cabin is a two-bedroom. My bedroom's upstairs. You can take Violet's old room downstairs."

This perks me up. "Really? Are you sure?" Ordinarily I'd want to thoroughly vet a guy before agreeing to stay at his place for any length of time, but it's gotten so chilly that I can see my breath, silver puffs disturbing the dust clouds. Besides, Aunt Violet liked him well enough to bequeath him half of Falling Stars. If he's good in her books, he's okay in mine. I'll have to find a way to scrub my brain of all associations with Jack McBride and the fact that he's a stone-cold stunner, of course, but that's small potatoes. It's been five seconds since I started seriously considering his offer, and in those five seconds I've spotted approximately three bats and four glowing eyes in the corner of the ceiling.

He turns his back. "I'll change out her blankets and pillows."

I'm reminded of Ruth saying Violet died in her sleep, full-body shuddering with goose bumps to think that I'll be lying in her bed. "Could you flip the mattress, too?" I call at his retreating back.

Wesley doesn't reply. He eases sideways into the passageway and disappears.

"Don't bother to wait up or anything," I grumble, picking my way along after. "Not like you'll care if I die." Just means he'll get 100 percent of the estate rather than fifty. Maybe I should be more suspicious.

I make slow progress. Play-Doh mega sets and bead bracelet kits wobble in my wake, glaring ominously down at my unprotected skull. I would hate to die by Etch A Sketch.

By the time I've made it out of the house, Wesley's long gone.

When I open the cabin's front door, there's a split-second flash of movement as a pull-down ladder folds up into the ceiling. Footsteps thud above, followed by stark quiet.

Violet's room holds few belongings, likely because she kept her hoard at the manor and didn't want to cross-contaminate. Or didn't want to make Wesley's life challenging by carrying the addiction over into his space.

It's spare but homey. A comfy queen bed, a dark cherry bureau, a lamp, a bookcase. There's an air of unfinished business about the room, however. It has the flavor of someone going to sleep in it one night, unaware they'd be gone the next day. My imagination is running away with me again.

I haul my luggage out of my car, too tired to properly unpack. I'm hungry and in desperate need of a shower, but first, curiosity niggles. I float over to the lilac stationery Ruth taped to the wall, and what I find there raises both eyebrows.

VIOLET'S DYING WISHES

IGNORE AT YOUR OWN PERIL

(I'LL HAUNT YOU DOWN, BESTOW 1,000-YEAR CURSES UPON YOUR BLOODLINES, ETC.)

Wish 1. Take extraordinary (extraordinary!) care to comb through *every single item* in the house before you decide to donate/dispose/keep.

Wish 2. Victor thought there was buried treasure out here but I never did find any. For the intrepid explorer, Finders Keepers rules apply.

Wish 3. Maybell, dear, I'd be thrilled if you painted a mural in the ballroom.

Wish 4. Movie night with a friend is sacred law, don't forget. Wesley, I'd love for you to make my favorite cinnamon-sugar donuts for the occasion.

I WALTZ INTO MY coffee shop in the clouds and *he's* already there, wiping down the counter with a damp rag. Everything goes soft and out-of-focus fuzzy, black and white like an old film. A dark vignette fades out all the people in the room but one, who seems to glow at the edges. He looks up at me, flashing a radiant smile he never shares with anyone else.

Today, Jack isn't a prince. He's a barista. We've enjoyed a will-they-won't-they dynamic for ages, but we've reached my favorite part of the love story: the sexual tension is at its peak and we've got nowhere to go but over the edge in a sensual, tour de force declaration of love. We know each other inside out by now. We trust each other and accept each other's flaws. I know he'll never hurt me, because in Maybell's Coffee Shop AU, hurting me is impossible without my say-so.

"Maybell," he says breathlessly, rushing over. "I can't hold it in anymore. The past few months have been unspeakable torture, and if I don't tell you how I really feel I will fall down dead right here and now."

"Jack!" I exclaim. "Whatever is the matter?"

He takes my hands in his. "When I look at you, I can't think straight. Aphrodite who? *You* are the goddess of beauty. Your mind is a splendor. It's impressive how you can do any calculation inside your head, like if I asked what fourteen thousand two hundred and eighty-seven times twenty thousand five hundred and forty-one is, you'd know the answer like that." He snaps his fingers.

"The answer is [redacted]," I reply humbly. "But I don't like to think of myself as smart. I'm just your average girl."

"There's nothing average about you, Maybell," he goes on, gaze yearning. He sweeps me off my feet, holding me princess-style in his arms. "You're compassionate and genuine and popular, all eyes on you every time you walk into a room. And *your* eyes! Incomparable. They're the prettiest blue, like the water in Sandals Resorts commercials. I hope I'm not gushing too much. But my heart can't take it any longer—I have to know how you feel about me."

"This is all so . . . unexpected." I am positively faint. To think I've been so consumed with my busy, successful café—the most successful café in this entire vague area, in fact—that I've hardly noticed what's been brewing between us, right under my nose. Or maybe I've been secretly pining. I haven't finalized the trope just yet.

"I love you, Jack McBride," I reply solemnly. "And I am ready to bear your children."

Everyone claps. I notice my parents in one of the booths, proud as can be. They're in matching white leather jackets that say WORLD TOUR on the back in rhinestones, and my mother (who's also my best friend) is beaming with happiness. She has everything she's ever wanted; she has only ever wanted the same happiness for me.

Color bleeds back into the scene, and for the first time, I realize we're standing in red rose petals that take the shape of a heart.

Candlelight dazzles off every surface. Jack's reached a level of hotness so severe that I have to shade my eyes, as his hair is dripping wet for some reason and he's wearing a loose white cotton shirt with buttons that come progressively more undone every time I look away. He grins seductively. "Well, what are we waiting—"

BEEEEEEEEEEP. BEEEEEEEEEEP. BEEEEEEEEEP. BEEEEEEEEP.

The café disintegrates. I spring out of my bed in the real world so fast that my foot gets caught in the quilt and I bang my elbow on the nightstand. "What the hell!"

The obnoxious beeping noise is coming from right outside the cabin, stopping when I throw open the front door. A bunch of men have marred my view of the lovely Smoky Mountains with two monstrously large containers that are about forty yards long each, sides emblazoned with WALLAND DUMPSTER RENTAL & WASTE SERVICES. It's eight a.m. I've been lying in bed awake and daydreaming since a quarter past seven, so I'm still in my pajamas, barefoot in the rain-soaked yard.

Wesley Koehler, mirror image of the starry-eyed barista I've unfortunately been forced to abandon, trots out of the house with a busted cabinet on his shoulders. I watch him balance the cabinet with one arm so he can free the other, shake hands with the guys, and throw it into one of the trucks as easily as if it were a loaf of bread. Wood splinters apart on impact. A small mushroom cloud of dust billows into the atmosphere.

"Hey!"

The dumpster-rental guys wave at me and climb into their vehicles, which look like the front parts of semitrucks but without the trailers, and peel out.

Wesley doesn't wave. He glances at me, then dismissively away, heading right back into the house. He emerges with one of the trash bags from the grand staircase, giving it a heartless toss. I hear glass breaking.

"Hey!" I roar again. "Now, wait just a minute!" I hurry into the cabin to forage for my shoes, discovering one in the living room and the other under my bed. No time for socks.

"Hold up!" I flag Wesley down, but he doesn't stop to listen. Just keeps carrying stuff out of Violet's house and throwing it in the dumpster. "Did you go through that first?" I inquire as he tosses another garbage bag.

He looks at me like I've unzipped my skin and shown him my skeleton. "Did I stick my hands in Violet's garbage? No. Why would I?"

"You don't know if that was trash!"

"Certainly smelled like it."

"Violet's dying wishes," I press urgently, following him into the house. "Didn't you read them? She wants us to inspect everything very, very carefully before throwing it out or donating or whatever. *Extraordinarily* carefully."

"Violet," he replies through gritted teeth, picking up a rust-eaten Weber grill, "liked to be difficult." The grill becomes smithereens.

"Okay, but—"

He walks away. Nostrils flaring, I hurry to catch up again. "I think we should honor her wishes and make sure there isn't anything valuable in these bags before we throw them out."

He gestures to the dumpster. "Be my guest."

When he comes and goes again, this time with an armful of clothes, I find my voice. The one I don't usually use because no one ever listens to it, or if they do, they laugh at me.

"I want to look through that," I declare firmly. "Can you stop for a minute? We need to discuss what we're doing." I can't help tacking on a *please*. It's why I'll never get ahead in life: I undercut myself with too many *please*s and submissive body language, my annoyingly timid *Okay, I understand, forget I said anything, let me know how I can help* that makes me mad at myself later.

"What *I'm* doing is clearing out this house," he informs me. By this point I've seen more of Wesley's back than his front, and in spite of the nice view I'm getting real tired of it.

He attempts to pitch a guitar case into the dumpster, but I tug it out of his grip. He capitalizes on my moment of distraction and disposes of the moth-eaten clothes I've just tried to save. "You've only been thinking about estate plans since, what, yesterday afternoon? I've been planning this for a year, since Violet first told me I was going to inherit everything after she died. I'm going to fix it up, raze five acres of land, and turn it all into a sanctuary for old farm animals."

"Into a *what*?"

Wesley shoots me a hard glare. I'm not prepared for it, for the horrible way it feels to have someone who *looks* like someone I thought I knew, someone who was warm and kind, direct such coldness at me. "What's wrong with an animal sanctuary?"

"What's wrong is that you've decided this all by yourself." Plus, I'm not living next to a literal pigsty.

"Why shouldn't I? Violet was my friend. I cared for her every day." He tugs the guitar case from me, opening it to reveal broken hinges and stained velvet lining. *See?* his expression tacks on smugly. "You, on the other hand? You're a stranger. You appeared from out of nowhere. No offense, but I don't believe DNA gives you seniority over me."

He's calling me an opportunist. Julie Parrish's girl, through and through.

"I know what improvements are best for Falling Stars," Wesley concludes pragmatically. "I've been suggesting them ever since I was hired."

"If Violet liked your suggestions, she would've implemented them," I retort. "I inherited half this place. And so help me, if you throw out one more piece of my rightful property without my approval, I'm going to take legal action." *Please don't call my bluff. I can't afford a lawyer.*

This stops him in his tracks. "I'm clearing out trash. Just trash, not anything that's salvageable. Is that not the obvious next step?"

He's got a point. I hate that he's got a point.

"What about Violet's wishes? Every little item, she said. *Extraordinary* care, she said."

He exhales through his nose, irritated. The irritation is contagious. "That wasn't serious. Movie night? Making cupcakes? Those aren't wishes, it's meddling from the afterlife."

"Donuts," I say, correcting him. "There's a thousand-year curse hanging in the balance. Sounds plenty serious to me."

"That's because you didn't know her."

Wesley isn't fazed by my crossed arms or formidable scowl. He chucks a cardboard box full of books with their covers missing and ignores me.

"Those can be recycled."

"I'm paying extra for the trash company to sort through it for recyclable materials. Part of the premium service package."

That sounds made-up. And possibly sarcastic. He's saying whatever he thinks will get me to stop talking to him.

It's a relief that I don't have to feel bad anymore about

intruding here, living in his cabin. He's been waiting around for my aunt to die so he could do whatever he wanted with her home.

I busy myself quality-checking holiday lawn ornaments. That's what I'm doing officially, anyway. Unofficially, I'm side-eyeing the muscles in Wesley's arms that cord and shift when he lifts heavy boxes, hunter-green shirt straining across his broad shoulders and back. His skin is tanned and freckled from an occupation that puts him center-stage in the sunlight, so when sweat crops up along his forehead and the bridge of his nose, he shimmers like gold dust. Whenever I'm warm and sweaty, my hair both frizzes out of its ponytail *and* plasters to my face, which goes as red as a stop sign. When I blush or get overheated, I don't get two cute splashes of pink on my cheeks. My face incites alarm. I blame the fact that I was born a redhead, which is my go-to piece of trivia whenever anyone mentions the strawberry highlights in my light brown hair.

I wonder idly if Wesley was born with dark blond hair, or if he's one of those blonds who had snow-white hair as a child. The idea of him having ever been a child is ridiculous. He looks like he was born with a five o'clock shadow and some sharp words for the nurses. I bet he refused to wear onesies because he found them demeaning.

I resent my intimate familiarity with what he looks like, which is at rotten odds with the coarseness beneath his surface. I know every inch of that face, thanks to my dumb, deluded self not running Jack's pictures through a Google reverse image search.

Physically, I speak fluent Wesley Koehler. Spiritually, he's a mysterious unknown. An enigma. That kind of face should come loaded with a cocky grin and eyes that twinkle with teasing humor. In the game of Who Wore It Better?, Jack wins, and he doesn't even exist.

Wesley threads his fingers through his hair, rumpling the every-which-way waves, darting a peculiar look in my direction, then away again. I watch him a while longer while trying to be discreet about it, but now his attention stays firmly fixed on his task. No *good morning*, no *how did you sleep*, no curiosity about me as a person and where I came from, no small talk between room-mates. No *bless you* when I sneeze. It's next-level rudeness.

It's a feeling too familiar to be mistaken. I'm unwanted in my home.

"Zero points for originality, universe," I mutter. "You've given me that story line loads of times and I'm still here." The Maybell Parrishes of the world are a gullible, often down-on-our-luck breed with determination that exceeds our talent, but at the end of the world, we'll be the last ones staggering through that field of zombies. Grumbling, shaking our fists at the sky, too bullheaded to know when to quit, with soft, stupid hearts that won't be jaded. Being delusional is our downfall but it's also our saving grace: we're deluded enough that we don't see why tomorrow shouldn't be better, even if the last thousand days in a row have been bad.

Our being equal inheritors of my aunt's estate is going to be a circus, I can already tell. But if one of us is going to give up, I know it won't be me.

Chapter 5

A FEW HOURS HAVE PASSED since I first began cock-blocking Wesley's mission to run afoul of Great-Aunt Violet's dying wishes, and I'm forming a hunch around how he justifies this behavior.

He and Violet were close, I'm guessing, being the only two people all the way out here, cohabitating in the very close quarters of the groundskeeper's cabin. When you live with somebody long enough, you pick up kernels of information about each other that lead to anticipating what the other person might say or do, how they might react in any situation. You learn their habits, you establish rituals. You grow comfortable. This spawns an easy rapport.

I didn't have an easy rapport with Violet, or at least I haven't had one in a long time. Our relationship was a chasm, basically. I sent a holiday card every year, because holiday cards were easy. *Thinking of you!* Short and sweet, with the thinnest slices of personal information. *Apartment-hunting again. Saw a sweater with jingle bells on it and thought of you. We sure are having a rainy month.* She replied with checks for twenty dollars and a few odds and ends: a bookmark with kittens on it; a newspaper feature on *My May Belle*, the historical Knoxville riverboat I was named after.

For birthdays and Christmases and Thanksgivings, I couldn't bring myself to pick up the phone. Too much time had passed, which led to awkwardness and putting it off even longer—and you see where I'm going with this.

What would I say? What if she didn't care about me anymore? Didn't remember me? Didn't want to hear from me? The possibility I might be accused of being a negligent niece—or worse, that she'd confess what a disappointment I'd turned out to be . . . my guilt grew steadily, but I couldn't face it, so I locked it in a drawer. Now I'll never get the chance to make things right with Violet.

Wesley doesn't carry any such guilt. Maybe he feels the inheritance was owed to him, after taking care of Violet. He must've had his hands full as a caretaker, because he certainly wasn't doing any groundskeeping. The landscape looks like a child's drawing of a tornado.

Maybe neither of us deserves the estate. But this is where I can make it up to Aunt Violet. I can honor her list. I owe her that much, at the very least.

It goes like this:

Wesley carries a crapload of stuff out of the house, and I make him put it in the Inspection Station (it's the spot near a shrub that's shaped kind of like a flamingo). I sort out anything salvageable into Keep and Donate piles. A sticker book I saved from the hoard has found new use designating what to do with it all.

Wesley delivers three more boxes to the Inspection Station and braces himself for interaction with a sharp inhale. "Does the yellow sticker mean 'donate'?"

"It means 'keep.'"

"I was afraid of that."

"Be reasonable. You can't possibly expect me to part with *everything*."

"*Me* be reasonable?" He points to himself. "Me?" Wesley leans across me suddenly, causing me to jerk back, and extracts a sweatshirt from the pile. It's older than I am, a paisley crime against fashion in brown, orange, and mustard yellow. "What are you going to do with this?"

"Not that it's any of your business, but I'm going to wear it." I'm still recovering from almost being touched by him, even though it was accidental and meant nothing. And also didn't happen.

"Really," he deadpans.

"It's vintage."

"There are, no exaggeration, hundreds of vintage clothes in the house. You've got to narrow it down. Be a little more discerning."

"Says who?" He isn't my boss. I've never seen this much *stuff* in my life, and I can't believe it's all mine. Most of my shirts have the Around the Mountain Resort & Spa logo on them, since I got a discount at the gift shop and gift shop clothes were a trendier, management-approved alternative to the staff uniform (blue pinstriped hat and overalls, which management stressed the importance of wearing while dodging the dress code themselves).

I grab a velour skirt from the box he just put down. It has a few holes, but I could patch them up easily with one of Violet's (twelve and counting) sewing machines. "Oooh, I want this, too." I swipe a Sonny & Cher shirt with a (broken) zipper that goes up and down the turtleneck and Wesley pinches the bridge of his nose.

What a Grinch. If anybody's going about this the wrong way, it is him, ignorer of Wish #1. Violet held on to her belongings for a long time, so I can't picture her being thrilled with our tossing out *too* much. If I can find a use for something, then I will. Wesley walks away shaking his head, and even though we don't know each other and his opinion shouldn't affect me, I can't help but feel like I'm failing a test of adulthood.

I was fifteen years old when my mother was thirty, so that number used to feel a lot older to me, practically middle-aged. Watching Julie's decision-making was a lesson in what not to do. I thought I'd surely be married to my soul mate by thirty, not necessarily with a teenage daughter in tow but definitely a slew of pets, living happily ever after in a cute cul-de-sac Cape Cod. I'd have a walk-in closet with sophisticated pencil skirts and chiffon scarves. A dependable best friend who was always there for me, thick or thin—a fiery, independent businesslady who brought out my sassy side (I hoped to develop such a side one day). We'd drink wine and laugh. Commiserate. She and her husband would double-date with me and mine, a perfect quartet. Perhaps she deserved it, perhaps she didn't, but I judged my mom back in the day because I compared our lives to these arbitrary markers of success and wondered how she could be so careless. Like she could have had it all, if only she'd wanted it enough.

I'm now at the age my mom was when I thought she was a letdown and it's terrifying to *still* be in this stage, bewildered, guessing my way through life on shaky baby-deer legs. No soul mate husband, no down-for-a-good-time best friend. Too many failures to speak of. So much of living is struggling instead of enjoying. And where's the utopia I thought society would have leveled up to by now? Somebody sold me a bridge.

To prove that I'm capable of parting with material possessions if I *want* to, I make sure Wesley watches me throw away two whole bags. The bags are actually filled with other bags, but he doesn't have to know that. When I catch his eye, I get that pang again. That *oof* right to the chest, when, for a split second, before the scowls and the curt responses, Jack McBride could be real. I miss knowing somebody out there cared if I didn't text for a couple days. My daydream world floats nearby like a lifeboat, ready and waiting for me to drift away, but I'm a masochist today. I want that pang again. I want to hold his gaze for just a little bit longer and pretend he's someone who cares. I am a sad, pitiful lady.

"When did she paint the house gray?" I ask.

Wesley frowns (it's his default expression, but he has the standard *I hate everything* frown and the deliberate *I hate you personally* frown that he goes back and forth between). "What do you mean?" Glances at the house. "It's always been gray."

He turns around, already moving beyond the conversation. How can he not be as lonely as I am? How can he not be starved for human attention?

"It was pink when I was a kid," I insist, unwilling to let him go.

The permanent frown doesn't abate but there's a subtle shift, agitation crossing into confusion. "How's that possible? I've seen pictures from ten, twenty, thirty, forty years ago—it's gray in all of them."

"It was definitely pink when I was ten."

The corners of his mouth turn down, hardening in place. He doesn't believe me. He thinks I'm off my rocker.

"That one isn't so bad," he says, eyes cutting to the pool of red sequined fabric in my hands. I didn't notice I'd drawn it out of the box. I glance down, and when I glance back up he's vanishing into the house.

"He doesn't want to talk," I say quietly to the dress, tilting its sequins this way and that to catch the light. "That's okay. We don't have to get along." It emerges sounding like a question, a common theme for me, so I say it again with confidence. "We don't have to get along."

I hate this gnawing sensation, that I am more alone than I've ever been. This is the first full day of Maybell's Fresh Start, so you'd think I'd be at the top of my game. I've inherited a (dilapidated) manor and two hundred and ninety-four acres of (completely wild) land with a view of the mountains, but I feel nothing. I haven't had a proper cry over Aunt Violet's death, either, which means there must be something wrong with me.

My absence from work today has been noted by Christine, who's sending increasingly threatening texts: You'd better be in the hospital. Gemma, too, who wants to know if I'm sick, and reminds me that if so, I'm already running out of sick leave, which isn't information she'd know. Paul definitely ghostwrote that text. I'm an hour away from that place, never to return again, so I'm free to give them a middle-finger emoji and block all their numbers from my phone. I don't know why I can't. I type out several responses but delete them all. Leaving all their messages ignored is probably the more chaotic choice—soon I'll be receiving "official warnings" sent to my company email that I won't check.

Next, I do what I always do and yet always regret doing whenever I'm spinning in lonely circles.

She answers her phone after six rings. "Hey, you."

"Hey, Mom." I put on my cheery, everything-is-fine smile even though she can't see me.

"You must be psychic, because I was about to call. I just listened to your voicemail." Her tone is a touch superior. "Too bad."

"Yeah, it's so sad." I realize I'm holding a box of White Diamonds perfume, and it's a mistake. My vision blurs. I'm in the kitchen with Aunt Violet, sifting powdered sugar over fudge brownie donuts, making a terrific mess, while she assures and reassures me how well I'm doing. Maybe I'll finally cry, and it'll be cathartic, and I'll be able to appreciate Falling Stars. Maybe it will all sink in.

"Well." Mom's cold detachment brings me back to earth. "She *was* old."

I swallow. "Still sad, though."

"So you've moved in already, huh? You find a job there yet?"

I'm abruptly reminded of why I don't call Mom often. "No."

"Oh, honey, that's not good."

"I only just got here. I'll find something soon." Hopefully. I don't want to think about applications right now, not when my employment history qualifies me to be a housekeeper and basically nothing else. "How've you been?"

"It's kind of an insult that Violet gave you the house, don't you think?"

The left-field question catches me cold. "How so?"

"The fact that it's trashed. Which! *Hah!*" Mom snorts loudly. "She thought *we* were trash. You and I." She's speaking faster; I can picture her on the terrace, half in the sun, one of her knees bouncing. "If I were you, I would have walked away. We're not the type of people to accept pity presents. That isn't how I raised you."

I don't know what to say.

"You couldn't pay me to live in that mausoleum," she continues haughtily. "No offense. I'm happy for *you* if *you* like it, but that could never be me. Never. And all the work she's just dumped on your plate? Inconsiderate. What an awful old lady."

"She wasn't awful."

"She nearly killed you."

"I was fine."

She blows cigarette smoke into the speaker. "That phone call still gives me nightmares."

Me too, because it signified being taken away. Aunt Violet felt it was her duty to let Mom know about the minor car accident—it wasn't her fault, the roads around here are loopier than a Slinky and neither of us saw the other car coming. The teeniest of swerves. The barest of guardrail bumps. We were okay! The other car was okay! Violet's trusty, clunky car absorbed the impact and we were fine, if a little rattled. Some light bruising from our seat belts and a few tears, but those were close-call tears. Happy-we-were-okay tears.

Mom raced straight to the Falling Stars, used the situation to try to extort money out of Violet, and it all went to hell. Each of them said the other was unfit to parent, but Mom was the one with legal rights.

"So damned irresponsible, driving when her eyesight was getting bad. And she really thought you'd be better off in her custody! Imagine."

I have. Vividly.

"You'd have turned out a mess." I hear a cigarette lighter click. "So. Totally trashed, then."

"Yeah. Can't hold out my arms on either side of me without knocking into stuff."

A peculiar pause. "What kind of stuff?"

I get that bad-faith awareness, the one that grips me every time we talk and makes my stomach churn—the one I forget about after we hang up because my brain is in perpetual repair mode and wants desperately to believe the best of people. "Vines, I mean. Just a bunch of vines. They've destroyed the windows and floors."

"Oh?"

I can see her wheels turning. She's considering driving out here. "The mold is wall to wall. And there're about a thousand rats."

"Eww. God." I envision the face my rat-phobic mother is making and can't help a slight smile. "You're the only one named in the will, then?"

My smile slides off.

"Ahh . . ." The part of my cognizance that registers Wesley and screams *OH MY GOD IT'S JACK* can't stop cataloging his movements, and my gaze tracks irresistibly to where his army-green Wellington boots are chafing a path through the yard. Back and forth he goes, house to dumpster, to house to dumpster, pitching armfuls of maybe, maybe-not junk. Not even discriminating. Could be throwing away antique buttons worth hundreds of thousands of dollars, but what does he care? "Mainly," I reply at length. I'm not getting into the two-inheritors mess—she'll suggest I take him to court, which Violet wouldn't have wanted.

"I'm assuming I didn't get anything, huh?" She tries to mask her hope with flippancy, but we grew up together. I can read Julie better than anyone.

"No. Sorry."

"Sorry? Ha! Don't be sorry for *me*. Bless your heart." Her voice picks up speed, antsier. "It was always a dump, anyway. If Violet had left *me* the house, there's no way I'd want anything to do with it. No thanks."

There's so much I want to say in reply to this. If it was such a dump, then why'd she leave me there for a summer? Also, it was definitely not a dump. I know I didn't invent how beautiful and clean it once was. *Also*, I haven't forgotten that Mom begged to live there, too, back when I was ten and she dropped me off. Violet wouldn't let her inside the house because Mom had tended to fill her pockets whenever she visited as a preteen.

"No offense, but the city's better," Mom's saying. "There's nothing out there in . . . what is the name of that dingy town? You *need* to come live here. I can help you find an apartment! We'll go apartment-hunting and shop till we drop, on Alessandro's Mastercard, of course." She rolls the R in *Alessandro*.

"Maybe I'll visit."

The ten seconds of dead air that follow are confirmation that this call is like every other call, in which she gushes about how much she wants to see me but stops short of solidifying real plans.

"I gotta go," she whispers. "Alessandro's home."

There's yelling in the background, and she ends the call without hearing *goodbye*.

I've never met Alessandro in person. She usually doesn't answer my calls if he's home because *he doesn't like kids, even adult ones*. It's why she hid the fact that she had a daughter from him for months—I'm a relic of her old life, which she's worked so hard to shed, and even though she does love me, she has been, from the start, bent on outgrowing her maternal role as quickly as possible.

It isn't that we never had any good times, it's that the good times, in retrospect, are kind of sad. Adolescent Maybell held tight to trivial, evanescent mother-daughter moments that made her feel warm, giving their memories a loving glow when anyone else would've found them depressing. It's rough when you have a nature that begs you to avoid heartache at all costs but also makes you wear your heart on your sleeve.

The jangling of drawers bursting apart in the dumpster jolts me to attention, and I fixate on Wesley. Sharing a house with a stranger who doesn't like me is a punch to the stomach: either I cooperate with him or I end up homeless. Again. At least I'm not embarrassing myself fawning all over him, since the Jack debacle left a bad taste in my mouth that, whether Wesley deserves it or not, extends to anyone resembling Jack. I don't look at him and hear angels plucking harp strings. I don't feel a hot surge of anything like love—I look at him and want to sock him in the throat. It's a nice surprise, personal-growth-wise.

"How are we going to live together?" I call out.

Wesley jerks. "What?"

"How does this work?" I take another stab at Authoritative Maybell and put my hands on my hips. "I get the first floor, you get the second?"

I'm not being serious, or at least I don't think I am, but he shrugs. "Sure."

"Who gets the third floor?" It's more of an attic, and largely unfinished, but still valuable real estate to stake a claim for.

Another shrug. "The ghosts?"

And off he goes again. I can't pin him to one place for the life of me. Fine! This is fine. I can get the ball rolling on my new life without him—it's not like I need his opinion or help. I've never had very much of anything, but I have resilience, and I have *this*.

I have memories of Falling Stars being beautiful. I can make it beautiful again.

It occurs to me that I forgot to tell Wesley thank you for letting me stay with him in the cabin. Or maybe I have every right to stay with him, since I own half of everything. *That's an entitled attitude to have*, I warn myself.

As I open my mouth to express my gratitude, he says, unprompted: "The house has always been gray."

My mouth closes. Purses. I fade from his notice once more, no more interesting than a piece of furniture waiting to be sorted into *keep*, *donate*, or *throw away*.

Stalking past him, I huff, "I did not make up that it was pink. I did not make that up." I stalk right into the foyer, where the path has been gradually widened (mostly thanks to him, I'll admit, since I've been preoccupied with expanding my wardrobe on the lawn), hoist a broken microwave into my arms, and stalk right back out.

Wesley shakes his head. Mutters something.

I ignore him, and it's empowering. *We don't have to be friends. We're only going to be living together, not like that means anything. We don't have to be friends.*

Wesley's muttering grows loud enough to form a distinguishable word. "Stop."

I do stop, but only because he's caught me by surprise. "What?"

He glares. Thrusts a . . . helmet? At me?

"Uhhh . . ." I look up at him, and he looks away, like he can't bear to make eye contact with me. From his perspective, I'm the usurper of a dream come true, a bigger inconvenience than all the water damage, broken windows, and split floorboards combined.

"I don't have a bike." Maybe there's one in the house. You know, I'm not giving Violet enough credit here. There's got to be at least ten bikes in that house.

"If you're going to be in there"—he points to the house, eyebrows clinching together, jaw hard—"you need protection. It's dangerous."

"*You're* not wearing a helmet."

He glares some more. Throws a shattered vanity mirror into the dumpster with unnecessary force, which might not have been intended as a threat but is for sure being interpreted as one.

"Fine, fine." I hold my hands up. Strap the helmet on. And I think: it really is a shame that we don't have to be friends.

Chapter 6

FOR SOMEONE WHO HATES having me around, Wesley sure loves getting in my way.

It's April sixth and I'm exhausted, heartstrings stretched until I've lost all emotional elasticity from the highs and lows of discovery and loss as I clear out Falling Stars. I am a sparking, smoking jumble of raw wires.

But I still haven't cried.

Why haven't I cried? I won't feel like I deserve this gift from my aunt until I've grieved the way a loved one is supposed to grieve.

So this is what it's come to: me sitting cross-legged in a circle of Hannobar mementos, immersing myself in Aunt Violet–ness, begging my heart to pick up any station other than the numb detachment I've been tuned in to.

Wesley's footsteps are getting stompier. I can tell he wants to say *Do you have to sit right THERE*, but he swallows the words. He presses his lips together to keep them from falling out as he grunts and sighs from heavy lifting, dismantling the living room furniture around me.

I *do* have to sit right here, in point of fact. This is the part of the house where I feel closest to Violet. My favorite hours on this earth were all spent in this living room, side by side with her, chatting about anything and everything. Violet was one of a kind. She didn't talk down to me, but she also didn't treat me like I was a grown adult. Mom went back and forth between extremes: one minute she'd snap at me that I needed to do whatever she said because I was a little kid who didn't know anything; the next minute she'd tell me too many details about one of her dates and if I made a face, I'd hear *Oh, grow up.*

"Oh, Violet," I say mournfully, since maybe a theatrical performance will bring the tears. "I wish I'd been able to say goodbye."

I can't help a glance at Wesley, whose expression is incredulous until he realizes I'm watching him. Then it smooths over, impassive. He's judging me.

"I wanted to call," I sniff. "It's complicated."

He says nothing. He gives up on trying to remove an unmovable floor-to-ceiling wardrobe that has stubbornly decided to fuse to the wall. It's an antique, white with a long oval mirror on the front. He shoots the bulky piece of furniture a glare and I have to admire its tenacity for winning that battle.

Wesley crouches in front of a table, beginning to do something to it with a screwdriver. I'd help, but 1) I don't think he wants me to, and 2) my back, legs, and arms are jelly from lifting and carrying so much junk these past few days. I'm used to hard work, but clearing out a house as big as this is a merciless beast. And we've only got about 3 percent of it cleared away. I'm so daunted by all we have left to do that I wouldn't mind screaming into a decorative pillow if they weren't all so musty. However, I am a Maybell Parrish, and Maybell Parrishes do not give up.

I'm sorting through papers, which are a rabbit hole of Victor and Violet Hannobar history. Deeds and documents, court papers and letters. So many letters.

My mouth curves into a smile when I select one, skimming the top line. It's so old that the paper is nearly transparent. When I hold it up I can see the writing on the back bleed through the front, rendering it all illegible.

"Did she tell you about how she and Victor got together?" I ask casually.

No response.

I glance up to make sure he hasn't left the room, which he hasn't. I frown, lowering the paper. "Are you going to ignore me forever?"

Sweat rolls from his hairline, down his forehead. His gaze lifts briefly to mine, impatient and piercing, before he continues focusing on his task.

It's been too long since I've felt heard by anyone, and I want to talk to somebody about Violet. Nobody else shares my memories of Falling Stars and my amazing great-aunt. I think that about half the people still alive who cared about her (or at least, he might have cared about her) are in this room.

"They dated when they were teenagers, but they went to different schools," I tell him. "Their senior year he broke up with her and she mailed him a *Sorry for your loss* card." It might be in this pile of cards I'm riffling through as I speak, actually. She saved hundreds of them, stacks tied with plaid Christmas ribbon.

"When they reconnected a few years later, he sent her a *Please forgive me* card."

I tug the end of a ribbon, a new stack fanning out across the floor. Jackpot. "In their early twenties, Violet and Victor were officially just friends, but obviously she was still holding a grudge about him dumping her, because she knew he was her soul mate. She knew from day one that Victor was the man for her, but teenage Victor was a little too slick and he wanted to play the field. Also, he didn't see it working out because, you know, he was Black and she was white. Interracial relationships weren't exactly smiled upon, even though their families liked each other."

Wesley, I notice, has been loosening the same screw for two minutes now. He doesn't want to appear like he's listening, but I know I've got an audience.

"Her letters were petty brilliance. *Hello, Victor. Would you be a dear friend and ask Henry if he's single? I'm dying to finally be kissed by someone who knows what he's doing.*"

I read a few aloud, but I have to keep stopping to laugh. Violet bedeviled Victor with recaps of all the dates she was going on with basically every other boy but him, and her signatures were a riot: *The Mighty & Majestic Violet Amelia Parrish, Knower of Her Worth, You'll Wish You Had This, Runner-Up Miss Good-Looking 1953.*

Victor wrote back with fevered desperation, penmanship atrocious to convey his passion, confessing how jealous she'd made him.

"Victor was working at his family's shop in . . . I think Cookeville." I squint. "Yeah. Cookeville. Once a week, Violet got dressed to the nines and flounced past his store, all carefree and stunning, rubbing it in. She'd send him photographs, too, of her posing on the hood of other guys' cars." I cackle. "She really let him have it."

I check on Wesley, whose gaze flickers away. He slowly removes the leg of a table and gets started on another one.

"Victor begged her to go out with him again. She dangled him on her hook for a month, but of course gave in, and eventually they got married on Starr Mountain in the middle of a thunderstorm—secretly, since they weren't legally allowed. The bride wore a ruby-red gown to match her hair." It's the reason I idolize nontraditional wedding dresses and why, if I ever do get married, I want to wear a bright color, too. "No one would rent them a house even when they applied to landlords separately, because everybody knew they were together. Her dad tried to buy a place for them, but the bank wouldn't give him a loan, either, so Victor and Violet had to live with her parents for years. Violet didn't give me a lot of negative details. She put kind of a glossy finish over the story, but by Victor's account they were pretty badly harassed when they lived in Cookeville. When his business made him enough money, they bought the most remote home they could find and got a pack of dogs to guard them. They got a real marriage license in 1967 but always kept their symbolic one up there." I point to the mantel. "It mattered more to them since they'd typed it themselves."

I browse through more letters.

"Dearest Mighty and Majestic Violet Amelia Parrish, Angel Among Mortals, Only Woman for Me: I am begging for another chance. You once called me the man of your dreams. Try to remember that!"

Wesley is looking sterner than ever. This must be the face he makes when he's firmly decided against feeling anything humor-adjacent.

I try another letter. I'll get him to fold.

"Violet, how long are you going to make me suffer? I can't sleep. I don't

eat. Your grandmother thinks you've put a hex on me and I don't care if you did, I just need you to either lift the hex or marry me. Love, your future husband (hopefully)."

He bites his lip.

"My beloved Violet, I saw you at the skating rink with James and my spirit has faded away to almost nothing. Remember that being good at tennis doesn't translate to being superior in other pursuits in the real world and I'm going to be a millionaire someday. Yours most sadly, Victor."

I stop cold at the curious noise that punctuates Victor's plea. "Was that a chuckle?"

Wesley's eyebrows slam together. He doesn't respond.

"Oh, c'mon," I tease. "You're so *serious*." That was definitely a chuckle. Or a mouse.

I don't think he's going to reply. At least a minute passes in silence. But then he ventures, almost reluctantly, "What made her say yes to marrying him?"

"He broke his ankle on a skiing trip, but Violet was told by their scheming mothers that he was dying. She made another boy she was dating drive her up to say her last goodbyes. She took one look at Victor in his hospital bed, right as rain aside from the busted ankle, and said, 'You can propose now.' He tried to get down on one knee, with the cast on. Aunt Violet could never finish telling the story because she'd be laughing so hard." I grin. "It was her favorite story to tell. Uncle Victor loved hearing it." I think he loved hearing it because it made his wife laugh. He was always just so *gone* for her.

I reach for another stack but snatch my hand away. My heart beats fast.

The Lisa Frank stationery. The diligent cursive with hearts dotting the i's.

From: Maybell Parrish
309 Ownby Street
Gatlinburg, TN 37738

There are twelve letters with twelve different return addresses, which, in retrospect, explains why I never got a letter back. I can't believe Mom posted them. She said she did, but I didn't believe her. Not when she hated Violet so much and hated how attached I got to her in such a short period of time. She wouldn't let me call or visit.

I begin to open one of the envelopes but can't complete the process. I stare at the off-yellow strip on the inside flap that a young Maybell licked and sealed, the stickiness long gone. I'm floored she got my letters. When did I send the last one? In my mind, I posted them all the way through my teenage years, but I only see twelve here and they're all from the Lisa Frank set. I rack my memory trying to recall when I stopped writing. All I can recall is that I didn't think it mattered anymore, that she probably never received a single one. I was careful not to say anything negative about Mom or anything negative about my life in general, since Mom was prone to snooping and I'd get in trouble over what she found if she didn't like it.

As I scoop up the letters to return them to their box, the sharp corner of a Polaroid scratches my palm. It's a picture of the manor, with a little girl in front. She's in corduroy skort overalls and a bucket hat, face rosy with sunshine, front teeth a little too big. I want to reach into the picture and give that little girl a hug, because I know why she's smiling so hard. She thinks she's there to stay. She wants her wonderful aunt to adopt her, so she'll never have to leave.

The house behind her is gray.

"I don't understand," I murmur, turning it over to the other side. There's a cursive inscription, but the soft pencil has worn away all but the letter M. "It was pink. Why do I remember it being pink?"

Wesley isn't looking at the photo. His attention is locked on another piece of paper that's tipped out of the stack: an old clipping from the *Daily Times*, dated 1934.

FALL IN LOVE WITH FALLING STARS HOTEL!
By Elizabeth Robin
THE DAILY TIMES

WE HERE AT the *Daily Times* covered the construction of Falling Stars Boarding House in 1884, when the newspaper was only a year old. It's fitting that on the fifty-year anniversary of that article, we're back with the first peek into the mansion's fresh revamp as a luxury hotel. Goodbye, outhouses and candlesticks, hello, twentieth century! The new proprietor has gone modern with an elevator and all-electric

The clipping cuts off after that. To the right, no bigger than two inches, is a black-and-white smudge of a house that I'd know anywhere. A glamorous woman with finger waves and dark lipstick twists her hand in hello under a wrought-iron archway that spells FALLING STARS HOTEL.

"I didn't know it wasn't always just a house," I tell Wesley, stupefied.

"I didn't know there was an elevator. When did it get taken out?"

"No clue." That's so fascinating to envision—an elevator here, in my *house*. "I wonder if it was still a hotel when Victor and Violet bought it. I think they've had this place since the seventies." I keep using the present tense. "Or, they *did* have it."

He doesn't find this as fascinating as I do, evidently. "Weird location for a hotel. Who'd want to come all the way out here?"

"We did."

He glances at me briefly, then scratches his jaw and lines up his screwdrivers in a neat row.

"It's pretty here," I point out. "Lots of hiking trails. Mountains to explore. I haven't checked out all the nearby towns yet, since I've been so busy. Any good restaurants or shopping malls within thirty miles?"

"I hate restaurants and shopping malls," he grumbles.

Jeez. "What *do* you like?"

If his scowl is any hint, Wesley doesn't like that question. It takes him two seconds to disassemble the rest of the table, and after he hauls it outside, he doesn't return.

BY EARLY EVENING, I can't take being in the house by myself anymore. I have to get out. A painful lump that's been rising up my throat since I found my old letters to Violet intensifies when I try to seek refuge in the cabin—her memory lingers there, too. Everywhere I go, a fresh wave of confusion or guilt or heartache follows, or a funny remembrance that sets me off-kilter because how can I laugh when it's all so terribly *sad*, so I decide to pour all of my attention into her dying wishes.

Wish 2. Victor thought there was buried treasure out here but I never did find any. For the intrepid explorer, Finders Keepers rules apply.

"I'm going to go digging," I call out to Wesley, who's sitting in his truck bed with a bowl of macaroni and cheese. I can only assume that the reason he's not eating in the cabin's kitchen is that I was just in there. He's been avoiding me all week. Any time I walk into a room, he finds a reason to leave that room. When I try to make chitchat, I get crickets.

He stiffens with his fork halfway to his mouth. "Digging up what?"

I ignore him. A taste of your own medicine is healthy, now and then. To the garden shed I go! I'm surprised dust doesn't shoot out in all directions when I open the door, since the groundskeeper around here obviously isn't doing much pruning. Imagine being a professional groundskeeper and getting paid to make someone's yard look worse. But inside, I'm surprised to find a tidy space. The door doesn't stick. Someone's been prowling around recently.

Wesley's invested a fortune in insecticide, I'll give him that. Along the dirty plywood walls are propped-up shovels, a million varieties of seeds, shears he doesn't use, weed killer he doesn't use, and a wheelbarrow piled with boxes. Shoeboxes, Amazon boxes, a round hatbox. I'm about to lift the lid of one when a shadow slips across my hands and it's whisked away, over my head. A large body towers behind me.

I duck, letting out an "Aghh!"

An unreadable face scrutinizes me, but says nothing.

I drape a hand over my heart. "How do you keep sneaking up on me like that? Please announce yourself!"

Wesley places the shoebox on a shelf out of reach, followed by the other boxes. His face is tight as his eyes sweep mine, estimating whether putting the boxes out of reach is going to stop me. It is. I'm curious about them now that I know they're off-limits, but scrounging up a stepstool sounds like too much work. Life is short, like me.

"Calm down, I'm only here for a shovel," I explain, barely managing to grab one before Wesley's silently edging me out of the shed without touching me, pushing a rake like a shuffleboard stick at my shoes.

Once we're out, he slams the padlock on the door closed and spins its dial.

I raise my eyebrows. "Seriously?"

His eyes cut away, as though he's bored, and he turns to leave.

"With an attitude like that, I'm not sharing any of the treasure," I call to his receding back. "Unless you want to help? Do you happen to have a metal de—"

I give up. He's heading swiftly back to the cabin, where I hope his macaroni and cheese is cold. A few beats pass. My hands are frustrated little balls at my sides, and it's like being picked on by school bullies again. "I liked you a lot better when you weren't you!" I yell once he's a good distance away. If he hears, he makes no indication.

Thwarted, I survey the overgrown woods and chew my lip. Fine. I always end up doing the lion's share of the work in group projects, anyway.

If I were a ridiculously rich person burying treasure (and you'd have to be ridiculously rich to pack some of it away in a hiding place), I'd bury it at the foot of a tree. I follow a trail into the woods, having barely begun but already tempted to write this off as a lost cause. Nearly three hundred acres of possible hiding places, and I don't even know what I'm looking for. I dig random holes, sweating, the skin on my fingers angry from gripping the handle. I am going about this uneconomically. But if I'm not actively dedicating myself to what Violet wanted me to do, how can I justify accepting the house? I don't deserve it. I haven't written, haven't visited, haven't cried. I don't have the right to be sad, either, since I was so flaky when she was still alive. I ran out the clock.

I use the shovel to make a shallow slice in the earth, then hop on and jump with all my strength. Down we sink, about four inches. Every time I hit a tree root I think I'm going to uncover a treasure chest.

I let the shovel drag the ground as I roam, searching for a big red X that marks the spot. That'd be too easy, of course, and if the treasure were easy to find, Violet and Victor would have found it themselves. I know when I've reached the part of the woods that has always been here when an old, old tree bursts out of the middle of where two paths fork. It's gnarled, bark peeling, draped with moss. In a smooth, whorled eye, a heart has been carved. Within the heart, initials.

I trace the engraving with my thumb: *V + V*. So touching I could melt, lasting evidence of love that's survived them both. What would it be like, to know love like that? To carve my name on someone else's heart? Mine has been dropped and broken a few too many times, held together with sheer, dumb optimism, a few ribs, and maybe magic.

The greenery around me shifts, trees shrinking down to houseplants in colorful planters. Yellow birch and blackberries flatten, becoming one-dimensional patterns on wallpaper. Cicadas change their tune, now a low melody wafting out of the jukebox, and my hands aren't raw and blistering from a shovel but from the spitting oil of a fryer. Between one footstep and the next, I disappear from the woods and rematerialize in my own little world.

"It's not your fault," Jack tells me, springing to my side.

My mind always, always misses its footing and lands on Jack unless I'm carefully, consciously choosing my steps.

I sigh, smoothing my hands over the familiar countertop in my café, the red vinyl booths, the cold window eternally spotted with rain. The thrashing sea of my blood pressure calms, settling into a still, waveless lake.

"Your aunt was in here earlier," he tells me soothingly. "She had to go, but she wanted me to tell you how happy she was to see you yesterday. How much she appreciates your visits."

A musical chime as the door opens, which another dimension might filter as the sound of leaves crunching underfoot as a woman walks through a forest. Who'd want to be her, though, when I can be this Maybell instead? When here I'm equipped with omniscience to kill the unknown in its cradle, and am the architect of every heart and every heart's intention?

I smile gratefully up at Jack, who will always listen, always put me first, never reject or betray me. "Thanks, I needed to hear that."

I serve donuts to friendly customers and chat with the inventor of Check Your References, an app that allows you to rate the accuracy of your exes' online dating profiles. She introduces herself as Gemma and tells me she can't wait to come back tomorrow for more of my wonderful cinnamon twists. I can tell we're going to be great friends.

I stumble over a broken floor tile, which transforms into a twig when I study it closely, and as quickly as I blew into the café, I drop out of it, landing hard on wet dirt and laurel.

In the dark.

"Damn it. Not again."

I dig in my pocket for my phone to check how long this time-slip lasted but come up empty. My phone's back at the cabin. And the cabin is . . .

I turn in a delirious circle, pulse thudding. It is dark and the woods are very, very loud all of a sudden. Only moments ago the only thing I could hear was the intro of a song called "Everywhere," which sounds like wind chimes and feels like opening a well-worn epic fantasy novel. Now I'm being swallowed up in the hoots of barred owls and small, furry footsteps. Bats' wings. An army of undead gem miners eternally seeking out the treasure, possibly.

"It's okay," I tell myself steadily, releasing a low breath that accidentally turns into a whistle. "You can't be too far out. You're still on the trail, so . . ."

I'm standing where the trail diverges in two. If I listen really hard, I think I can hear the universe laughing. Along with more twigs snapping.

This is when I remember the dense black bear population in this neck of Tennessee.

My kneecaps liquefy.

I'm imagining the thud of heavy paws, I try to convince myself, regretting that I seem to have dropped my shovel somewhere and can't use it as a weapon. I'm surely imagining how the sound grows closer. I squeeze my eyes tightly shut, as if that'll rearrange reality to be more to my liking. Taking away one of my senses makes it worse, my hearing sharpening to compensate. I am not imagining the footsteps closing in.

Closer, closer.

I want to run but my arms and legs lock up instead; what a terrible way for me to learn my instincts in the worst-case scenario are all wrong. I'm frozen in place. I'm going to get mauled by a bear and I'll just stand here and let it happen without making so much as a squeak. Even the bear will be confused.

And then there he is.

He gazes down at me, moonlight dusting the curves of his features. Bears don't have wavy blond hair or cotton T-shirts. I'm so happy to see Wesley Koehler that I'd cry and leap at him, if only I could unstick my feet from the ground.

He waits. Watches. I still can't talk, and he chooses not to.

Finally, my voice starts working again. "I've grown roots," I say weakly. He must think I'm a huge baby. I can't deny he'd be right. Tonight I'm sleeping with all the lights on.

Slowly, he holds out his hand, palm up. I examine the pale fingertips from a slight distance, as if this might not be real, but his gesture has a strange effect on my muscles, freeing them. I'm moving before I know it.

I lay my hand over his, which he tugs lightly, reeling me in. Once I'm safely at his side, he lets his hand drop, then motions for me to proceed down one of the trails.

His pace is measured so that I can keep up, the trail just wide enough to accommodate both of us walking side by side. It's full dark now. I dearly hope I am not hallucinating this rescue, which seems like something I would do were I being eaten alive by a bear and decided I'd rather not be present in the moment. Out of the corner of my eye I glance at Wesley, who's staring straight ahead. I don't think my imagination could paint the tension he radiates, though, his awareness of me but refusal to glance my way. Annoyed that he had to stop whatever he was doing and come save me from being killed by elk or falling rocks or a river I didn't see coming.

I don't think my imagination would have the bandwidth, while I was spurting blood like a fountain, to generate realistic details like the small tear in his sleeve, the smear of dirt on his arm, the nick on his jaw from shaving. When my arm accidentally brushes his, I don't think I imagine how his hand clenches. If I were making this up, the least I could do as a gift to myself would be to design a Wesley who smiled at me. And carried a military-grade flashlight.

We still haven't spoken when we emerge from the woods, the tide of trees pushing us out and dumping us right on the cabin's porch. The television is on, subdued voices bumping up against the door. He swings it open. There's a plate on the coffee table with a meal only half-eaten, handle-end of the fork lying in sauce as though dropped in a hurry.

I open my mouth to say *Thank you for finding me, for leading me back*, but Wesley doesn't grant me the opportunity. He yanks the cord for the pull-down ladder and climbs up to his bedroom. Only when I'm directly behind him do I notice the back of his shirt, which reads KOEHLER LANDSCAPING, fabric darker from saturation. His nape glistens. It's cool enough outside that the tip of my nose is numb and my teeth are chattering, but Wesley, not even wearing a jacket, is drenched in sweat.

THAT NIGHT I DREAM in black and white. I open the cabin's front door to find that all the trees are gone, only gently sloping hills and prairie smoke flowers everywhere, everywhere, as far as the eye can see. They slant over and under one another in the breeze, each monochrome tuft a happy wave hello. The manor soars larger than life, laced up with climbing roses rather than creeper vines. There's a wrought-iron archway in front—FALLING STARS HOTEL—and beneath, in vivid color, Wesley waits for me with an unreadable expression, hand outstretched.

I sit up straight in bed.

Chapter 7

KNOW WHAT WE SHOULD do with Falling Stars."

"Animal sanctuary," Wesley replies mechanically, sipping his coffee. I've sneak-attacked him in the kitchen at seven a.m., an hour before I usually get out of bed. I don't want to think he intentionally gets up an hour before I do to avoid bumping into me, but my skeptical side has its third eye narrowed.

He observes the donuts curiously, which I baked in the midst of a planning frenzy at four in the morning specifically for the purpose of buttering him up. He reaches for the plate.

I open my mouth and a single word pops on my tongue like a bubble. "Hotel."

He retracts his hand. I watch his guard rise like defenses around a castle. I am full of similes when I haven't had much sleep.

"You know?" I'm already botching this. "I want to make the house a hotel again, like it was in that newspaper you found."

"I didn't find that newspaper, you did."

I'm trying to make this his idea, so that he'll be more receptive to it. It requires logic gymnastics. I stack my fingers together on the tabletop like my imaginary businesslady BFF. "Falling Stars Hotel, two point oh. It's the perfect idea."

"A hotel," he repeats.

"Yes."

Our stares lock, and it's unsettling how much his attention weighs when he decides to pin me with it instead of looking right past me like he generally does. He has long eyelashes, brown at the root and fair at the tips. The freckles on his cheeks, the gold locks of hair curling every which way above thick, stern eyebrows—the effects of each detail pool into an exceedingly distracting portrait that will derail me if I don't fight hard against the current.

"No," he says, devoid of emotion. Wesley does not need or care to be liked at all; I doubt my opinion could touch him. Those who care less always have the upper hand.

I've only ever wanted to be liked, and I've only ever wanted to be liked by absolutely everybody I come in contact with, however temporarily and inconsequentially. It's my most dominant and simultaneously weakening driving force, which leads to my toning down various wants and needs in order to make myself digestible, easy to get along with. The essence of Maybell Parrish is painfully sensitive, and if you touched it, it would retract and try to surrender. For better or worse (and I've certainly tried to be anyone but myself), I am a wobbly white flag.

No. Just like that.

My natural reaction is to say okay and pack myself up nice and small and out of the way, too unobtrusive to be a bother ever again. But even though my idea is only a few hours old, it is burning up in me like a fire demon. I *want* it. Nobody can make it happen for me but myself.

I lean forward, matching his determination. It surprises us both. "Yes."

"You're suggesting that instead of living in the house myself, I let a bunch of strangers sleep in it. There is no possible way you can convince me to agree to that."

"Let me try."

He welcomes the dare, gesturing for me to go right ahead. I'm abruptly jittery—he doesn't realize how much voltage it took for me to push back and I'm crackling now with an excess of electrical energy my body isn't used to supplying; I have to grip the seat of my chair to keep from jumping out if it. I can play it cool.

The sales pitch I've spent the morning rehearsing is dust in the wind. My mind is a wide white void.

"I really, really, really want it," I plead, throat scratchy.

I watch my flow of power redirect in midair. Wesley leans back in his chair, crossing his impressive, tanned arms, siphoning it off. My brain blinks. *Forearms.*

Shh, I scold myself. *Not now.*

"Do you know what kind of an undertaking this would be?" he inquires placidly.

I have found myself in a job interview without warning. The most important interview of my life. I am wearing a Sonny & Cher shirt with a broken zipper and there's a streak of flour in my hair. I should have an overhead projector beaming pie charts onto the wall and more than five hours of sleep on deck.

"Actually, yes. I have experience in the hospitality industry."

A modicum of my power changes hands, passing back to me. "I was an event coordinator at a hotel. One of the biggest hotels in Pigeon Forge, Around the Mountain Resort and Spa." He can't deny that I definitely worked there. No one alive has more Around the Mountain Resort & Spa merchandise than I do. It's all I have to show for a decade of hard work, along with a text message from Paul that landed half an hour ago: You're fired. I've been expecting it. I'm surprised it took him this long to swing the axe, actually. But I'm a Goody Two-shoes to the core, priding myself on my strong work ethic, and reading that message threw me into a cold sweat. I'm still keyed up over it, stomach playing badminton with my breakfast.

Wesley acquires a calculating look, rubbing his chin. "What kind of events did you coordinate?"

Ahhhhhhhh. A fine question. I am fine with this fine question.

I flash a winsome grin to conceal how badly I need him to say yes. "All sorts. I planned an indoor fall festival in September. Very large-scale." It's technically true. I did plan a fall festival, with the works: Scarecrows, fog machines, hot chocolate and cider. A booth where you can bob for apples and then decorate them with chocolate, caramel, and candy. Hayrides. Halloween-costume and pumpkin-carving contests. Cozy, family-oriented activities appealing to all age demographics. It took me two sleepless weeks to crunch budget numbers, reach out to local vendors who might contribute supplies, and put together a seamless proposal. Haggling for discounts, bargaining, exhaustion slumping me over the keyboard, discovering I was more likely to persuade contacts over email than by phone, especially if I changed my signature to the gender-ambiguous M. Parrish.

The project didn't clear the first hurdle, which was getting a sign-off from Christine, my co-coordinator. I cried in my car during lunch break and loathed myself for it. Mean Christine has probably never cried when somebody told her no. She probably just jammed a nail in their tire and then felt better.

With my own hotel, I can green-light any project I want. No overhead management to tell me my ideas are too big or impractical, that I'm being idealistic or missing the forest for the trees . . . I snap off that dark trail of thought, the condescending internal voices that bubble up.

"Okay, so you do have some experience, then," Wesley concedes grudgingly.

"Mm-hmm!" Lying doesn't come easily to me or sit well with my conscience, so I hope I sound suitably innocent.

I prod the plate of donuts closer to Wesley, my resolve ironclad. He'll be more congenial on a full stomach, and no one can be grumpy when they're eating jelly-filled donuts. It's biology.

He takes one. Polishes it off in three swallows. "That's good."

It ought to be, with all the blood, sweat, and tears I've put into mastering the recipe. "Baking donuts is a hobby of mine. They're almost as delicious as Violet's, I think." I feel myself starting to glow with pride and take it down a notch. People call women who brag about their accomplishments *unlikable*. "Hers were legendary."

"Violet used to bake?"

His gaze slides to the purple sheet of paper taped to the living room wall, then back to me. There's a strange glint in his eye.

"She loved to bake." I can't believe he doesn't know. "She never made donuts when you lived with her?"

He shakes his head. Taps the back of his hand. "Arthritis made it difficult for her to do anything in the kitchen. I did all the cooking, except when I was away on a job, and then Ruth helped out."

"Oh." A little sliver of my heart chips away.

"She liked to watch baking shows on TV, though," he adds thoughtfully. "The holiday ones on Food Network were her favorite."

I realize he's sidetracked me from my hotel pitch, and come at him from another angle. I am a confident, capable event coordinator. I deserve this promotion to hotel manager after all the hard work I haven't been allowed to do. "The hotel will be a reliable source of income," I point out. "Keep in mind that Violet isn't here to pay your salary anymore."

"I make a decent income doing landscaping for businesses. Violet hasn't paid me in half a year, thanks to QVC, Home Shopping Network, and the catalogs they kept sending. I don't have many enemies, but if I ever meet Lori Greiner . . ." His face clouds.

Oof.

"Well. Just think of all the money you'll save on gas if you don't have to do all those landscaping jobs. From here on out, it's only the easy streets for you. No effort, no involvement required with the hotel. Simply live your life and rake in a percentage of the profits." I'm offering him a kingdom here and he doesn't even appreciate it.

"I enjoy those jobs. Like the golf place one?" He takes a casual sip of coffee. "With that woman, Gemma, who's the reason you have a picture of me at my brother's wedding on your phone. The *why* of which you still haven't shared."

I flush, praying to all the Norse gods and a few Greek ones to shield him from reading my mind.

"I haven't forgotten that," he finishes impassively.

I do a flawless impersonation of Wesley by opting to ignore what he said. "By the way, I wanted to say thank you for finding me last night." I bestow upon him my best damsel-in-distress smile. "Saved me from being eaten by Bigfoot."

"Sasquatch inhabits the Pacific Northwest and eats a vegetarian diet," he replies mildly. "Like me."

I.

What.

"What?"

"I'm a vegetarian," he responds in the voice of a patient kindergarten teacher. And then this man helps himself to another donut. Is he trolling me? I think I'm being trolled, but I can't tell. My Myers-Briggs personality type is INFP. We give too many people the benefit of the doubt.

"Anyway," he continues, "you're welcome. But please don't make it a habit. I don't want to attract bears to the house by having food wandering around out there."

"I'm food?"

"You will be if you keep getting lost in the woods. That's their home out there, not ours."

How does he keep rerouting this conversation? "It's a big house. There's plenty of living space for us along with the guests."

"I'll never agree to it."

"I'll never agree to the farm animal sanctuary, then."

Checkmate. He arches a brow, jaw tensing.

"I know you haven't factored my opinion into your plans," I go on, watching in real time as he reckons with my unavoidable influence over his life goals, "but I'm co-inheritor, buddy. Your personal remake of *Charlotte's Web* isn't happening without my consent."

"These . . ." He sounds strangled. "This isn't comparable." Wesley and I are both leaning forward now, nearly nose to nose. A crumpled napkin peeks from his fist. "You want a hotel, which means *people* in my *living space*." He doesn't hide the pure revulsion such a scenario inspires. "An animal sanctuary won't affect you at all. They'll be living outside."

"I'll have to smell it."

He casts a withering look up at the ceiling, grinding his molars.

Maybe I'm playing dirty, but it isn't fair that he gets to make all the decisions. "Fine. The hotel won't affect you, either. There's enough room on the first floor for plenty of guest rooms, which we've agreed is *my* floor. You'll get to keep the second floor to yourself and be as people-hating as you please."

He leans back again, mouth turning down at the corners. He's trying to figure out how to argue this, but he also doesn't want me interfering with his dream of filling our yard with geriatric goats. This must be what shady blackmail dealings in white-collar offices feel like.

"So you'd be turning the sunroom into a bedroom," he says shrewdly.

"I don't know. Probably."

The frown intensifies, like he's trying to solve a tricky math equation. I'd laugh if there weren't so much at stake. "I want the sunroom."

"Why?"

"Because I want it."

Leverage! I love leverage. "I'll give you the sunroom for the cabin."

Wesley balks. "Why?"

I could do tons of things with this cabin. If I hire another manager, they could live in it. Or I could use it for a bridal suite, since Falling Stars would make an amazing wedding venue. But if I tell Wesley I want to throw weddings at his house, he might flip the table.

"Because I want it," I reply evenly. His lips press together. I mimic him, sensing I am close to a resolution here, close to winning.

He tries to silent-treatment me into giving up. It almost works, but my discomfort with long silences prompts me to react strangely and I throw both of us off by giving him a wink.

He stares at me, wide eyed, like I've grown another head. "What the hell was that?"

"A wink?"

"Winking is weird."

"You're weird."

"That's a bizarre thing to do, shutting your eye at someone."

I shrug. "It can be kinda hot, I think."

Wesley is visibly uncomfortable, but the wink is effective. "Fine, you've got a deal. I get the animal sanctuary, you get your hotel. Which is a terrible idea, by the way." He's already getting up and leaving.

"Is not!" I sing at his retreating back, counting the donuts remaining. He ate three. I'm taking that as another win.

IT'S THREE DAYS AFTER we struck a deal and we haven't agreed on a single thing since. Also, the manor is trying to kill me. All I want to do is love it, and it responds by raining plaster over me and moving the broom and dustpan so that they're never where I last put them. Every time I open a window to get rid of the thick dust-and-lemon-Pledge cloud that hangs at nose level, I hear a rattle and glance over to watch the sash juddering back down. I've had two pairs of rubber gloves disintegrate on me somehow, but luckily the hoard replenishes itself and more pairs of gloves reappear on the living room mantel. Along with a bottle of ointment, which has helped heal the blisters that stupid shovel gave my fingers.

Wesley is going room by room upstairs and getting rid of broken stuff first, or stuff that's rusted, expired, ruined from water damage, etc. After the obvious trash is dealt with, he sorts through whatever's left. I, however, choose to tackle the hoard all at once, which results in a million piles whose purposes prove difficult to keep straight. We keep ramming into each other at the front door and in the yard, arms too full, each refusing to offer the other one assistance if an item is dropped. I rubberneck at whatever he tosses in the dumpster, but if I pick through his half of the house in addition to mine, this clean-out is going to take years.

Whenever I brush past Wesley, the image of him beneath the iron archway in my dream flickers to life, those eyes probing mine like I might offer the answer to a long-held question, or I remember him in the dark woods beside me, a solid protector, and it's annoying. I don't want to associate soft feelings with this person who scowls at me all day.

"What do you want the sunroom for?" I can't resist asking at one point, as we're passing each other in the foyer.

"Why's my picture on your phone?" he shoots back so quickly, he had to have been already thinking about it.

I grumble as I skulk away and he takes off up the stairs. I am incredibly glad I called dibs on the first floor, because I can't imagine what running up and down the grand staircase is doing to his calves.

Actually . . .

I try to steal a glimpse, but he's too fast for me.

The next time we bump into each other, it's because he's got a busted armoire and can't fit it through the door. I could help, but he didn't help *me* when I was trying to roll up a rug and he watched me wrestle with it. So I lean against the wall and cross my ankles, observing.

"Hmm. Having some trouble there, partner?"

He grunts, shoving harder.

"Please do take care not to scratch the door frame."

He rolls his eyes. "Why not? We need a new door frame, anyway."

"Okay, well. If you scratch it, you'll be responsible for putting the new one on." I don't know why I'm feeling particularly argumentative today.

"Try worrying about yourself," he suggests. "You're going about this so inefficiently, it hurts."

"I'm being *thorough*. What would Violet say if she saw you treating her belongings like this? So callous."

I think the reminder of Violet is going to stick him where it hurts, but he doesn't care. "I informed her myself of exactly what I was going to do with her belongings. I told her several times, after she told me I'd inherit it all. At any rate, I don't see her here. She doesn't have to deal with this mess. We do." I notice how he glances furtively up at the ceiling, as if the ghost of Violet Hannobar might be bobbing around up there, keeping an eye on us. Maybe she's the one who tripped him on the stairs earlier when I hollered up that I'd discovered his little secret (it was the remnants of a bacon sandwich, to which he'd sputtered, red faced, that it was vegetarian bacon; I took a bite and spat it back out, confirming he was telling the truth).

He's taking forever with the armoire. He has to stop for a break at intervals, sweat rolling down his ruddy complexion, flecking his shirt. "Need some help?" I ask. I'm an angel.

"No."

Lord, he's stubborn. "I wasn't going to help, anyway."

"I know. Can't wait to see you try to drag the pool table out of the billiard room by yourself."

I point my nose higher in the air. It was already up in the air to begin with, because I have to yank my head all the way back to look him in the eye (it's rude that he won't at least slouch), but I've got to make myself as big as I can. An equal voice. "I'm keeping the pool table."

"Yeah? Along with all the pets you've got living in it?"

"What pets—" I scrunch my nose when understanding dawns, and he almost grins—I can see one forming, but he tamps it down.

The armoire door swings open, trash skidding out.

"Oh!" I exclaim, bending to pick up a box. "Hey, I've seen these on commercials!" I dig a wire head-scratcher out of its packaging and inspect the thing. It looks like a broken whisk, but if I fit the prongs over my scalp, it's . . . "*Ooooh*, that feels nice." Wesley watches in bemusement as my hair becomes a tumbleweed.

"That's from the second floor," he tells me, "which puts it under my jurisdiction. You can't have my trash."

My inner raccoon sulks. "You can't use my kitchen, then."

"There's a kitchenette upstairs. It's in better condition than yours, actually."

I press down on the armoire to make it heavier. He twists away from me, and it's just the right angle to finally squeeze them both out the door. "Thanks!" he chirps. I make a truly ugly face at him, and it happens again: that almost-smile. He fights it and wins. I think he's under a curse—if he laughs, he'll die. This is a sensible explanation to me. It isn't that I'm not a joy to be around, it's that he'll literally die.

Chapter 8

MAYBELL'S COFFEE SHOP AU has a musty odor to it, and there are a few trash bags building up along the wall.

"What's going on in here?" Jack asks, waltzing over.

"I'm renovating."

He nods, skimming the café. "Looks bigger."

"I let out the seams of the walls to give us a few extra feet. I'm thinking about adding a hotel to the café. What do you think?"

"I think that's the best idea I've ever heard in my entire life." He brushes a strand of hair out of my face. "But I'm not surprised. Your ideas consistently amaze me." His voice drops an octave. "So when are you going to let me take you to Venice on my private jet, you beautiful genius?"

I sigh. For whatever reason, Jack just isn't doing it for me today. I'm finding his presence grating. "Rain check?" I propose, and his hopeful smile crumbles. He's devastated, of course. Jack's been chasing me for months.

The red light on the rotary phone flashes: *IRL Calling*.

"Anyway, life's pretty hectic right now," I tell him, swiveling to check on the batch of apple fritters in the oven. "Let's try this again another—" Oh, that stupid red light won't stop flashing.

I send the call to voicemail. "Maybell!" an aggravated voice blares through the speakers.

"Raghh, I was just about to leave, anyway! Give me a minute to wrap this up—goddamn it!" I've burned my apple fritters. Here! In my magical coffee shop where nothing ever burns! I whirl again and wipe away the café with a swish of my hand. Wesley's knocking on my bedroom door.

"Are you in there?" he asks. Rudely.

I bolt out of bed, too fast, giving myself fuzzy brain static. Every time I'm interrupted mid-daydream, it's an embarrassing reminder that I've once again lost touch with reality. I become irritable. "What?" I yell back.

"Sorry to bother you." His tone is *testy*. If I ever need a rather large stick, I'll know exactly where to find one. "The dumpster guys are going to be here in thirty minutes to pick up their containers, so we have to make sure we've got the house cleared out as much as possible."

"I've got my half cleared."

"Are you sure? It looks like there's plenty of trash left."

I open the door. Wesley backs up two steps. "That's not trash," I reply nicely. "It's all stuff I can keep or donate."

"That reddish-purple sofa's seen better days. I mean, there are springs coming out and . . ." He trails off as his gaze zeroes in on my chest. Or not my chest, but my necklace. My blood can't tell the difference and rises to the surface, splotching the area in question.

I'm wearing Violet's pendant, which I found under my bed

along with a dust bunny and a colored pencil. It's stamped with the number *51* to commemorate either Violet's fifty-first birthday or her fifty-first wedding anniversary, and I rummaged up a chain for it so that I can keep something precious of Violet's close to my heart.

I watch the muscles in Wesley's face go lax, the raw grief he exposes for only a second before sending it back into hiding.

"Anyway." He clears his throat. "Thirty minutes." His eyes drag down my outfit. "Not too late to add more to the dumpster."

Message received, and unheeded. I'm wearing gems from my hoard haul: cowboy boots, a turquoise bolo tie, a rhinestone peasant top, and gold culottes. I can't imagine wasting all these interesting statement pieces. Everything I've ever heard about fashion sense is wrong. Less isn't more; more is more. "What?" I say sweetly, adding a sun hat with cherries and a veil to my ensemble. "I *told* you these clothes were still useful. And you said nobody would ever wear them. Pah!"

He winces. "It hurts to look at you."

"You made me burn my apple fritters, so we're even."

"When did I do that?" He perks up, sniffing the air. "You made apple fritters?"

"Here." I hand him the hat. He eyes it like I'm offering a dead skunk, not taking it from my hands. I try to put it on his head, but he's too tall. I play a game of horseshoes, which one of us finds very amusing.

It lands on his head after seven tries. "Need to get a picture of this." I dig out my phone.

"Another one for the collection?" He isn't being mean, I think, but he does take the hat off and pushes my phone away. "I don't like having my picture taken."

"Why not?"

"Just don't."

"Are you in witness protection?"

He shakes his head, walking away. It's been less than three minutes and he's already done with me. "Why is that where your head goes?"

I follow him to the house, trying to catch up but never quite able to match his pace. It's like he's trying to escape or something. All the more evidence that he's in witness protection.

I pounce on him in the kitchen, which is starting to resemble a kitchen again. Wesley's only half-hidden by boxes and storage tubs, 80 percent of which are filled with plastic ladles and spatulas. I don't have the heart to get rid of good ladles and spatulas. Or the salmon dish towels, which are a little bit moth-eaten but could still be useful if I ever need to clean grease off the bottom of my car. And a few broken cups, which I can give a second life to with a craft project of some sort. I'll get into the world of mosaic-making.

"What's that?" I poke at his thermos of sweet tea.

"Poison," he mutters. "So don't drink it."

"I'm not going to drink your tea. Imagine that: me putting my mouth on somebody else's thermos." I glance at the lid and imagine it. "Chill out."

"If you knew it was tea, why'd you ask?" He turns to lean against the counter. The window above the sink is right behind him, transforming whatever's written on his face into an indecipherable silhouette.

"There's nobody else around here to talk to. I don't know how you can be so quiet all the time, unless you're arguing. You're the most argumentative and the least talkative roommate ever."

He doesn't reply, face tilting up. I think he's underlining my point. And surveying me, it feels. My skin goes hot and itchy.

I don't like loaded silences. When someone is quiet I tend to assume they're thinking unpleasant things about me, so I have to stem that flow by distracting them with conversation. Conversation proving I am an all-around great person and definite friendship material. "I don't know anything about you, really," I ramble. "Which is weird, don't you think? If we're going to be living together for . . ." I haven't considered how long we might be living together. If neither of us ever wants to give up Falling Stars, we could be puttering around the estate together as geezers. He's already grumpy as a young man—I can't imagine what kind of sunshine his nineties have in store for us.

Still no reply.

"Silent treatment again?" I shift into a defensive pose, arms crossed. "Very mature." I think he knows that lounging in front of the window turns his face to shadow, all the light hitting me and lighting me up instead. Vulnerability and uncertainty creep in.

"You should see what your face looks like," he muses after a spell. His voice sounds different. Smokier. The volume hasn't changed but the words register in my ears as coming from point-blank range; we're not close at all and yet we could be standing in a tight closet, his mouth right above my ear. A shiver rolls down my spine. I hate to think what my face looks like *now*.

I have no response to this, so I stomp off. I could be wrong, but I'm pretty sure I hear a dark laugh curling after me.

I'M STARVED FOR HUMAN attention and Wesley's the opposite of a warm friend, so I call my mother. When she doesn't answer,

I find Ruth's phone number on Violet's calendar, which still clings to the fridge in the cabin. The box for April twenty-eighth is scrawled with unsteady writing that unintentionally carries into the twenty-ninth: *Dr. Porter 1:45.*

I wonder if anyone's canceled Violet's appointment with Dr. Porter. It's unnerving to think about her standing here marking the calendar with April plans that will never come to fruition.

"Hi, this is Maybell," I practice while the phone's still ringing. "I'm calling to check in!" I don't know why I'd check in with the home health aide of my dead aunt, or if she'd care, but it's too late now.

She doesn't pick up. I'm both relieved and disappointed.

I poke around drawers and cabinets in the cabin. Fold my laundry. Tweak the arrangement of hoard baubles on a shelf in my room. It was ludicrous of Wesley to think we should throw out the snow globes that lost their water—they look like magic crystal balls now.

I pick up an old note I brought with me when I moved here: it's from Violet, one of her rare responses to my holiday cards. *I'm so happy to hear from you! I hope you enjoy your holidays and are doing well. Love, Violet.* This note proves I wasn't a total letdown. She still loved me. Or maybe she was just saying that . . . maybe she was just being nice . . . except she left me the house, so she probably did love me . . . except she left it to Wesley, too . . .

I'm still carrying the note around, lost in my daydreams, when Wesley's voice blooms unexpectedly over my shoulder and I scream. "Aghhh!"

He jolts back. "Jesus."

"Stop sneaking up on me! For the love of god!"

"I'm not! I've been standing here for like five minutes. How did you not hear the microwave beeping?"

I'm in the kitchen, evidently. Wesley's eating leftover DiGiorno, shoveling it into his mouth while it's still steaming.

"Oh."

He jerks his head at my note. "All I was saying was that I wrote that."

"You what?" I flip the note over, as if there might be a second one on the back.

"I wrote that on Violet's behalf. I remember assuming it was for one of Violet's old-lady friends, because of the name Maybell." He shrugs.

"What's wrong with the name Maybell?"

"Never said there was anything wrong with it," he replies lightly. "Anyway, got a couple moving trucks coming to haul furniture and big-ticket items away to auction. Violet was a packrat, but lucky for us she had some good stuff hidden here and there. The jewelry should go for a high price, especially, and if we're thrifty we might be able to use all that money to fund renovations."

"I'm going to advertise an estate sale," I inform him. "For the items that you thought were too inconsequential to take to auction in Maryville." I try not to come off as accusatory, but it's a sore subject. I get the feeling Wesley wages an eternal battle between needing to be the wallpaper and having to be the centerpiece. He takes charge in situations even when he doesn't want to and I do. Let me be the centerpiece! I'd love the opportunity to shine. "There's so many products still in their boxes, brand-new, that it's stupid to not try to sell them."

"Here?" The pizza he's holding up goes sideways, a mushroom sliding off. "An estate sale here?"

"Yes." I can't resist. "Your expression. It's like if a person could be crispy."

"Crispy?" He makes a face.

"*There's* your other expression. You have two of them. One is crispy and the other is sour milk." I point, grinning. "Wait. That's a new one. *Mystified.*"

It's like he waves a wand over his face, how rapidly it goes blank. "Your expression is—" he begins, then clams up.

"Go on," I dare him.

"Never mind." His cheeks are turning pink. Not mystified, not sour milk, not crispy. One might almost think Wesley Koehler has become embarrassed.

It makes me want to poke the bear. "What were you going to say?"

"Nothing."

He stomps off, and I laugh. He stomps harder.

It's all fun and games until he tracks me down after the trash has been hauled away, tossing me rubber gloves and a mop. "Hope you don't mind getting your hands dirty, miss big-shot event coordinator."

I'm stretched out lazily in an empty claw-foot bathtub that inexplicably sits in the center of the ballroom, reading the smutty parts of one of Violet's old Harlequins. He glances at the cover and a muscle in his cheek jumps.

"I've been getting my hands dirty since I got here," I retort dryly. "You aren't the only one who's made a few trips to the dumpster, sir."

But I don't think I've appreciated the irony until now, easing the gloves over my fingers, that I'm being forced into taking up the housekeeper role again. I wish we had the budget to hire a professional cleaning crew, but we've got to save money wherever possible and that means fumigating, painting, scrubbing, bleaching, patching, all by ourselves. My gaze darts to the ceiling corners, where Violet might be watching us and, it can only be assumed, laughing wickedly. I am starting to visualize her with horns instead of a halo.

"Don't mix chemicals. Make sure to keep the windows open while you clean. If you pass out, it'll take an ambulance half an hour to get here."

"Thanks, man." I give him the thumbs-up, but my gloves are too long, so it just looks like I'm holding out my hand at an odd angle. "I'm aware that mixing chemicals is a no-no, but it's good to know if I pass out you won't even drive me to the hospital."

"You're the one who pointed out I could be saving money on gas," he replies, leaving me to single-handedly fix up the first floor. It isn't fair. He's going to get his floor done so much faster, since he's got all those muscles to help out. I think his workout regimen involves deadlifting logs.

You know what sucks? Not having the electricity turned on yet. If I could run a vacuum hose along the baseboards it would save my back from having to stoop and scoop debris into a dustpan every five seconds. I think a cat's been living in here, too, because whenever I work the broom I see little cat hairs floating away from me, *refusing* to be dustpanned. The walls in the west wing aren't that bad, but they do bear plenty of scuff marks. If I can rub those off, that'll save me a paint job.

I run to the bottom of the staircase and scream up: "Have you seen the Magic Erasers?"

At first, I think he's ignoring me. But then a heavy object clatters between the floors, between the walls. I open the broken dumbwaiter in the foyer to find a chunk of brick that sloughed off the chimney, a piece of paper taped to its front. *NO*. In aggressive capitals.

"You couldn't have just yelled that?" I holler up the metal chute. "This required more work than saying no!"

I close the door and a minute later the dumbwaiter rattles again. I pull out a remote control for a toy airplane. The message taped to this one reads: *will you bring me the lysol wipes*

This man's unbelievably stingy with his decibels and he's got to have the best-preserved vocal cords ever. When he's a hundred years old he'll be able to sing like the Mormon Tabernacle Choir.

Grumbling, I grab the wipes from the kitchen, which is operating as our home base for cleaning supplies, and run them up the stairs.

"Down here," he calls from the end of a hallway on my right, sticking his hand out a door to wave. I don't make front-door deliveries. I chuck the wipes like a football right as he emerges, which means the package hits him in the neck. "Ow!"

"Sorry."

"What'd you do that for?"

"I said sorry! Why didn't you just go get them yourself?"

He frowns and rolls his shoulder, which in my opinion is a little dramatic. I didn't hit his shoulder. "My legs are tired."

"So are mine!" They aren't, truthfully, but my arms and back are, so I want credit.

"You're not the one going up and down stairs all day."

"If you let me have a few rooms on this floor for my guests, I'll be your errand girl," I offer. "You'll never have to come downstairs again."

He tuts. "Not a chance."

This is when my attention homes in on the pile of used-up Magic Erasers in the room he just vacated. They're sitting in front of an ornate ivory wardrobe that matches one I've got downstairs, its built-in oval mirror reflecting my fury. "You *liar*."

Wesley follows my line of sight. "Oh, *those* Magic Erasers. Sorry. I just used the last one."

I seize the Lysol wipes from his hands and throw them down the dumbwaiter.

He has the nerve to go, "I didn't really want them anyway," at my back as I march off, stomping hard enough to rain more plaster below onto floors I just swept.

THE COMMUNAL MOOD IN Falling Stars spikes in temperature from rankled to downright irate when we decide to work right through lunch and dinner, subsisting on Violet's expired pretzels and Wesley's sweet tea, which he doesn't know he's sharing.

Night's falling, but I don't want to be the first one to give up. I've stolen a few peeks and I know he's got four rooms upstairs totally spotless. But what's the point of a billion rooms if you aren't going to hold on to any furniture to put in them? It's freaky empty up there. Even your thoughts would echo.

"We'll have to get the electricity turned back on again," Wesley shares when he finally lumbers downstairs for the last time. I know he's finished for the day because he's brought all his trash bags down with him. They reek powerfully of bleach, which knocks me back in time to Around the Mountain and its persistent chlorine smell.

Thank god this day is over. I drop my extendable feather duster, sagging along a wall.

"After the auction and estate sale, I hope we'll have enough money left over to dig a pool," I muse aloud.

A choked laugh bursts from Wesley's throat. "We'll be lucky if we make enough to cover all the costs for new flooring, new windows, new pipes, new drywall—the only pool you can afford is one of those round plastic kiddie ones from the dollar store."

"Pessimist."

"One of us has to be realistic."

"I get it," I groan. "You're Mr. Reality Man and you have no tolerance for good vibes or whimsy, but you know, dude, you're really starting to bum me out."

"Mr. Reality Man? What kind of superhero lottery did I lose? And for your limited information, you aren't the only one who wants this place to succeed in some capacity." As an animal sanctuary. Which will not, by the way, turn a profit. How am *I* the impractical one here?

He continues to tally up costs. An electrician. New insulation, which he tells me will save us money on heating and cooling in the long run, which I already knew. Mansplainer. I suggest solar panels and he's visibly jealous he didn't think of it first. "Should fix that dumbwaiter," he mentions. I want to crack a joke using the word *dumb* but I'm too tired.

"We'll need to hire a real landscaper," I say, adding to the list.

"*I'm* a real landscaper."

The waist-high grass twenty feet from Falling Stars doubles over in laughter. "Are you, though? The grounds are a mess."

"It's an ecosystem."

Lazy justification for a mess. "When *I* stayed here," I reply airily, and he's heard me begin enough sentences this way that he's already rolling his eyes, "the yard was immaculate. Neat hedges.

Short grass. There were violets and roses and all sorts of beautiful flowers that you could actually see, not covered up by weeds."

"Those aren't weeds." He gestures to the wall, as if I have X-ray vision and can view what lies outside. "That's Cain's reedgrass. Smoky Mountain manna grass."

"Well, it looks awful."

"Ugh. I can't—you are just—" He shoves a hand through his hair. At the rate he's doing that, he's going to end the week with bald patches.

"What? It does. Don't you know anything about gardening? You want to get plants that are pleasant to look at. Tulips. Snapdragons. I'll send you a link."

"Violet specifically instructed me to grow those plants in large quantities because they're endangered species, along with Virginia meadowsweet and spreading avens and Blue Ridge catchfly, because conservation is more important than the useless aesthetics of neat hedges. I'll send *you* a link."

"Oh." I stand tall, but I don't feel it.

Wesley takes all the height I've just given up and adds it to his own, towering over me. "Nature conservation was important to Violet. I don't know if it was when *you* stayed here, but she hired me after she heard about the diminishing numbers of Fraser fir and ginseng being poached from the parks. She felt it was her responsibility, with considerable acreage at her disposal, to replenish what humans have destroyed." He's getting all worked up over this. "Is it pretty? Not necessarily. Sometimes chaos serves a larger purpose."

"But you want to raze it, you said. For your pig nursing home."

"First of all, this is not the first time you've mentioned pigs," he tells me, vehement. "When did I ever say pigs? Not that I'm not

going to get pigs, but you keep going back to that one animal—"
He waves a hand. "Never mind! I'm not razing all of it, just a few
acres, and none of the endangered plants. Some of the property is
wild but can be altered without hurting the environment."

"So . . . some of the property is simply neglected, you mean."

"You think that's neglect?" He angles his head, facial muscles
clenching, and takes a stride toward me, then another, getting up
close in my personal space. Oh, wow. When his eyes flash like
that, they don't remind me of root beer or bronze coins. They're
daggers glinting in starlight. He's never invaded my personal
space before, as if I am an ogre to be shied from, so I must have
really touched a nerve. "You have no idea how much work I've put
into that land. Weeding out invasive species and adding flowers to
attract endangered birds. Over a hundred boxes put up for native
pollinator bees. There's a method to the madness."

I don't have anything intelligent to say. "Okay, but it still
doesn't look good."

If I could read auras, I think Wesley's would be black as the
night sky right now. His wild stare fixes on me for a tick too long,
which sends my nervous system spiraling; my automatic reaction
is to smile, and he definitely takes it the wrong way. He stalks off
and doesn't speak to me for days.

Chapter 9

WISH 3. MAYBELL, DEAR, *I'd be thrilled if you painted a mural in the ballroom.*

Wesley was right: there isn't going to be enough money in the budget for an in-ground pool. I'm gratified, however, to report that the estate sale netted a nice chunk of change. Which Wesley didn't help with. At all. He hid up in his bedroom the whole time and wouldn't come down even when I tried to tempt him with vegetarian hamburgers, because he thought it was a trap. (It was. I needed help lifting a chair into the back of a teenage girl's truck, but he saw us struggling from his window and came out to help. He made up for the moment of niceness by glaring excessively.)

If I can't offer my guests a refreshing swim in a pool, they can at least stand in the ballroom and marvel at my giant painting of a waterfall lagoon.

I'm having trouble making the paint do what I want with it; it's dripping down the wainscoting instead of staying put. I try to blend colors à la Bob Ross and they're too faint, more like the memory of color than true pigment. My trees are pale green blobs. I can't get the branches to distinguish themselves, so I add black for definition and end up with bigger blobs. I've got enormous, washed-out black blobs on either side of a blue smear that's supposed to be a waterfall.

"What do you think?" I ask aloud. It gets lonely, so I like to imagine that Violet and Victor are hanging around, keeping me company. Victor's finally out of his stuffy old bedroom I still can't bring myself to enter, relaxing with some ghost magazines in the library. *Good Housecreeping* and *(After)Life*. Victor loved his magazines. Whenever I see a *TV Guide* at the grocery store checkout, I'm transported back to the ottoman at Victor's bedside, reading him the "Cheers & Jeers" section. His favorite show was *The King of Queens* and he told me, every single time I watched an episode with him, that *nobody has range like Jerry Stiller*.

"Perfection," I reply to myself, because that's exactly what Victor would have said about my disaster mural.

Violet, I think, would gently tell me I'd done a good job, and then at one in the morning I'd walk in on her redoing my efforts. "Thought I'd help just a *tiny* bit," she'd say guiltily. Then she'd distract me with spontaneous chocolate chip pancakes. She made them for dinner sometimes, as a special treat, which I thought was the most incredible thing. Chocolate chip pancakes for dinner! In our pajamas! *Don't tell anybody*, she'd mock-whisper, even though the only other person at home was Victor and he loved to encourage the indulgence in special treats.

"Violet, I think I should have hired a professional for this," I say. The summer I lived here, I found a *Garfield* comic book in the library and promptly zipped through a comic-drawing phase. Violet and Victor were overly complimentary of my clearly plagiarized comic strip about a lazy rat who loved spaghetti, and made me believe I was a genius. Maybe Violet asked me to paint a mural because she thought I'd grow up to be more talented.

The sky in my mural looks like the sea, and the lagoon looks like . . . someone who doesn't know how to paint tried to create a lagoon and didn't take her time with it. I don't have the patience to nurture the skill required for this.

When I was a kid, this room was the one and only fragment of Falling Stars I privately thought could be improved. When you tell a ten-year-old you have a ballroom, she's going to picture the one from *Beauty and the Beast*. And then when she finds out the floor has shaggy peach carpeting, the windows are adorned with heavy floral drapery you'd find in a Best Western, and the piano isn't even an old-timey-looking piano but rather an upright piano that belongs in a church—well, that child is going to be underwhelmed.

"We'll get a proper *grand* piano," I murmur, dabbing my paintbrush into a blue puddle. "Or a harpsichord. The carpet needs to be ripped out, for sure. You can't throw a lively masquerade ball in these conditions."

"A lively *what*?"

I twist on my stool, paintbrush dribbling cerulean across my skirt. Wesley needs a goddamn bell around his neck.

"Uhh . . ." I cast about for a good lie. You can't have a ballroom and *not* throw a holiday masquerade ball—the idea is madness—but he needn't know this particular event is on his horizon until the day he walks in and gets a load of me and my forty finest guests outfitted in Regency attire. Because yes, costumes are absolutely necessary. "A baseball. I want to throw a baseball."

He raises his eyebrows. I smile with all my teeth and start

estimating how much work it would be to put down a baseball diamond on the property. Everything I know about baseball can be traced back to that scene from *Twilight*.

Then his gaze skids onto the mural.

Okay, so it doesn't look like an expert did it. I'm not an artist, except when it comes to flavors, icing, and sprinkles. But he doesn't have to look at my painting like *that*, with his lips closed around an unspoken *Hmm*.

"At you," I snap. "I'm going to throw a baseball at you, if you don't change your face."

Wesley endeavors to change his face. "Are you using watercolors?"

"Yeah."

He appraises the wall as if in pain.

"Why? Does it matter?" I love watercolors. They're so dreamy and serene.

Groaning deep in his throat, he throws his head back and walks straight out of the room.

I stare after him. "Does it *matter*?"

I squint at my painting, straining to view it through someone else's eyes. It isn't recommended. I slip back behind my own eyes again and ponder the merits of paint-by-numbers wall hangings. Would that be considered cheating?

Wesley returns with a large, rectangular plastic tub loaded with bottles of craft paint. "Whoa!" I paw through the rainbow of colors, some brand-new, some a quarter full, with rivulets of dried paint encircling the caps. "Where'd you find all this?"

"Upstairs."

I shake a bottle of sunflower yellow. "These are fresh, though. Do you think Violet—"

"These are acrylics," he interrupts quietly. "I think you'll find them easier to work with."

"Okay, great." I squeeze some admiral blue onto a paper plate. "Thanks."

Wesley leaves, and he's right, the acrylics are a way better medium. The paint stays where I ask it to, thick and vibrant. I begin to hum, swishing my brush, until Wesley reappears and plucks the brush from my grasp. I frown at my empty hand, still in midair, until he prods a new brush between my fingers.

"Use this one," he tells me, and disappears again.

But not for long.

Every time I turn around, he's hovering in the doorway. I can't focus while he's doing that. *"What?"*

He looks like he wants to backseat-paint so badly and can barely hold it in, pressing his knuckles to his lips, other hand cupping his elbow.

"Nothing," he mutters.

I lower my brush, which has smoother bristles than the last one and applies paint more evenly. "Come on, spit it out."

"It's just . . ." He begins to point, then tugs his fingers through his hair sheepishly.

"Listen, if you happen to have any tips, I'm all ears. I don't know why Violet asked me to paint a mural. I haven't painted since art class in high school."

Wesley loses his hold on his restraint and drags over a chair, positioning it two feet from mine. He second-guesses the distance between us, then drags it another foot in the opposite direction.

"Are those supposed to be trees?" he asks benignly with a motion toward my green-black blobs, to which I can't help but laugh.

"If you have to ask, I guess they're pretty bad."

"No! Not bad. Not at all." Lies. "Here, try this." He plucks two brushes with flat, fanned bristles from the plastic tub, one for him, one for me, and dips them in water. Wipes the excess carefully against a paint-stained rag. "These are perfect for coniferous trees." He dabs his into hunter-green paint and then creates a realistic fir tree in seconds, like it's nothing.

"You don't always need to have your brush loaded with paint," he says. "If you let it fade out, you end up with softer branches. Then you come back, like this, with a little bit of yellow. These brushes are handy for grass, too." He demonstrates, barely tapping the bristles against the wall but managing to leave behind feathery strokes of yellow-green grass.

I copy him. "Ahh! Look at my tree! I made a tree!"

"Very good," he replies, even though his tree is much better.

"Would you mind helping me?"

Wesley doesn't take any convincing. He asks what I'd like him to do, and I put him on tree duty. I try to mirror whatever he does on my side of the mural but keep stopping to watch him work. He makes all sorts of trees, using different brushes for the trunks, for different textures. He knows exactly which brush is the right one for the result he wants. Which colors to use. "You're really good at this," I say.

He grumbles noncommittally, arm stilling its movements. It takes him a while to get back into the groove, and as I watch his progress, I also watch his cheeks and neck redden.

I can't believe it. He's self-conscious.

"No, seriously, you're an actual artist," I force myself to tell him, like I'm trying to pet a dog who might bite me. "You're legit."

"Not really." He squirms.

"You must paint all the time, then? To be this talented?" There are a few landscape paintings hanging up in the cabin, but I assumed he or Violet bought them.

"I'm not . . . I'm not that good." Wesley rubs the nape of his neck. I think complimenting him is making it worse. It's so humanizing, to see this giant starchy potato get all pink and flustered simply because I'm bearing witness to his fluffy trees. It makes me want to compliment him more, which is a disturbing development.

"Anyway." He rolls his shoulder and tries to twist himself so that I can't see his face. "Light. And shadows. Um. So, look, there's the sun, so . . ." He darts me a sidelong look. "Pay attention to the art."

"I am."

(Awful, is what I am, but in my defense he walked right into that one.)

His blush is furious. You could fry an egg with it. "Look at my brush, please. You're missing important techniques here."

He adds whitecaps to the waves, and reflections of overhanging trees. I imitate him. He isn't as precise anymore, fumbling with the paint bottles, knocking over our cup of water. He mutters and grumbles and, honestly, looks completely miserable. I have never seen him like this. I'm so startled that I don't know what to say.

"Thanks for teaching me," I say, nodding at the wall, where a waterfall lagoon mural is slowly emerging from the mess I made. "I appreciate it. You must have taken quite a lot of pity on me and my painting abilities to help out somebody you hate."

It's a joke. It's mostly a joke.

Wesley swivels his head, eyebrows knitting. "I don't hate you," he says slowly, like it's obvious.

"Kind of thought you hated everybody," I say. It's another sort-of joke that falls flat.

"No." He looks hurt. "I liked Violet. I like my family."

This piques my curiosity. "What's your family like? Are they all giants?"

"My mom's four eleven."

"Holy cow, your dad must be Paul Bunyan."

His grunt tells me this conversation is closed. Then, a few minutes later, after I've forgotten and moved on: "I'm not that tall. The national average for men in the Netherlands is six feet. If I lived there, no one would even notice me."

I stare.

He swings away.

"Could you teach me how to draw a pirate sh—" I begin to ask, but Wesley drops his brush in a fit of frustration, rising from his chair.

"I'm not any good at this." He sounds so resigned. And sad.

"What?" Not any good at this? What in the hell is he talking about? "Are you kidding? You're amazing at this!"

"No, I'm not," he mutters under his breath, cleaning up after himself jerkily. I can tell now that staring bothers him, but it's impossible not to.

"Wesley." I stand up.

"I should be cleaning. I'm too busy for this, I shouldn't be messing around." He holds out a hand like a stop sign, as if to say, *Don't you dare move. Stay where you are.* "You've got this," he assures me, gravely serious. "You're doing great." He keeps his hand up—*Don't come any closer*—all the way out of the room.

I gape at the doorway. Then the mural.

"Okaaaaaay."

I keep going for about two minutes longer, but concentration's a pipe dream. I've got to go see what's up with Wesley.

I find him in the kitchen, standing at the sink rinsing out his paintbrushes. I can't tell if he's hanging his head because he's upset or just tired, but he isn't his usual rigid self tonight.

In this silent house, my footsteps are an uproar. Wesley glances my way, eyes shuttering. We're hungry and exhausted, a dangerous mix. We're sick of requesting constant approval over every renovation detail when it comes to our own home, which we are each being forced to share with a stranger. Or not a stranger, anymore, not really—but certainly not a friend. He makes his distaste for my company crystal clear by finding any excuse to exit a room right after I've entered it and responding to my attempts at conversation with apathetic monosyllables.

"You all right?" I ask. I can't help it. I'm an incorrigible peacemaker.

"Fine." He shuts the water off, even though his hands still have paint on them, and begins to leave. He's an incorrigible room-leaver.

"Have you seen the new box of garbage bags?" I ask before he can perform one of his vanishing acts. "I need to bag up about a billion paper towels. Cleaning out vents is disgusting."

Without turning fully around, I know he's gone stone-faced. I can tell by the shape of his profile, the minuscule jut to his chin. I hate that I pay close enough attention to be able to tell. "New bags are at the cabin. On top of the fridge."

"Why'd you put them all the way up there?"

I'm trying to lift the mood with a little light ribbing, but Wesley's too distressed to realize it.

"The top of the fridge isn't *all the way up there* to me," he replies tartly.

I don't think I like his tone. "Not everyone's as tall as you are."

He's the ungrateful kind of tall. If I had that sort of height, I'd be a blessing upon the earth. I'd hang tire swings and save cats. Ask my neighbors if they needed their curtains taken down to be washed.

"Not my problem. You should have eaten more vegetables when you were a child."

I glare at him, which he doesn't see, because he's refusing to look at me. After a short miracle of getting along, showing me kindness, he's reverted back into the grouch he's been from the start. When I get my hotel up and running, I'm putting families with small, loud children in the bedroom directly beneath his. There will be complimentary trumpets and kickballs.

"For someone as beautiful as you are, it's a shame you're such an insufferable ass," I blurt out angrily.

Stillness rings. "I'm not that bad, you know," I continue. "You are constantly turning your back on me, ignoring me when I'm around like I'm a punishment to talk to, and it makes me feel like shit. You make me feel even lonelier than I already was."

I can't believe I said that. I can't believe I said that out loud. But if I'm shocked, he is *floored*.

His eyes are saucers. I'd give up the left wing of the hotel to know what's running through his mind.

"Whatever!" I shout, embarrassment joining my anger. "I won't bother you anymore, then. Go ahead and be alone."

I spin on my heel, leaving him behind. From another room, I hear him yell out: "I was just kidding about the vegetables thing! Maybell! That was a joke!"

I slam the front door. A section of door frame splinters apart.

"Damn it."

God, I have had it with today. With this week. Month. Year. Maybe Falling Stars is cursed. My phone starts to vibrate in my pocket and I decide that if it's that telemarketer from Lancaster, Pennsylvania, who's been calling me for two years nonstop, I am going to give them hell.

"Hello?" I bark into my phone, marching stiffly across the dark yard back to the cabin.

"Maybell?"

I stop short. "Ruth!"

I don't know why my attitude does a one-eighty. Too many years spent using my customer service voice, I suppose.

"Hi! Sorry it's taken me so long to return your call. I've been swamped." Right. Violet probably wasn't her only client, and being a home health aide must be a demanding job. "My son moved back in with me, my mom decided to visit for the next few weeks unannounced, and I just found out my daughter dropped out of culinary school to get away from her ex-boyfriend."

I feel stupid for having called days ago, wasting her time. "Oh my gosh. You're so busy—I didn't really have anything important to say—"

"No worries, I'm taking a drive right now to escape the madness. So, how are you settling in?" She's bright and cheery. Friendly. It's nice to know *some* people still know how to be.

"Fine, fine. Settling in fine!" I chirp. "Everything's great. Fixing up the manor."

"That's wonderful! I'm so glad to hear it." She genuinely sounds glad, too, which makes me smile. "How are you and Wesley getting along?" There's a cautious edge to her question that tells me she suspects we might not be.

"We're not," I reply baldly. "He's driving me nuts."

"Ah, well." Ruth is warm. Sympathetic. "Don't worry, it probably won't be long before the house is good to go and you'll be off the couch in no time."

"I'm not—"

"The plaid is quite an interesting choice," she continues. "The couch, I mean. Wonder where Wesley got it from. It was so *strange* when I visited. Eerie to walk in and not see Violet's hospital bed taking up the whole living room anymore."

"Why'd she have a hospital bed in the living room?"

"Where else would she go?" I hear an ignition spur to life on the other side of the phone. "I'm just glad she had *a* room there, you know? The way she was living before Wesley moved in was . . ." She audibly shudders. "It took plenty of convincing on his part to get Violet out of that house, but he hated her sleeping there. Fire hazard, you know. And unsanitary. We're lucky nothing fell on her. Then he got in touch with some doctors, brought me on board."

I wheel around to peer up at the second floor of Falling Stars. All the windows have gone dark but two. In one yellow rectangle, a tall, broad silhouette looks down on the lawn. His body curves away slightly, as if preparing to make a quick getaway, but I don't move and neither does he.

"Wesley's the one who contacted you?"

"Before Wesley, Violet hadn't been to a doctor in years. This woman was in her late eighties, mind you. Had nobody. I don't like thinking about it. We tried to convince her to let us clean up. Let us donate all the stuff she didn't need. She couldn't bring herself to part with anything, kept saying we could get rid of it after she was gone if we hated her belongings so much. A benefit of moving into the groundskeeper's cabin was that it's only a one-bedroom, which meant no extra space to fill up with Amazon splurges."

My attention wraps around *one-bedroom* and squeezes tight. "What about the bedroom upstairs?"

"The what? Hold on, Maybell." I hear a window rolling down. "I'd like a number one, please. With cheese. No pickles or onions. An apple pie, too. Oh, and a Cherry Coke! Thank you very much." To me, she adds, "Are you talking about the loft? Honey, that's a closet."

I stare at the silhouette in the window for one beat. Two beats. Three. The light gutters out, taking Wesley with it.

My thumb is already hovering over END CALL. "Thank you so much for calling me back, Ruth, I really appreciate it. Good luck with everything."

"Good luck to you, too. I'm going to park five houses down from mine, listen to a podcast, and enjoy my food in peace."

"You deserve it. Thank you again for talking to me."

"Anytime, Maybell. Don't be a stranger."

Hanging up, I walk calmly into the cabin. I'm not going to go into his bedroom. I'm not. It's an invasion of his privacy.

I grab a chair and clamber up, but only because I want to see if I can reach the cord on the ceiling. I won't pull it.

As it happens, I *can* reach it. Just to experiment—I'm not actually going to go up—I grab the ladder and slide it down.

Maybe I'll climb a little bit, but not all the way to the top. This is Wesley's *bedroom*. It is indubitably, 100 percent, no-gray-area, none of my business.

Up at the top, I press on the ceiling and it gives way, a warped square of thin wood that pitches forward easily. Invitingly. A wave of hot air slams me upside the head.

I suck in a sharp breath, pressing a hand to my mouth. Oh my god.

It's not a bedroom.

Exposed beams, exposed insulation, exposed wiring, dust motes eddying in stagnant air. A small window with a hand towel stapled to its frame to block the light that would stream in at sunrise and aim directly at the bed, which isn't a bed at all. It's a sleeping bag on the floor.

A sleeping bag that takes up the *entire* floor, the bottom six inches of it curling up the wall because there's not enough floor for it to lie completely flat.

A miniature desk fan blows loose sheets of paper as it oscillates, plugged into a surge protector along with a small table lamp resting on a stack of books. There's a flashlight and a wallet. Three neat piles of clothes at the head of the sleeping bag, functioning as a pillow. Headphones attached to a thin cord that snakes beneath a laptop. A half-empty cup of water.

It's stuffy, cramped, the ceiling too low—Wesley would have to duck or risk hitting his head, even in the middle of the room, where the vaulted roof slants up to its highest point.

I lock gazes with a familiar pair of blue eyes staring out of Wesley's sleeping bag and sway, overtaken by dizziness.

It's me. *I'm* lying in his bed.

Chapter 10

A TWO-DIMENSIONAL MAYBELL PARRISH PEERS out at me with colored-pencil features, wearing a sunset-colored ROCKY TOP TREE HOUSE SPLASH ZONE racer-back tank, four black hair bands like bracelets tracking up the left wrist. Glow-in-the-dark nail polish. She's up close, so close that I can make out the strawberry tints in her wind-disheveled brown hair that you don't notice unless she's standing in the full sun. Faint reflections of trees flash in her round glasses, but she's staring right at me with a guarded expression, and my stomach hits the floor because I know exactly what she's thinking. I know exactly when she was thinking it, and where she was. It was the day I came to Falling Stars.

I was thinking, *You look just like a lie I know.*

The hairs on my neck rise, but at the same time I flush, an extraordinary awareness pumping through me. I feel like I've had a mask ripped off my face. It would appear that the man who ignores my existence 99 percent of the time has an eye for my every tiny detail. He must have a photographic memory.

There are other sketches in pen, pencils, and oil pastels, of Falling Stars and the woods and flowers I don't know by name, strewn haphazardly; I envision Wesley with the artwork on his lap, back a crescent slope, profile close to the page. The instrument in his hand races feverishly across the paper in elegant, expert slashes, capturing a flashbulb moment in time. He has to get up suddenly—maybe he checks the time and it's almost eight in the morning, which means I'm going to be opening my bedroom door soon and coming out. If he wants to avoid bumping into me all day, he's got to get moving. He rises. The papers go sliding everywhere.

I'm kneeling on Wesley's sleeping bag, the hard floor beneath it pinching my knee, when the top half of him emerges three feet away from me without warning. I'll never understand how someone of his size can move without a sound.

"Oh!" I hasten to stand up, but my shoe slides on the slippery material and I knock into his stacks of clothes. Boxers and rolled-up socks topple off, which, in my panic, I pick up and put back. I am touching his underwear now. Wesley's eyes are unusually hollow; he watches with a drifting, faraway expression, saying nothing.

"I'm sorry." I have no excuse to be up here, so I don't even try to come up with one. There is no talking my way out of this. He looks so lost. This looks so bad.

It feels really, really bad.

I straighten the drawings. When the drawing of me passes into my hands Wesley drags his face away from me to focus on the wall, forehead furrowing. He's still standing on the ladder, gripping either side of the hatch with pale knuckles.

"I . . ." My mouth opens and closes, heart accelerating so fast my chest is overheating. I'm up to my ears in broken pieces of apologies, swimming in them, but I can't link any of them together.

He begins to sink back down the ladder.

"Wesley?"

I hurry after him, the front door snicking closed just as my shoe hits the second-to-last rung. "Wesley!" I open the door, jumping off the porch.

"Please don't!" he calls through the dark. "Don't follow." His voice grows fainter, ebbing toward the manor. "Please."

There is pain in that *please*. I grow roots.

Within minutes, a light in a window upstairs winks on. There's nothing for me to do now but go back inside the cabin, back into my room, which I realize the moment I cross the threshold is Wesley's room. I have been living in Wesley's room.

I have been sleeping in Wesley's bed.

What a weird, surreal night to top off a long, tense day. I'm not dragging and drained anymore. I'm jumpy, my mind spinning out, heart pulsing like it's ensnared in someone's fist with inadequate room for expansion.

I lie back on Wesley's bed to reevaluate my entire life.

The *why* takes a while to fight to the surface, bogged down with other memories trying to push their way up. I think about that first night here, when I discovered the manor was unlivable and my cabin had a man in it, who'd inherited half of everything. How I needed somewhere to sleep and absolutely had to get away from him, this person who was the unwitting face of a scam. I told him I'd sleep in the filthy manor and . . .

That's when he invited me to stay in the cabin.

I bungle my way into the shower, consumed with figuring this out. I forget to rinse out the shampoo before massaging conditioner into my hair. I scrub my face, discovering I'm still wearing glasses.

He hesitated.

Before he invited me in, he hesitated. I thought then that it was because he was reluctant to have me in his house, taking it personally when perhaps I shouldn't have—I was a stranger, after all—but now I can see he hesitated because there was nowhere for me to go. There was only one bedroom. He'd turned Violet's makeshift room back into a living room, which by that point I'd already seen.

I don't dry and comb my hair, leaving it wrapped in a towel. My skin's still wet as I pull on underwear and an oversized shirt, tripping dazedly back into bed, *into his bed*, letting my head fall heavily onto the pillow. His pillow. His only one. I roll over, maybe but maybe not imagining that this pillow smells like him, and the comforter, too. And the floor and the walls and now, me. It's ridiculous. I don't know what Wesley Koehler smells like.

Petrichor and the smoke of a candle blown out. Blue Head & Shoulders shampoo that stings your eyes when it runs down your face in the shower. That's what he smells like.

I am ridiculous.

I think about his lie that the cabin was a two-bedroom—that odd shadow to his features as he told it, making sure he got a head start back to the cabin while I picked my way carefully through the unfamiliar maze of Violet's hoard. He's a minimalist. Who wouldn't be, honestly, after living with Violet? He didn't have much to grab from his room when he beat me back there to supposedly change out her bedding. When I opened the front door, he was already ascending the ladder.

I grapple for another explanation while knowing there isn't one.

All I can see are the blue eyes of that drawing staring at me, in the softest strokes of colored pencil, so realistic and detailed. When I woke up this morning I thought I didn't know anything about Wesley, but now I know even less than *that*. Less than nothing. He's an artist? He sleeps in a closet and draws lovely pictures of flowers? Saves little old ladies from the monsters they built?

I need to lie down, I think, while already lying down.

Knowing I'm in his bed is doing peculiar things to my skin. I cannot remain still.

I'm keyed up and pacing my/his room, stopping periodically, helplessly, at the window to lift the curtain. The lights in the other house have gone out. He's got a few rooms up there clean enough to live in, and the utilities are back on, so I guess that's that. I'm not moving in until it's been visited by an exterminator and reinspected for mold, so if I play my cards right I've got the cabin to myself for the time being.

Every minute is at least two hundred seconds long. *I need to lie down*, I think again, hovering at the window for another half hour, waiting to see a dark shape lumbering back across the yard that never comes.

I'M GETTING LOTS OF work done at the estate now that I have absolutely no one to talk to. Gemma's stopped texting me *Where are you?* and *I miss you* GIFs of miserable people sobbing, probably because I logged on to Facebook after a long social media hiatus and liked somebody's post. Now she's seen evidence that I'm ignoring her, after her ego's probably gotten its hopes up that I've been taken out by a tragic accident she can use as an excuse to bail on work for the rest of the day.

It's stormed hard for the past two days, just me and Wesley and the rain. I've spotted him hefting large bags of potting mix and topsoil as well as planters into the sunroom, which he must be planning to use as a conservatory. He's probably also planning to padlock the door to keep my guests from enjoying it. Seems like a Wesley kind of move.

Since I can't get within thirty feet of the man, I left an exasperated note on the grand staircase at the manor yesterday afternoon for him to find.

> *I'm so sorry that I went upstairs. It was wrong of me to snoop.*
> *I've been trying to apologize but whenever I call your name or*
> *try to walk toward you, you disappear. It's going to be*
> *profoundly difficult to live together if one of us is always*
> *pretending the other one is invisible. The enchiladas I put in the*
> *fridge at the main house are vegetarian, by the way. I noticed*
> *you didn't eat any, but please don't let perfectly good food go to*
> *waste just because you're mad at me. I promise to respect your*
> *privacy going forward and hope we can put this behind us.*

Stiff and formal, but as apologies go, not too bad. An hour later, the note was gone. I thought he was going to keep ignoring me, since he didn't come find me yesterday and hash this out.

Then this morning, in the same spot where I left his note, a white sheet of sketch paper appeared.

I'm not mad at you. I'm avoiding you because of what you saw in the loft. It's embarrassing. I'll be fine, I just want to be left alone.

Sorry about the enchiladas. I didn't know they were vegetarian or that you were okay with me eating them. I thought you were probably mad at me.

I'm beginning to see that he isn't a hash-this-out sort of person. He's an avoid-your-problems-forever sort of person. In this case, the problem is me. The *I just want to be left alone* is making me come out of my skin because I don't know if I'm physically capable of leaving anyone alone when I know I'm responsible for them feeling bad.

Wesley's slippery as a ghost, gone every time I turn the corner. I've never been able to stomach people's being upset with me, *needing* that resolution. If he would let me get close enough to apologize, the dynamic could at least return to the way it was. Sure, he was grouchy, but when he avoided me it was a different sort of avoiding. Like a preference rather than a necessity. It's as if I've walked in on him naked. The power balance has shifted.

I pluck a sheet of lilac stationery out of a rolltop desk and write.

Hey,

You don't have anything to be embarrassed about. I'm grateful you let me stay in your room, putting yourself through a lot of trouble to do so. I know you've been sleeping at the manor for the last few days, but if you want you can have your room back and I'll sleep on the couch. Also, I didn't see many of your drawings when I was up there but what I saw was impressive. You don't have to be embarrassed about those, either. I'm sorry again for snooping.

Anyway, I saw something you didn't want me to see, so I'll tell you about something that's embarrassing for me, too. It's only fair.

When I was fourteen, my mom and I stopped in at a diner in Lexington, Kentucky, right after she bought a lottery ticket. She put the ticket on the table between our plates, waiting until we were finished eating before scratching all the tiny Christmas trees off with a quarter. It was fun to pretend the ticket might land us a million dollars. We talked about what our dream home would look like. After we were done eating, she scratched the ticket and won six bucks, which she spent on two slices of apple pie.

We left the diner, never went back again, but for some reason I thought about it a lot. It cheered me up to remember sitting in that booth, hoping that the ticket to an amazing new life sat right in front of me, waiting to happen.

The first version of a café I'm always daydreaming about was based on that diner. I've remodeled it so many times since then, evolving the décor to suit whatever my tastes happen to be in the moment. I like to imagine all sorts of swoony romantic scenarios taking place there. The climax in every rom-com movie, basically, when the hero thinks he's going to lose the girl and he professes his feelings with raw, desperate honesty. I daydream about fun banter, too, even mundane afternoons where all I'm doing is decorating donuts with colorful icing and sprinkles. But my favorite daydreams are those fast-paced ones where the stakes are high, when even I don't know if the hero *and heroine will get together because I get so carried away. Even though I'm the heroine in this fantasy, so I control it all.*

This is something I've never told anybody, so now we're even. But if you tell another soul about Maybell's Coffee Shop AU, I will cut you.

—M

The front door closes right as I'm penning the last line. I glance at the window and there's Wesley, taking to the woods. He skulks off into his self-made nature preserve every time the rain lets up, probably to escape all the fumes from our cleaning supplies. Or me. Probably me.

I could leave the note on the staircase for him to pick up when he returns, but my feet have other ideas. They decide they want to go on a walk, too.

Off I dash, waterlogged grass squelching under the oversized boots I saved from the dumpster. We're teetering on the precipice of April, nearly ready to hop into May, the weather warming up. I lower the hood of my rain slicker, overhanging boughs catapulting raindrops from leaf to leaf.

He's soundless, but the footprints give him away. They lead me to the trickle of water, a creek cutting through heavy green foliage. There are signs along the paths, wooden slabs nailed to tree trunks I was too distracted to notice the last time I was in the woods. Their edges are sharpened into pointing arrows, handpainted with monikers like *I Spy Something Blue Trail* and *Say Goodbye to the Sky Lane*.

The path he's chosen, *You Are Here*, isn't one I've explored before—my heightened fear of being mauled by bears has prevented me from getting too adventurous—with an old stone bridge that I think used to be part of a road but is now overgrown with moss. I stop to remove my glasses, lenses steamed up with my breath from the exercise.

Wesley's trail of footprints ends here.

I glance uneasily over the sides of the bridge. The water's high from all the rain we've been getting, pouring swiftly between rocks, over dips, gurgling and eddying. He wouldn't jump in, would he? The water's too cold for swimming. Sunlight takes a while to reach the ground here, moist stones dappled with soft green, atmosphere cool and peaceful. Otherworldly. I peruse beds of fallen pine needles for a shoe-shaped disturbance but find nothing. It's as if Wesley sauntered across this bridge and straight through an invisible portal. He's in a medieval forest right now, taming a wild unicorn, and I'm standing here studying pine needles like they're a Rorschach test.

A bird's nearby trill jerks my head up. It's a very helpful bird, giving away the location of another creature up in the branches, and if looks could kill it would be roasted on a plate with carrots and potatoes.

"Ahh. There you are."

"No, I'm not."

Wesley's lounging in a white oak towering directly over me that's got to be hundreds of years old, one of the thick, lichen-scaled boughs bending like a hammock to fit him perfectly. Its roots burrow into the bridge like clamping fingers, tendons, and bone. From my position on the ground he's about eight feet up, watching me with *Oh, no* written all over his face.

"There's no escaping me," I tell him. It comes out sounding disturbingly ominous.

He sighs. "I know. You're inevitable."

I don't know quite what he means by that, but now that I've got him good and trapped I'm going to make him read my letter and restore the balance. "Here." I wave the lilac paper. "This is for you."

"What is it?"

"Oh, come on. It won't bite."

I reach up on tiptoe, he reaches down, and in that flicker of brief contact with both our hands on the paper, his eyes meet mine and something very like fear seizes them. But when he blinks, it's gone.

The base of the tree has a springy cushion of moss around it, which I decide to plant myself down on while awaiting my *I forgive you, you are thus absolved.*

Suppressing the urge to stare at him with laser eyes while he reads is killing me, especially given that he's reading about something private. My instinct is to distract him from this new information he's likely going to use to make fun of me by chattering, lessening the impact, toning it down into nothing at all, just having a laugh. As if there are several levels at which one could process the letter, and if I can bring him down to the shallowest tier he'll *know* it, but he'll know it *less*. Which probably does not make sense.

I have to look.

He's still reading, and wouldn't you know it, he's frowning. This isn't one of his signature frowns, so I don't know how to decipher it. I review my selection of modes, slamming the one that says PANIC.

Oh god! Why didn't I share a less personal story? I've got loads of embarrassing stories in me, high-resolution reels that play behind my eyes every time I lie down to sleep. I could have told him about the time I set off a firework upside down. Or the time I bought a hot dog at Chickamauga Lake and got attacked by a seagull. Or when I strangled myself with a dress that didn't fit in a dressing room at Target and wore myself out trying to wrench myself free for close to an hour before another lady helped me pull the ripped dress over my head and, while doing so, commented that I wasn't wearing the right underwear for that kind of dress.

The nose of a purple airplane swats me on the forehead. I blink.

"Sorry."

New writing in black ink spreads over one of the airplane's wings. I unfold it. He wrote back?

He wrote back.

AU?
> *The enchiladas were good. Thank you.*

That's all he has to say? I squint up at him. "You have a pen on you?"

"I always have a pen on me." His arm dangles over the edge, pen slipping from his fingers, letting it tumble down into my lap. Well, all right then.

AU = Alternate universe, I write back.

He reads it, then responds aloud, "What's it like?"

"My coffee shop?"

"Yeah."

I can't get a read on whether he's only asking for details so he can laugh at them, or if he's sincerely curious. Not that it matters. It doesn't matter what he thinks of me.

I close my eyes to visualize my café, but for a split second, I see the cabin loft. I think it's safe now to admit that I low-key, secretly, sort of care what he thinks. I think maybe he cares what I think about him, too. And isn't that something?

"What the café looks like on the outside is hazy, but there's a big pink neon sign," I tell him, eyes still closed. In my mind, I push open the door. "The door chimes when you open it. A wave of cool air hits you, like when you've been out in the rain and walk into an air-conditioned building. It smells like cocoa powder and cinnamon."

"Do you make donuts there?"

"Yes." I feel myself smile. "The best anyone's ever had."

"That's true in this universe, too."

It is true that I crave that validation. It is also true that praise makes me squirm. "The floor is all shiny aqua tiles that go halfway up the walls. The rest of the walls are pale, pale purple and decorated with mirrors of all shapes and sizes. Succulents in hanging baskets. Travel posters of fictional lands. There are tons of big, leafy green plants everywhere. I kill every plant I touch in real life, but here I have a green thumb." I open one eye, chancing a peek up at Wesley. He's writing on the paper, a small smile creeping over his face. One corner of his mouth hooks back slightly, unconsciously. I talk faster.

"There are red vinyl booths and a black countertop with bar stools. An old-fashioned cash register. A jukebox. Fairy lights. A display case full of donuts."

"What kind?" he interrupts.

I'm a pastry junkie; I could write sonnets about *what kind*.

"Cinnamon sugar, chocolate strawberry mousse, caramel and peanut long johns. Fudge brownie with powdered sugar."

"Nice."

"Cinnamon rolls," I go on. As I talk, the talking becomes easier, and why should this embarrass me, anyway? My café is spectacular. "Bear claws. Beignets. Pumpkin and cream cheese. Butterscotch pralines. Mexican hot chocolate. Donuts with every filling imaginable: raspberry, apple, lemon curd, blueberry." I'm making myself hungry. "There's an old rotary phone on the counter that flashes red when it's time to go back to the real world. Beside it sits a frosted cake stand especially for Lamington donuts. Half are covered in traditional coconut, the other half chopped hazelnuts." I realize I'm gesturing, as if he can see what I'm pointing at, and that Wesley's smile has gotten bigger.

My thoughts run into each other, a thirty-car pileup, totally arrested by that smile.

I have seen Wesley mildly amused, but I have never seen him *enjoying*. I react with a powerful expanding of pressure in my chest: my body is double-gravity heavy, immobile, never to move again. But my heart is a balloon.

"So?" I wheedle. "What do you think?"

"I think," he replies softly, "I would like to walk into that alternate universe and buy a cinnamon roll from you."

"Anytime," I manage to reply, swallowing. "We're open twenty-four hours."

"Busy, busy." His demeanor turns pensive. "Do you make coffee cake?"

I flourish a hand. "Look at that, it just appeared on the menu."

"Sweet tea?"

"Sir, this is a coffee shop. Not that I ever concentrate too much on the coffee aspect of it; I guess I get preoccupied with the donut part. We offer coffee, water, chai, and hot chocolate." I tick the options off on my fingers. Whenever I daydream, the drinks materialize out of thin air in chunky earthenware mugs. I don't travel lovingly through the entire process like I do with baked goods. A girl's got to have priorities.

"Look at that." He flourishes his hand, too. "Sweet tea just appeared on the menu."

Wesley is playing with me?

My grin widens. "It did not."

"Right above the macchiatos. Don't you see it?" He is watching me with a very serious expression. Neon pink from that revolving sign in a faraway land casts out its light all the way to here, glowing upon his cheeks. I've seen this expression on him before, but I didn't know the difference between his *nice* serious and his *intimidating* serious. "The customer's always right."

"So they are. Go ahead and have your sweet tea." I hear a clink as the mug is put down on the counter. The jukebox comes alive, unspooling nature sounds: whistling birds, a babbling creek.

"Thank you. Oh, wait. *Ohh.*"

I look at Wesley. He's on the opposite side of the counter in my dreamland, seated atop a stool. He's high in a tree, smiling down at me. Either scenario is equally confounding, and both are true. "What's wrong?"

"You didn't put enough sugar in this. Someone should really teach you how to make sweet tea."

Wesley is playing with me.

I take the mug back, peering inside. "Looks okay."

"Why do you even have it on your menu if it's going to taste like this? Honestly."

"Ah, I see what's happened. I mixed up the tea with that big jug in the back with the skull and crossbones on it. Three big X's." I make slashes in midair. "Whoops."

"I'll leave you a positive review with my dying breath. For capitalism."

"See, that's really me, though. Whenever I eat out at restaurants, they could serve me a bowl of rocks and I'd say, 'Thank you so much!' People in the food industry don't get paid enough for all they put up with. I'm not about to make their job worse. Give me rocks, I'll tip twenty percent."

He shudders. "Restaurants."

"You've mentioned that before. You don't like them." I study his face, his gaze locked on mine with the faintest trace of trepidation. "Any reason why?"

"I like the part about eating food I didn't have to cook," he replies. "Not having to wash any dishes? Great. But then they destroyed the idea by letting people in."

Something about the quick cadence of his words, how easily they roll off his tongue, tells me he's leaned on them at least once before. A rehearsed justification. But I'm delighted, anyway, laughing, and it shakes the leaves. We both tip our heads back. It's raining again, fat drops jumping across the canopy far above in a frenzy. Wesley meets my eyes, his smile still warm. The aroma of cinnamon and cocoa powder drifts on beyond reach, pink neon chinks of light magicking back into sunbeams of an eerie golden green. The color of the sky before a storm.

"Time to head back, looks like," I say reluctantly. I should try to dampen how disappointed I sound, but I don't have the heart to.

"Watch out," he replies. My limbs are rusty, the bottom of my jeans cold from sitting on the ground. I scramble away right in time for him to jump out of the tree and land with a hard thud beside me.

We race across the stone bridge, rain pelting faster, while I don't pay a single crumb of attention to where we're going. Wesley could probably navigate this wood blindfolded; he doesn't second-guess his steps, taking one turn, then another, hand hovering over the small of my back as though I might get lost otherwise. We're soaked and shivering when we make it back to the manor, but at least I've got my rain slicker. Wesley isn't wearing a jacket. His hair is dripping, shirt clinging to his skin. It's glorious.

"I'll light the fireplace," he says, which is completely unnecessary because we've got gas heating.

"Ooohh, good idea."

He hurries into the living room. I peel off my jacket, comb my fingers through my shaggy hair, and kick off my boots. I'm following after him when he passes me, threading back into the kitchen. He grabs a broom.

"What do you need that for?"

"Sweeping?" He jerks his head toward the ceiling. "Heading back up. Break time's over."

I don't know what I was hoping—actually, yes I do. I was hoping he'd light the fireplace and we'd talk more. I want to see him smile again. I want the unexpected warmth of talking to Wesley, and Wesley talking to me, just as much as I want warmth from a fire. I've only gotten a taste of it.

"Oh."

His arm brushes mine, just barely, a microscopic touching of skin cells, as he exits the room—*Unintentional, Maybell, that was definitely, probably unintentional*—but unintentional or not, I am stock-still for the next twenty seconds, forgetting where I am and what I'm doing. What *am* I doing?

I amble into the living room, trying not to be disappointed. That's when I see the letter I wrote him, which was last seen up in a tree. He's scribbled on it.

Not a scribble. A sketch.

Scratchy lines for shading, no border, one of the table booths interrupted by words: *AU? The enchiladas were good. Thank you.* A freehand sign with my name on it, and a half-eaten donut on a countertop. A vintage telephone. It's my coffee shop. He's drawn my coffee shop.

And inside it, two people. A chill steals through me—not at all an unpleasant one—when I recognize that he's positioned us exactly the way I envisioned. I'm behind the counter; he's seated opposite, in the second-to-last stool. We're leaning toward each other slightly, enough to notice. He's exaggerated the messiness of his hair while downplaying his broadness and height, as though he views himself as smaller and slighter than he actually is.

I can't stop staring at miniature illustrated Maybell. She's a quick sketch, not detailed like the photorealistic drawing I found in the loft, but I like the friendly touch he's imbued me with. The twin spots on my smiling cheeks, the rogue wave in my hair on one side that doesn't match the other. I told him about Maybell's Coffee Shop AU to restore the balance, to send us back to where we were before. I think we might have accidentally turned down a different fork in the path. *Let's See Where This Goes Road.*

SOMEWHERE FAR ABOVE THE clouds, glittering in stars and nebulae, a neon sign spins leisurely outside a cheerful little haven where everything always goes according to plan and nothing un-expected ever happens.

With no one around to watch, the sign buzzes brighter, brighter, brighter, sparks flying. The walls tremble. A giant white oak tree surges out of the prefabricated floor, dead center in the middle of the café. Its great roots unfurl, wending their way up the walls, clamping down between framed mirrors. Each facet of glass reflects a pair of questioning brown eyes, an in-spite-of-itself smile, an open, outstretched hand.

Chapter 11

*T*HUNK.

It's a quarter to midnight, so either that was one of my tired synapses misfiring or there's a possum in the newly fixed dumbwaiter. I crack it open veerrry slowly and am both relieved and puzzled to be wrong. An ordinary spiral notebook sits inside—snapped up at a back-to-school sale by Violet, surely, the bottom-right corners curled up, pages crinkling when I flip them. A message from civilization! I'd almost forgotten I'm not the last person on Earth. Scrubbing tubs with bleach for hours will do that to you.

The first line of the first page is dominated by a cumulonimbus scar of ink trying and failing to conceal the original header: *Hey Maybell,*

He's opted to cross out the poor, harmless greeting, cutting right to: *What station is that*

I snort.

Clicking the pen he lodged in the metal spiral, I make my

greeting extra large: *HEY WESLEY, I'm listening to WKCE. Also, you should know that I've got the entire east wing spotless, including the library. Beat that.*

I send the notebook back up, then get cracking on the west wing, which isn't quite as scary as the east wing was. Over here, Violet stacked storage tubs in the hallways rather than inside the rooms, blocking them off before they could fall prey to the hoard. Opening each door reveals a pocket of cold air that smells about two hundred years old. I'm burning through Glade PlugIns and Febreze like nobody's business, but it's a crypt in here. The smell has seeped into fabrics—curtains, wall hangings, carpets. I love these fabrics because of their historical value, but if I get them adequately cleaned I think they'll disintegrate. They have to go.

The notebook is back in the dumbwaiter when I pass by again, with a response from Wesley.

I've got both my wings spotless, except for two bathrooms and one last bedroom I'm trying to get unlocked. Don't worry, you'll catch up in a month or two.

This spurs me to up my game. I grab my mop and run into a bedroom, ready to work through the night if it means I'll beat him. The door sticks initially, frame warped from all the shrinking and expanding over the years, the fluctuating temperatures. Having the heat shut off for so long has given some of the doors funhouse-grade leans.

The carpet in here is thick, soft, frosted in gray dust that compresses white in footprints I leave behind. Dust coats the heavy, bulbous television set and twin bed, the duvet cover I once thought was patterned with half-moons but now see are peach slices.

I spin 180 degrees, watching a younger version of myself sit down on the ottoman next to the bed. I'm showing Uncle Victor my comic strip. *You're so talented*, he says. He's got a grave, serious voice that acts like a gavel, pronouncing everything he says to be the word of law. It also acts like truth serum. When Victor turns his solemn brown eyes on you, all your secrets come tumbling out. Aunt Violet hovers behind me. She'll wait until I leave before trying to cajole him into eating more, but I'll catch wheezy bits and pieces from down the hall: *Stomach's bothering me. Please, sweetheart, I can't.*

He died not long after I left Falling Stars. Judging by Violet's magazine stockpile that dates back twenty years, that's when she started accumulating so much stuff.

The oxygen machine is gone. When I was a kid I didn't think about why Violet and Victor had separate bedrooms, but my guess is she couldn't sleep with the sound of that machine. I pop open the VCR to look at what he last had in there: a home-recorded *Casablanca*. Recent tapes in the stack next to the TV are all home-recorded, too, inscriptions written in green permanent marker: *Moonstruck. Quigley Down Under. Planes, Trains and Automobiles.* Everything is as he left it on his last day here. His sweaters are folded in their drawers, photo albums still on the lower shelf of his nightstand—the top one, avocado green, filled with Polaroids of their numerous yearly trips. They loved visiting new countries, trying the local cuisine, staying in family-owned inns instead of chain hotels to absorb more of the culture.

The wristwatch in his catchall dish is no longer ticking, its battery having quit at 5:12. I'm about to leave, closing the door behind me, when I notice the three large rectangles on the wall above his bed. I'm sure I've noticed them at another point, but they're interesting in a way that only an adult who's foraged between couch cushions for pennies to buy something off the dollar menu can appreciate.

They're framed collections. Coins on beds of red velvet. Vintage stamps. Signed baseball cards in mint condition. I take a step forward, studying them. Holy *crap*.

"Maybell!"

I jump, spinning, almost running face-first into the wall. "What?" He's upstairs. He can't hear me. "What?" I call, louder.

No response. This is one of Wesley's signature moves: he'll call my name when he needs something, but when I yell back *What?* he goes radio silent, forcing me to go to him to see what he wants. Or I don't have to go to him, I suppose, but I do anyway. One of these days I'm going to yell and make him come to me instead.

I pull open the door, but my head is full of coins and baseball cards, so I open the wrong one. It's Victor's closet. I gasp out a breathless "Ooooohhhhh."

Bzzz, bzzz.

My phone's vibrating. I send it to voicemail, then receive a text. This is Wesley.

I'm still staring at my phone in surprise when the number flashes across my screen again, buzzing in my hand. I answer it. "Hey, come up here," Wesley says into my ear.

"How'd you get my number?"

"Why do you have a picture of me on your phone?" he shoots back.

Ugh, not *this* again. Cherish the past, Wesley, because the grace period for treating your feelings with kid gloves has expired and you're not getting away with throwing that picture in my face to avoid answering questions you don't like.

"Why did you have a picture of me in the attic? Hand-drawn, which is even more questionable than a real photograph taken from your brother's *public* Facebook page."

His mutterings fade; he's lowered his phone, probably making a face at the ceiling.

"I can't go upstairs because I just made the most magnificent discovery," I continue airily, confident that our stalemate has divested him of that particular weapon. "Come down here and take a look."

"My discovery is better."

"Sincerely doubt it. I found a *Christmas tree.*"

Five seconds pass. ". . . So?"

"So, it's one of those fancy ones! With fake snow! It's got to be like ten feet tall. I found it in Uncle Victor's closet."

"I don't see what's special about finding a Christmas tree."

This man has no soul. I begin heaving the tree out of the closet. The branches have been smoothed down so that it takes up less space in storage, but it still scratches the frame up as I ease it out. And it's unexpectedly heavy. Fake snow showers my hair and shirt. "My uncle Garrett was right. I *did* grow up to be a tree-hugger."

"That's great. Come upstairs, you've gotta take a look at something."

"Can't. I'm putting the tree in the ballroom."

"Right now?"

"Yes!"

"It's April. Actually, no, it's technically May now."

"Christmas is a state of mind, Wesley."

"Why do you sound so terrifying when you say that?"

This thing weighs about as much as a real tree. I grunt as I drag it down the hall, careful not to bang into any chandeliers. There's a medieval iron one in the kitchen that's my favorite, with candlesticks going around the circular rim. "I . . . just . . . want . . . to . . . see," I bite out. Pine needles jab my hands.

"In May."

"I'll put it right back." I've reached the ballroom. It's in a state of chaos because whenever I find something cool, I bring it in here. It's going to be my favorite part of the house after I'm finished making it magnificent and less like the set of *The Nanny*. So far I've got a hodgepodge of candlesticks, clocks (all kinds: grandfather, cuckoo, carriage), old books, sculptures, wall hangings, fancy pillboxes, a barrel I might try to convert into a table, and a tangled heap of silk wisteria. I don't know what I'm going to do with everything, but somehow I *will* cram it all in here and make it fabulous.

I was right; the tree looks amazing in the ballroom. I plug it in and voilà—soft white lights glow to life, casting a small golden halo onto raised plaster roses on the rococo-style ceiling.

My high-pitched "Ahhhhhhhhhhhh, I love it!" earns me three thumps of a broomstick rapping from above.

"Your problem is that you love everything," Wesley complains.

"My one flaw."

"I've seen the furniture you're trying to repurpose for your hotel. None of it matches."

"The beauty of themed rooms," I reply. "I'll never get bored, because every room will be different."

"Are you coming now?"

"Patience. I think I saw a tree skirt in the closet . . ." I rummage in Victor's closet, which looks like a snow globe from all the white fluff. I find the tree skirt, along with a large silver box that makes me squeal with delight.

"Oh, no. What is it now?"

"Nothing! I'll be there in a minute. Ten minutes, tops."

He sighs.

"It's an emergency."

His voice goes low, suspicious. "You found ornaments."

"I did! They're wonderful. Weslcy, come look at these ornaments. Ohh, here's a little drummer boy. Ohh, here's Rudolph. Ohh, it's the whole set from *Santa Claus Is Comin' to Town*! Ahhhh!"

"Please. My ears."

I grab a chair from where I've got it positioned by the wall, next to Wesley's tub of paints and my three-quarters-finished mural. My attention's temporarily waylaid by a new development in the waterfall-lagoon world, thrashing on stormy waves. "You painted a pirate ship." Thick, sinewy tentacles, pearlescent as abalone shells, lunge out of the water to grip the *Felled Star*'s stern, ready to devour.

"I hope you don't mind."

"Is that the kraken? That is *awesome*."

"Are you about done down there? You're going to want to see this, I'm telling you."

"Just a sec." I climb onto the chair and stretch, hanging a particularly handsome ornament as high up as I can manage. It's a glass sphere the size of a softball, splotched with gold shimmer. A plaid bow rests inside, the same ribbon that Violet used to bind her stacks of letters—

"Wait a minute."

"I've been waiting for seventeen of them."

"There's a paper in this ornament." I jump down, wriggle the top off, and shake it until a rolled-up piece of paper slides out. "Like a message in a bottle." The ribbon's stiff, permanently crimped after I loosen the tie, smooth the paper against my knee. "I think it's a map."

"Of what?"

"Not sure."

I've got to show him this. Hard to believe I was tired earlier—I'm *wired* now, thundering up the staircase two steps at a time, crashing into a brick wall that's been unexpectedly erected on the second floor.

The bricks are softer than they look, absorbing my muffled "Oof." And an "Mmpphhhhh," which might or might not be caused by how good it smells.

"Sorry." The brick wall grows arms, gingerly tipping me back with the tips of its fingers. Has Wesley always been this tall? From down here, the top of his head is in the stars. I'd have to break my vertebrae to see his face.

He takes a blundering step away, raking a hand through his hair. "Can I . . . see it?"

Instead of handing the map over, I scoot next to him so that we pore over it side by side. "I'm pretty sure these are trees." I point at a jumble of broccoli florets drawn in blue pen.

Wesley analyzes the map closely, raising it higher. Our height difference means that the half of the paper I'm still clutching is bending significantly downward. "This is the manor here," he murmurs, pointing at a blue square. I'm distracted by his large hands with short, square nails as he skims a finger to a second, much smaller blue square next to the manor. I've seen these hands halve an apple without a knife, and they're the same ones that paint miniature pirate ships. "This is labeled 'shed,' but that doesn't make sense. The shed should be over here." His finger dances an inch to the left.

"The cabin used to be Victor's work shed," I reply. "Maybe that's the cabin, not the garden shed."

He nods. "That has to be it. All this over here, I don't recognize." He circles an area that says *prairie smoke field*.

"That used to be a field, yeah. Back before Aunt Violet was anti-lawn."

"Pro–natural habitats," he replies with emphasis. "Everyone with a yard should designate a natural growth area, to be honest. Put up a small fence around it and just let—"

"Yep, sure," I interrupt. "Look at those X's! It's like a traditional pirate treasure map." There are five of them, scattered wildly all over the property. It would be an exhaustive trek to get to all of them, any potential treasure buried under the X's hidden by more than shallow mounds of dirt by now. This map is at least two decades old. There could be whole adult trees growing over the tops of those X's.

"Violet's second wish," we say at the same time, meeting each other's gaze. I'm suddenly aware of how close we're standing—so is Wesley, and we spring apart.

"Violet said Victor thought there was buried treasure," I explain unnecessarily. "Maybe these are a few of the spots where they thought treasure might be located. Being older, and Victor's health being the way it was, I guess they'd gotten to the point in their treasure hunt where they were theorizing instead of doing any physical digging."

"Mm-hmm, mm-hmm," he replies quickly. "Makes sense. I'll just pocket this map, then . . ." He starts to slide it into his pocket, but I snatch it up.

"Not so fast."

"Finders Keepers rules apply," he says with a teasing half grin. "That's part of Violet's dying wish. I don't know about you, but I'm morally obligated to honor her terms."

"I'm the one who found the map."

"And tomorrow, you'll find that all the shovels have been hidden. Somewhere you'll never be able to reach, like the top of the fridge. What are you going to use to dig up treasure, a spoon?"

"Maybe. I'm a Maybell Parrish. It's tradition to do everything the hard way."

His eyes flicker with amusement in the shadowy corridor. "Are there a lot of Maybell Parrishes running around out there?"

"Maybe." I bite my lip, trying not to dwell on that tonal shift in him, where it feels like he isn't merely tolerating me anymore. This is . . . friendly. It's nice. I'm dreading him taking this budding niceness away, putting *that* out of reach. "Here, I'll make a deal with you. If you do all the digging, I'll bring you along and we'll split the treasure fifty-fifty."

"This mythical treasure," he adds, in a way that tries to be skeptical but wants to believe.

"This treasure that could be real. There's no reason to think it shouldn't be."

He frowns, thinking. "Okay. But not for another week, all right? Are you willing to wait until Saturday? I've got a landscaping job in Gatlinburg that'll take up most of my time from the third through the seventh."

I stick out my hand for him to shake. "Deal."

"And now." He keeps my hand encased in his for a few seconds longer than necessary, then squeezes lightly before letting go. "Come on." He jerks his head, already walking off without me.

"Ah, yes. The monumentally important discovery of yours, which you incorrectly believe is more impressive than a Christmas tree."

"A Christmas tree in *May*."

"You seem to be stuck on that."

But then I shut up, because he leads me toward an open door that is essentially a portal to the past. A ruffled white and pink blanket on a canopy bed, pillows smaller than I remember. Everything smaller than I remember, in fact. A white dresser. A pink vanity table. A shelf of my old favorites: The *American Girl* series, with Molly's books taking the special number one spot. *Dear America* books. *The Princess Diaries. A Series of Unfortunate Events.* And hanging on the wall across the room from my bed, a very old postcard in a wooden frame with no glass.

Season's Greetings from the Top of the World!

Two red-cheeked, bundled-up kids play on an old-fashioned sled in front of Falling Stars Hotel, snow covering the ground, roof, and distant timberline. The hand-painted postcard is bordered with holly. Victorian lamps flank a wrought-iron archway dressed in red and green garland, cardinals perched atop.

The house is pink.

Not because it truly was, but because the artist painted Falling Stars at sunset, taking creative liberties with pigments. In 1934, somebody made Falling Stars look just as magical on the outside as it felt to me on the inside, embedding that magic in my brain, literally shining a rose-colored light on all my recollections of this place. I can see now, from an aged and experienced perspective, that gray stonework lies beneath the wash of sunrise.

"Oh," I say softly.

"I know. Memory is a strange thing." He steps closer, sliding his hands into his pockets. "This used to be your room, I take it?"

"Yeah." I barely hear myself, taking the picture down off the wall. It leaves behind a small imprint untouched by dust. "I can't believe none of this has changed."

We lock eyes and I know we're both thinking the same thing. Violet kept my room this way in case I ever needed it again.

"There were a couple others that I think used to hang up, too, but fell off the wall." He takes two more postcards from the dresser, handing them to me. Their condition isn't as good—one's half missing, advertising the *biggest victory garden in the state of Tennessee!* The other's severely water-damaged: BUY WAR BONDS.

I can't stop staring at the postcard, filling all the way up with emotion. My throat is raw, eyes burning. He nudges it. "You know, I think I like it better like that."

"Pink?" I sit down on the bed, laugh hoarsely.

"The house does need a paint job anyway."

I quirk an eyebrow. "You'd let me paint the house pink?"

My mind is a fanciful storybook that loves symbolism and parallels. It invents romantic notions, where there often aren't any, in everyday life situations. It has led me to perceive many a man in a nobler light than he deserved, and it's told me bad situations were *meant to be* as a coping mechanism to make them bearable. Wesley is watching me with a glint in his eyes that draws an imaginary parallel line into the misty past, X marking the spot on Victor. I think of how Victor used to look at Violet with a similar expression, like he knew an extraordinary secret and she was the only other person in the world in on the secret with him. I think of the incredible, million-to-one odds that out of all the pictures Gemma could have used to catfish me, she used *his*.

Wesley smiles, which sends the warning sirens blaring. I'm reading into coincidences. The universe is chaos and coincidence. If it were operating with any intention, it would be cruelty.

"Not by yourself," he says. "I'd help you paint it. We'll put some gold touches around the windows and doors, too, like the way the light hits it here." He taps the postcard, but I don't tear my gaze from him. My heart is thumping fast, fast, racing right toward a cliff. A little bit of friendliness doesn't mean anything more than that. I'm a danger to myself, my imagination running away.

I nod mutely.

"As someone who likes paint," he says sheepishly, refusing to simply say *As an artist,* "I think the project will be kinda cool. Trying to make the house look like it's sitting in a perpetual sunset."

"Yeah," I force myself to say. "That would be wonderful."

I thank him for the discovery, clutching it as I depart. I am nearly in the clear when my Achilles' heel is attacked—he's turned on Christmas music at top volume, *sleigh bells riiiing* following me down the stairs.

Chapter 12

THE FOLLOWING DAY, I head over to the manor to get to work and it's a relief that Wesley's away doing a job. Why did I think friendship with Wesley would be a good idea? It's a *terrible* idea. I'm going to catch a crush on him. He's dreamy, but until now his grumpiness has saved me from making an idiot of myself. If he shows me the barest hint of warmth, my weak knees will buckle like clockwork. It's my worst habit.

Right now, a crush swelling with the most dangerous undertow I've ever laid eyes on flits at the horizon, tearing it up at warp speed, but I've still got time. I've got willpower. I am resolving myself here and now to keep my distance, which should be easy enough. Wesley loves distance! We'll ignore each other. Wesley loves ignoring each other! I've picked so many insensitive, cold hearts to give mine to, but his is a new record. I'd be the least safe in his hands: What if we dated and it went south, as most relationships do? We share a house! Neither of us wants to give it up. I'd be living directly under my ex, unable to escape him. If he cheated on me like most of the others did, that would ruin Falling Stars for me forever. It'd be too painful to stay—I'd have to give up the hotel of my dreams. Unacceptable.

I can't decide if that scenario is better or worse than another contender: that I'll develop feelings, and those feelings will be unrequited.

I've got to stamp out those feeble quiverings *now*, before they become a problem. He's gone and dug a tent out of storage—one tent, singular—to use on Saturday, as he casually mentioned the trip will take us all day and most of the terrain we have to explore will have to be trod on foot. If it gets late, we'll camp out. In the same tent. Together. Maybe he's able to be blasé about it because he finds me so unattractive that I'm not even a shadow on his radar; I'm like a shovel, just part of the expedition gear. Or maybe he plans to seduce me. I envision us lying next to a roaring fire as he feeds me s'mores . . .

"You don't like him," I tell myself sternly. "He's a grouch."

I walk into the ballroom, determined to lose myself in cleaning. The first thing I see is the handmade tinfoil star that's appeared at the top of my Christmas tree, which I'm not able to reach. Someone has indulged my untimely holiday spirit.

I groan louder, spin on my heel, and walk right back out.

"He doesn't like me," I growl at myself. "I'm just the pesky equal inheritor. The necessary evil he can't get rid of, so he's sucking it up and making the best of a bad situation." I smack my face lightly. "Even if he *does* like me, it doesn't matter. Doesn't change the fact that muddying those waters is a bad, bad, bad idea."

Think long-term, Maybell. Priorities. Eyes on the prize.

I open the dumbwaiter longingly and despair that it's empty.

He made me a *tree-topper*. It's even better than a store-bought one, with its cute little irregular edges . . . I have no willpower at all.

I smack myself again.

There's only one tried-and-true method to escape dwelling on this. I pace back and forth, giving myself a workout, mentally reaching for the door of my café. It won't open.

A sign on the door reads OUT FOR LUNCH.

"Can't stop me," I grumble, probably losing it, as I pick the lock and the door in the clouds shoves open with a tinkling chime.

I definitely didn't put all these ferns here. Moss creeps up tables, swarming napkin dispensers and condiment bottles. I hack vines out of my way, sidestepping HAZARD signs, breaking a sweat to get behind the counter. A gurgling sound of rushing water is coming from the jukebox. My doting parents pop their heads in, concerned. "Are you open?"

"Yes! Just give me a minute. It's . . . ah . . ."

"You've got a forest," Mom notes, eyes large as she stares around.

I scratch my head, three small birds circling. I'm going to get cited by the health inspector. "It would appear so."

A familiar figure nods politely to my mother as he saunters over, making himself at home on a stool. "What are you doing here?" I exclaim, dropping a pot of coffee. Glass shatters everywhere. "Oh, goodness. So sorry, that's never happened before."

"Hi, Maybell."

"Hi . . . you."

He grins wider, propping his chin in his hand. "Not gonna say my name?"

"Don'tseetheneedto," I mumble under my breath. "You really shouldn't be here right now."

"Why's that?" He flicks open a menu. "I'll have one of these." Taps the Grumpy/Sunshine Platter: a frowny face of blueberries and banana slices on French toast with a sunny-side-up egg.

"I don't serve French toast and eggs!" I grab the menu from him, panicking. "Where'd that come from?" Other options I never approved write themselves into existence. *Forced Proximity Pancakes. World's Biggest Cinnamon Roll: Recommended by the chef! Crispy outer layer conceals a soft, delicious center.*

"Slow-burned toast," he begins to read over my shoulder. I snap the menu closed, my cheeks hotter than a stove. "Did I just read something about a secret baby?"

"We're all out of toast. And secret babies. You can have a donut. We serve *donuts*."

"I'll take your special of the day." He points at the chalkboard menu on the wall behind me. "*Opposites Attract: coffee cake and sweetheart tea.* Aw, isn't that cute." A dimple pops in his cheek. I die.

Fireworks begin flaming up behind him, huge heart-shaped bursts that transform into confetti. He turns. "What was that?"

"Oh no." My heart sinks. Flutters. I wring my hands. "It's happening."

A skywriter zigzags through the clouds outside the window, barely visible between dense branches. I leap in front of it to block the view, shielding the banner proclaiming *MAYBELL LIKES—*

He spins back toward me and tosses his head, giving me a knowing look. He has no idea how sensual it is. The tingles that course through me course through the electricity, too, popping breakers. "Oh, yes. It's inevitable, isn't it?"

I kneel (or collapse) to clean up the mess of glass and coffee, but it dawns on me that I don't have a broom and dustpan here. I glance sadly at my *5,840 days without an accident* sign as the number switches to *0*. What is going *on* around here lately?

He leans across the counter, surveying me on the floor. I wish it would open up and swallow me. "You all right down there?"

"Fine," I reply faintly. "It's fine, I'm only dead." It was the dimple. It killed me.

RIP, me.

"Did you fall asleep like that? Odd place for a nap."

The fireworks shape-shift into a chandelier, and as he extends a hand to help me to my feet I'm zapped out of the café. This is IRL Wesley, gripping my hand in his (*oh*, his hand is strong) and standing me upright in the real world. He hands me my glasses, then holds up a white paper bag. Gives it a shake. "I finished early for the day. Brought home some—"

"Ahhhhhhh-ahh," I interrupt. He cannot finish that sentence. If that bag has pastries in it, I'll swoon. *Resist! Resist!*

I stare into his eyes, which are sparkling like fire agate. Do ordinary eyes sparkle like these? These are chocolate and hazelnut. Smoky earth. They would make angels weep and they're boring into mine, calmly oblivious to the truth that I'm spiraling, demanding no answers as to why I was lying on the floor with my glasses off.

"You look feverish," he murmurs, gaze dropping from my eyes to my lips.

My default recording plays itself, lacking air. "I had red hair . . ." I wheeze. "When I was born."

"Oh, really?" He should be stepping away, but he doesn't know it. He keeps getting closer, filling in the distance as I shuffle backward step by step. There's nowhere safe for my eyes to rest. I look at his hair and words like *gilded* and *Apollo* explode in my mind as I imagine plunging my fingers into the wavy strands. I look at his eyes and hunger. Forget his mouth.

His *mouth*. It's too late, I'm looking.

"I have to use the bathroom," I blurt. "It's going to be a while. Don't wait up."

Wesley smiles confusedly, eyebrows knitted, as I dash away. "O-kaay?"

I throw myself into the bathroom and give up on life. This is bad. It's so, so bad. All it took for me to flush my sense down the toilet was an attractive man cutting a star out of aluminum foil. Surely I am not this weak.

I check my reflection in the mirror. The Maybell I find opposite me is a damn disappointment: chest heaving, red and blotchy all over, hairline damp. I'm a certified mess. I check the window, that threatening horizon looming closer—a stone's throw away. I'll be fine. I only need some space. Until Saturday, I need to avoid all interaction with Wesley, and thinking about him. We're talking zero-tolerance policy. Total ban.

Or else I'm screwed.

I SUCCESSFULLY EVADE WESLEY for the rest of the day, citing an upset stomach. The next morning I've got a new bottle of Pepto Bismol outside my bedroom door. He doesn't initiate any more contact, thankfully. And sadly. Maybe he hates me now? Maybe he was *just about* to like me, but I ruined it, which I should be grateful for, because IT WOULDN'T WORK ANYWAY, MAYBELL. Maybell Parrishes don't cycle through the five stages of grief. We burrow into the denial leg of the journey like tourists overstaying our welcome and live there forever and ever. We also chug peppermint hot cocoa whenever we're drowning in dramatic passions (I'm on my third pint of the day) and mythologize ourselves in the plural.

But on Wednesday, Wesley texts me. It's a serve I didn't expect.

He's snapped a picture of my recent addition to the ballroom mural: the tiny *My May Belle* chugging along near his pirate ship. I didn't consult wind patterns before painting it and the two boats are on track to smash into each other.

He adds this question, sans punctuation: Why did you add an e

I look up the Wikipedia page for *My May Belle*, a showboat that cruises the Tennessee River in Knoxville, and send him the link.

A young Julie Parrish had dreams of sailing away on that riverboat, I type. When she was pregnant with me she tried to run away from home, but the sheriff found her and brought her back. My name was supposed to be May Belle, but Mom was loopy on pain meds when she signed the birth certificate.

Growing up, she built up this boat in my head until it was larger than life, the pinnacle of Southern charm, telling me we'd go there someday to have lunch in big Kentucky Derby hats and white dresses. We finally went for my thirteenth birthday, but her boyfriend at the time's daughter came along and I got jealous of the attention Mom gave her, then subsequently moody. Mom tended to be extra-specially nice to the kids of her boyfriends, trying to win them over. I ruined the day for everyone.

I like Maybell without an e, he types back.

I went once, I tell him. I told the staff what my name was and they gave me free dessert.

The occasion had been so talked up, so looked forward to, but ultimately I remember regular old Happy Meal dinners with more fondness. I think my mom was trying to re-create a pale image of her own childhood nostalgia.

Is there a story behind the name Wesley? I ask.

He replies: I was the fifth son. They ran out of names.

A minute later, he tacks on: My mom had a dream while pregnant that she was putting wooden letters above the crib. They spelled out Wesley.

Aww, I like that story.

Better than my brother Humphrey's. He was named after the paramedic who delivered him in a Walgreens parking lot. Then he sends another photo of the mural, playing a game of Can You Spot the Difference? A dark shape in the water swans away from the kraken.

Is that a sea snake?

The Loch Ness Monster, he says. She's real and she's out there.

I'm about to respond when I get a grip on myself and turn off my phone before temptation destroys the shred of self-control I'm clinging to. *Distance. Space. Eyes on the prize.* If I want to ward off a crush, it's the only way.

I'm not so strong that I don't duck into the ballroom a few hours later and paint a small island in the lagoon, complete with a palm tree and a tiny man laying out for a tan. When I check it again on Thursday, Wesley's given the tiny man sunglasses and a sunburned nose. I also find two miniature people, a man on board the kraken-caged *Felled Star* and a woman waving a handkerchief at him from the deck of *My May Belle.*

. . . .

I STRAIN TO IGNORE the mural all day Thursday, but on Friday I'm swept away by a marathon of Hallmark movies and it punctures a hole in my already flimsy self-discipline. I take pity on the pirate, about to be sent to the ocean floor courtesy of an enormous sea monster. *My May Belle* throws a life preserver out. I dot all the trees with tiny silver stars, even the palms.

Wesley notices immediately, adding ornaments and lights. We take turns sneaking into the ballroom to add more and more, until it doesn't resemble your average waterfall-lagoon mural so much as Neverland. I have a sickness. I'm communicating with Wesley more now than I was when we were verbally talking.

We've both fully moved into the manor, he into my old bedroom and me right below in a guest room. I hear his footsteps above at night as he paces out of his room down the hall, then it falls quiet, then he's pacing again. I can't fall asleep until he's completely still, not because the noise bothers me but because I get caught up in visualizing him, wondering what he's doing, what he's thinking about.

He texts on Friday night. Want to head out at 9 am tomorrow? Or 10, if 9 is too early?

This is the part where I should cancel the treasure hunt, apologies to Aunt Violet. She'll understand if we don't carry out this wish.

I reply: All packed and ready to go at 8:30. Just filling some virtual shopping carts with all the decorative rugs I'm going to buy with the solid gold bars you're digging up tomorrow!

I'm about to turn off my phone, to be on the safe side, but he responds swiftly. My brother Casey built my landscaping website, and he's making one for my animal sanctuary. He offered to make a website for the hotel if you want. Unless you've changed your mind and realized a hotel would be awful.

I sit up so fast that if there were water in this claw-foot tub I'm lounging fully clothed in, it would have gone sloshing all over the ballroom floor.

He's told his brother about my hotel. His brother knows I exist. I wonder if Casey is the one who got married in that black-and-white photo of Wesley in a tuxedo, but I can't pose this question without Wesley pressing the sensitive topic of my having seen that photo in the first place.

That would be fantastic!!! I say. What are his rates?

He replies so quickly, he had to have had the response typed up and ready to send. I've identified the font they used in your postcard as Fanal, in case you wanted to use it in brochures or advertising. Thought maybe you'd be interested, since you like the postcard so much. I tried my best to color-match the house. If you want to imitate sunset, we'll need a few different colors. These ones are the closest match I could find. What do you think? He includes links to three shades of paint—Bermuda Breeze, Raspberry Mousse, and Oxford Gold.

Neither of the pinks he's chosen is quite identical to the hotel in the postcard, but my heart has taken too many arrows for me to dream of doing anything other than enthusiastically agreeing. He went to the trouble of researching the font. Color-matching the house. This surly giant buttoned up in ten thousand buttons, who likes plants more than people, is going to paint his house pink because a woman he's only known for a month mistakenly thought Falling Stars was supposed to be that color.

"You don't like it?"

I jerk my head. Wesley's in the ballroom.

I grip the sides of the bathtub and steel my spine, praying I don't look anything close to how I feel. "Huh?"

"You didn't reply."

I glance at my phone. The time stamp on his message shows he sent it fourteen minutes ago. I've been staring moonily into space for fourteen minutes.

"Sorry, I got distracted. Those shades are *perfect*, thank you. And thanks for looking up the font, too. That's a good idea, going old-fashioned nostalgia for advertising. Playing up the historical . . . ness." My voice is squeaky, words rushed.

Lying in a bathtub in the middle of the room feels a great deal different when I've got a man towering above me. He tilts his head as he analyzes me, gesture revving my pulse. "What?" I ask lowly, nervous. Wesley's gaze sweeps over me: my knees are bent, heels propped up on the lip of the tub. My sundress has slid down to midthigh, and while I wouldn't think twice about showing this amount of leg on any ordinary day, the position I'm in leaves me feeling exposed as well as uncharacteristically lewd.

His lips press together. I used to think that was a sign of annoyance, but now I'm not so sure.

I cross my legs in a stab at modesty, but the action makes my hem slip down even farther and I hurriedly smooth the material back up my legs. Wesley revolves to face the wall, rubbing his jaw with one hand. I am burning all over.

"Eight thirty a.m., then," he says, voice gravelly.

I sink down into the tub, skin scorching. "Yep."

My face hidden by porcelain, I glance at the wall in time to watch the profile of his shadow turn, throwing another look back at me. He's got a fist pressed to his mouth.

"I gotta . . . I'm going back upstairs." He sounds weak.

"Yep," I repeat, an octave higher. "See you in the morning."

I see Wesley well before morning. He visits me while we're asleep.

I'm back in the ballroom, standing above him. He's the one in the tub now, sprawled out lazy and regal, wearing a pirate costume. He holds out his arms for me to climb aboard. "Time for your bath, Maybell."

I wake up at 8:29 Saturday morning hot, sweaty, and doomed. Nothing like a sex dream between friends to speed up the unavoidable: I've got a full-blown crush.

Chapter 13

NOT TO BE DRAMATIC, but I would rather drink battery acid than be in the throes of a crush.

Crushes are fun in theory (ask me about my many dreamland husbands), but in reality, they're energy vampires that are more trouble than they're worth. The preoccupation is exhausting. I get sick to my stomach from swallowing too many butterflies, I lose sleep, my already intrusive penchant for fantasizing levels up a thousand degrees. I start worrying too much about whether my hair looks perfect or if I'm talking too loud, and prescription-strength deodorant becomes the safety pin holding my precarious shit together. All this emotional work, only to always end up being hurt by it? When I drag a glance over my dating history, the polls are conclusive. Nothing good *ever* comes from a crush.

Wesley's wearing a knitted white cardigan this morning, lounging against the wall and peeling a banana, when I stroll into the kitchen with my camping gear. Cardigans are my kryptonite. I don't know how he knows, but he knows. What am I talking about? Of course he doesn't know. He doesn't *care*. Oh lord, this is already wretched.

He makes a *come here* motion and shows me one of the X's on the treasure map. "I figured we'd start over here, then work our way northeast. The truck won't be able to pass beyond this point"—he raps a cluster of trees—"so I hope you won't mind carrying the pack with our food and smaller supplies?" His questioning look prompts me to nod.

Wesley's pack is considerably larger, containing our tent and sleeping bags. He'll also be toting a shovel. I think about the roll of toilet paper in my pack and regret every choice I've ever made that's led me to this point.

"Great." I unscrew a bottled water, proceeding to chug the whole thing.

"Hey." He bends his knees and tilts to look me in the eye, the ghost of a smile quirking his lips. "You all right? You good?"

"Yep."

The playful light in his eyes falls flat. "You don't want to?"

"Are you trying to talk me out of this?" I pick up my pack, narrowing my eyes at him jokingly. "That treasure's mine, Koehler. Let's roll."

The smile returns, bigger now. "Okay, *Parrish*."

It's shaping up to be a balmy spring day, and the drive is gorgeous. Wesley's pickup barrels through tunnels of green, bright and rich, like being inside an emerald. Irises and bleeding hearts are in bloom, garden-variety flowers petering out the farther we go, overtaken by native plants. He calls them all by name, pointing out lady's-slipper orchids, phlox, silverbells growing directly out of cracks in the road. We'll eventually have to get the road repaved, as it looks like it's endured several earthquakes and an apocalypse. The prospect makes me a little sad. I'm starting to like the wildness of Falling Stars, nature reclaiming what we stole.

All too soon, we're parking in a field and Wesley's killing the engine. "This is it," he announces, opening his door.

"Already?" I grab the map, calculating how far we are from the first X, then how far away the second X is from the first. There are five potential treasure sites. Over two hundred and ninety-four acres.

"Hope you're wearing hiking shoes."

I am. With special Dr. Scholl's socks that are supposed to prevent blistering. The last thing my dumbass libido needs is for my feet to give out on me, leaving Wesley responsible for carrying me home.

"Hope you're wearing shovel-digging gloves," I counter.

"Hands are already callused." He raises his brows, a touch haughty. "I'm in landscaping, remember? No stranger to shovels."

Oh. Right.

I have no business dwelling on his callused hands, or how sturdy and capable he looks when he shrugs his pack on. I bet he could lift me up on his shoulders right now without a faltering step. If I'm going to survive this, I'll have to pretend he isn't my hot exploring companion but a . . . guard bear . . . or something. A bear with the stubble of a beard and minty mouthwash on his breath. And a *cardigan*. Oof.

I'm fine. I'm fine! I'll fight this off like an infection.

"So, Koehler," I begin casually as we slip into the trees. Effortlessly casually. Breezily, in fact. "How'd you get into the landscaping business?"

"I grew up on a farm. Tell me about your dad?"

I nearly walk into a tree.

"Sorry." He looks it, too. "I didn't mean to put it so bluntly. It's just, I've been wondering. I know the name Parrish came from your mom's side of the family. You've never mentioned your dad . . ." His face is reddening.

He's awkward, but I'm about to be even more so. "I don't know who my dad is."

"Oh no, I'm sorry. I'm not the best conversationalist—I'm much better in text messages and notes left in dumbwaiters."

"It's all right." I offer him a rueful smile. "You want to hear something bonkers? Whenever I think about my dad I picture Mick Fleetwood. You know who I'm talking about? One of the guys from Fleetwood Mac?"

He laughs. "Are you serious? Why?"

I know this sounds ridiculous. And illogical. "Mick Fleetwood was about forty years old when I was conceived, and also, he's *Mick Fleetwood*. I know he's not my father. And yet."

He arches a brow. "And yet?"

"It's funny what the human brain does with one little puzzle piece when it's missing the rest of the picture. My parents met at a Fleetwood Mac concert. She was more of a Johnny Cash girl, but her friend had an extra ticket."

Wesley's eyes are fixed on the forest floor, a wrinkle in his brow. "Mm."

"That's all she's told me about him. Fleetwood Mac's the only piece of information I've got, so even though my dad was probably some scrawny teenager, all my life I've pictured the middle-aged guy on the cover of the *Rumours* album." Which I bought with my first paycheck, and have memorized. "I think he must have blue eyes, though, because mine are blue and Mom's are green."

"My parents have been together since middle school."

"*Wow.*"

"Yeah, it kind of sucks for all their kids that our parents found their perfect match so young. They think it should be that easy for everyone. All I ever hear when I visit is that the clock is ticking and I'm going to die alone."

I wince. "You're not going to die alone."

He shrugs. "I'm fine with it if I do."

I sense that he's starting to clam up, so I change the subject, digging my compass out of my pocket to pretend I know what I'm doing when I aim it this way and that. I got the thing from a box of Lucky Charms when I was a kid. "You sure we're not gonna run into Bigfoot today?"

He knows what I'm doing, but it works—he grants me a side-long almost-smile. "You haven't been paying attention in class. Sasquatches don't live in Appalachia."

"Sasquatches, the Loch Ness Monster," I remark, unable to hide my curiosity. "Do you believe in them?"

"Will you laugh at me if I say yes?"

"I would never."

He considers this. "Then I might believe in them. Or I might believe in the *possibility* of them. Wouldn't it be incredible, if these creatures are real and they've successfully eluded humans all this time? I mean, humans have taken over everything. We cage animals, we pillage, we destroy."

I raise my eyebrows.

"Meanwhile, here are these other ancient beings who just want privacy, and they've outsmarted us," he goes on. "A giant middle finger to the assholes who've ruined their habitats." He frowns, coming to a standstill. "I'm sorry for saying *assholes*."

I shake my head, suppressing a laugh. "It's fine."

"I don't like to swear in front of ladies."

"It's *fine*. I swear all the time. Anyway, you were saying . . . ?"

"I got carried away. I won't curse again." I throw him a dour look and he continues: "Okay, so these people who hunt for Nessie, who have their own TV shows dedicated to getting video evidence of the supernatural, it's all a money grab. They desperately want to find them, for money and clout, but if they find Sasquatch, if they find Nessie, that means the end of those creatures' way of life. They'd never have peace again. If they're legitimate, scientists would get tons of funding to do a real search, forcing them out of hiding. It's not in their best interest to be found—which means the hunters don't care about these creatures, really. It makes me happy to think they're out there existing, that they'll never be found by those they don't want finding them."

"You don't want to find them?"

"I do want proof," he admits, "especially of the Loch Ness Monster. That's my favorite myth; there's a ton of evidence to back up its existence, and not just the existence of one, but probably more. Maybe even more than a handful. *But*, I only want proof because I really need to know these myths most of the world doesn't believe in have gotten away with it. That they've pulled off the greatest trick ever, living so stealthily that they've become legends and to believe otherwise nowadays makes everyone skeptical. I want to believe there are still wonders out there left unspoiled." His face hardens. "But I wouldn't interfere. I wouldn't so much as take a picture of a Loch Ness Monster. I'd never violate its right to privacy."

"You wouldn't tell anyone?"

"I wouldn't tell a soul. Not a single soul, not for a billion dollars." He glances at me, expression unsure. "You want to laugh."

He is wholly misinterpreting my smile. I have never adored a speech more than I adore Wesley's talking ardently about mythical creatures with longing in his gaze. I have never had reason to hope the Loch Ness Monster exists, and now I'm 100 percent invested. I need Nessie to be real, for Wesley.

"Not at all," I assure him. "I believe in things, too. Like, all the UFOs that have been spotted? I think we probably have aliens walking around on Earth." I shrug.

His eyes light up. "Right? It makes sense! I think extraterrestrials are here, too. Maybe hiding in plain sight, looking the same as we do, or possibly shielded from the visible spectrum by advanced technology. Or, the government has them in captivity but they're not telling us because it'll expose the inhumane experiments they're performing on them." He slows down. "Look."

It's the entrance to a caved-in mine. The mine's drawn on the map, too, right next to the first X. It's barbed-wired, boarded up with a rotted BEWARE sign. I wouldn't have noticed it, obscured by a mass of thorny vines.

I whistle. "Nice catch."

We drop our bags and stretch our limbs, my muscles sore already. After I strike gold and become a billionaire, my first purchase is going to be a track extending all the way out here, with one of those San Francisco trolleys to go with it.

"So. Aliens. Area Fifty-One," I mention as we forage with our noses to the ground. I'm pleased I can contribute more to the alien conversation, wanting to keep the topic alive when it brings out such a marvelously, talkatively zealous side of Wesley. It's clear he's given myths and conspiracies a lot of thought.

One side of Wesley's mouth hooks back in a grin. He reaches toward me, hand grazing my chest as he touches the pendant on my necklace. It lasts only a second, then he lets go, gaze averted to the ground. As soon as I can breathe again (it takes several seconds), I touch the pendant myself and it hits me.

The engraved *51*.

On this jewelry that I thought was Violet's, since I found it under Violet's bed, which was actually . . .

"This is *yours*!" I cry.

Wesley bites his lip to keep back another grin, but it escapes. "Yes."

I gape at him openmouthed. "Why didn't you say anything? I thought it belonged to Aunt Violet."

"I know."

"I thought it was for her—for her fifty-first anniversary or something!" I sputter.

"I figured. Violet bought that for me as a present. It was an *X-Files* key chain; we used to watch that show together."

"And here I've been wearing it! Well, don't I feel stupid." I immediately reach for the back of my neck, fumbling with the clasp, but his hand shoots out, fingers closing over mine.

"No, keep it," he tells me earnestly. "Please."

I grumble, embarrassed. It's good I can look away, busying myself studying the ground for any markers, any disturbances that might hint at treasure in the vicinity.

"I like that you wear it," he tells me in a tone so soft and genuine that my chest cavity feels hollowed out. "For months, I wasn't able to find it. Then one day, there's that missing piece of my key chain around your neck."

"Wesley."

He stops. I raise my arm to a tree with a trunk curving into the shape of an S, the side facing us scratched with a large *X* at eye level.

Wesley stares. "Well, that was a lot easier than I thought it'd be."

"No kidding. An actual X?" I glance from the tree to the map and back again. "They guessed the location with perfect accuracy."

He unzips the outer pocket of his bag and withdraws a tool that resembles an oversized box cutter. Then he presses a button and waves it over the grass at the base of the tree. "What's that?" I ask.

"Handheld metal detector."

"Ooooohh, aren't we a Boy Scout." I'm teasing, but he nods in the affirmative.

"Eagle Scout." He scans my face, adding wryly, "I was super popular in high school, as you can imagine."

To look at him, you'd think he *would* have been super popular. A hot jock type. But Wesley Koehler isn't anything at all that he seems.

Every new detail about him makes me want to know more. "Did you grow up near here?"

A small light on the metal detector flashes green as it beeps. He switches it out for a shovel, then juts a thumb. West, according to my compass. "In Stevenson, where my family still lives. You won't have heard of it, it's a very rural town."

I'm amazed that he knows which direction is west without looking up. "I bet you were big into FFA in high school." He definitely seems like the Future Farmers of America type.

"I got detention for being late to English all the time because I was taking care of other students' plants in our ag class's garden."

"Giving those kids A's they didn't deserve, I bet."

"Worth it. None of them knew anything about tomatoes."

The tip of his shovel clinks against something underground. We lock eyes. "Aye, here be ye gold, matey," I say, dead serious.

Wesley snort-laughs. We kneel, dusting dirt away, and wrench a dinged-up cookie tin out of the ground. Royal Dansk Danish butter cookies.

"Not quite a treasure chest, is it?" I observe doubtfully, the bars of gold in my mind shrinking down. Maybe it'll be gold coins instead.

"Hey, I like cookies. I'll take it."

"Mmm, decades-old cookies." I try to prize the lid off but it's rusted shut. I hand the tin to Wesley, who pops its lid off in one easy motion. I'll be honest, it makes me a little bitter.

"Well, it's not cookies."

It isn't gold, either.

I lift an art deco diamond ring from its bed—a faded washcloth—and twist it to catch the light. Wesley selects another piece of jewelry, an engagement ring with a large emerald flanked by two diamonds on a gold band. The third item in the tin is a diamond bracelet.

"Holy cow!" I exclaim. "I bet these are worth a crap-ton of money." I pick up a small white card that has one line on it in gold typeface: *We'll always have Paris.* "Interesting."

Wesley eyes the card from opposite me, reaching for it. "May I?"

I hand over the card, trading him for the emerald ring. The metal is cold as I slide it over my finger, mentally pressing PLAY on the scenario of standing on the Pont des Arts in Paris while a man on bended knee proposes to me with such a ring. Below us, the Seine glitters.

"This is extraordinary," I murmur, trying on the bracelet.

"We have to check the others. What if there's treasure in one of the other spots, too?"

Wesley nods. "We should definitely check them all."

IT ISN'T LONG BEFORE I'm regretting that bottle of water I chugged right before we left. I order him to stay put on the bank of a stream while I find somewhere to relieve myself. Paranoid he'll see me from across a football field's worth of distance, I get hopelessly lost in the weeds and don't stumble my way back for thirty-six minutes. Wesley rises from his designated rock on the riverbank when I emerge, face white with panic. His hair is a mess, like he's been running his fingers through it nonstop. I notice he has rerolled his sleeping bag to compress every molecule of air from it and tucked it into the top of his pack along with the many bells and whistles he's also reorganized during my absence. "I was about to go looking for you! I was prepared to get slapped for it, too, depending on what you were doing when I found you, but there are *bears* around here. Don't wander so far."

I wield my trusty can of bear mace that I pray I won't have to use, smiling. It hurts. My left cheek said hello to a briar a little too closely and got clawed. "I'm all good!"

"Here, you should put on more bug spray. It's been a few hours." Wesley starts fussing with Off! Deep Woods and a creamy green ointment that smells powerfully of mint. I wrinkle my nose as I slather it on, but it's not good enough for Wesley and he makes me slather it on even thicker until I'm head-to-toe green goop. I've never felt so unattractive in my life. Wesley stands back, appraising me with satisfaction. "It'll keep the ticks off you," he says, painting himself into Shrek.

"I smell foul."

"Better than getting Lyme disease." He tosses me a canteen of water. Wesley puts conscious effort into avoiding single-use plastics and wouldn't be caught dead with Aquafina. "Drink all of this, so that you don't get dehydrated. We've got a long hike ahead."

"Thank you, Eagle Scout." I pat his shoulder in a friendly way. His shirt is damp with sweat. "You too, mister. Have a canteen."

"I drank two of them while you were gone. Do you want to sit for a while? Take a break?"

"I'm ready to keep going if you are." There's no stopping me now. I've got gold fever. "Gimme that map."

He gives me the map and a granola bar. "To keep your blood sugar stable until we stop for lunch." He tries to be discreet about watching me eat it to make sure I finish the whole thing, but his long legs propel him at a brisker clip and being ahead of me, he has to keep twisting to see what I'm doing.

I can't even pretend to be annoyed—it's just so nice that someone cares. I peel the granola bar open, savoring it in tiny bites.

It takes close to two hours to reach the second X on the map, leading us to a long-abandoned rail yard. The metal detector is useless here, with scrap metal all over the place making it scream its head off. We toe aside unattached rails, pick up spikes and drop them into the weeds. Axles. Piston rods. A crushed lump of metal I'm calling a whistle, even if it isn't. We complain about mosquitoes and how it shouldn't be this warm so early in May until we're sick of each other and ourselves. Then, marvel of marvels, I find our hard-won loot inside an old switch lantern with its blue lens busted out. Probably from all the rocks we've kicked.

"This can't be it," I say, holding up the treasure. It's a cassette tape.

"Has to be. There's nothing else here."

Also, the only marking on the tape's label is the letter X, in blue pen.

"Maybe it's a decoy," I reply slowly. "Maybe somebody got to this treasure before we did and replaced it with a cassette tape." I can hear my incredulity. "For some reason."

"Maybe it's unreleased Beatles recordings," he replies mysteriously.

I brighten, giving his forearm a series of rapid pats. "Hey! What if it isn't music: what if it's a *secret murder confession*?" I rack my brains, trying to remember where the Zodiac Killer lived. "Are there any famous unsolved murders around here?"

"Let's keep going," he suggests, plucking the tape from my fingers. "Maybe we'll find something better at the next spot."

We break for lunch on a soft hilltop, the heat of the day swelling to a crescendo. Our peanut butter and jelly sandwiches are warm and mushy, but I've worked up such an appetite that I inhale mine in three seconds flat. I didn't pack enough water, so to ration it out Wesley offers to split a canteen. Every time it's my turn to take a swig, I get the world's most pathetic thrill out of knowing our mouths have both touched the same spot.

Getting up after my legs have had a chance to rest is torture. "Aghhhh," I groan.

Wesley gives me a once-over. "You want to sit for a while longer?"

"Nope." I meet his concern with obstinacy. "Unless you're getting tired."

"Pshhhh." He grins, and off we go. I have to grit my teeth for the first few minutes, before my muscles loosen up and cooperate again. My back isn't as compromising.

I shift the weight of my pack for the tenth time in as many minutes. Wesley's slightly ahead of me, so he shouldn't have noticed, but he tugs it off my shoulders, slinging it over one arm to lump my burden with his. I try to protest, but he shakes his head.

There are biting winds in my hollow chest cavity now. Sharp, silvery arctic winds. A crush's physical effects are just as intolerable as the emotional ones.

We find the third X at two thirty in the afternoon, in a wishing well. It isn't a proper wishing well. It's a decorative lawn ornament, with cute wooden shingles and a charming bucket you can pulley up and down. When we come upon it, the bucket's at the bottom. We crank it up, set aside clear plastic operating as a protective cover, and lift out two plastic-wrapped photographs.

One of the photos is of Uncle Victor, before he got sick, standing in front of the mirror that's built into the white wardrobe in the living room. His clothing and the salt-and-pepper hair tell me it was taken in the eighties. He's squinting with a Polaroid camera held up to one eye, flash brightening as he presses down on the shutter release. His other hand is in front of him, pointing down at the floor. The other photograph is exactly the same, identical down to the ghostly lens flares, except Victor's pointing upward.

I get full-body chills.

"This is weird. I think Victor knew a little more about this whole treasure legend than he was letting on." I shake my head in disbelief.

Wesley's not studying the photos. He's watching me. When I look at him, he scrubs his hands over his face, messes up his hair, and groans into his steepled fingers, "I have a confession to make."

Oh no. For a moment, the possibility that this is all made up, that Wesley put these treasures here, floats to the surface. But then he shows me the card from the first treasure: *We'll always have Paris.* There's print on the back, which I didn't look at before.

HOLLYWOOD ICE, FINEST CELEBRITY IMITATION JEWELRY. *THE CASABLANCA COLLECTION.*

My jaw goes slack. "So the jewelry is . . ." I can't bear to finish the thought.

He bites his lip, rueful. "Fake. Yeah."

"*Casablanca* . . . That movie's in Victor's VCR."

"Violet watched it every year on her wedding anniversary. I knew as soon as I saw the card that this must have all been planned by Victor. I'm thinking he buried it a long time ago, to lay the groundwork for a buried treasure urban legend. Either that or he thought of all this while he was sick and got someone to help him. A gift for Violet, to find after he died."

"Oh." I am feeling extremely stupid for getting so excited over the jewelry. The rings and bracelet are pretty, but they're costume jewelry. Probably worth about fifty or sixty bucks, if they're from a legitimate collector's edition. "I thought it was real treasure."

"I should have told you. It's just that you might have wanted to turn around and stop looking, if you knew this wasn't real."

And he wanted to keep going?

I want to ask why. I'm afraid he'll give me an answer.

Wesley tips up my chin with a fingertip, willing me to meet his eyes. They're flooded with guilt, and if I weren't already kneeling on the ground, that touch would have tripped me. But then he second-guesses it, letting go. "I'm sorry."

"No, it's all right. It's . . . sad that Violet never found this." After her husband died, she started filling up the house with junk to replace him. I think it's likely that she didn't put up a Christmas tree or ornaments ever again, so Victor's surprise went undiscovered.

I am horribly disappointed on his behalf, and devastated on hers. If she had known he'd left her something like this, maybe it would have changed her grieving process. Maybe she wouldn't have built the hoard monster that bricked up the door to Victor's bedroom, keeping his secret dormant until after her own death.

I gather up the rings and bracelet, the cassette tape, the photographs. "They *are* real, though," I tell him after a while. "They're not diamonds, but to Violet, this would have been better than treasure. And this was one of her dying wishes." I stand up, slipping each piece carefully back into my bag. "We might as well see it through."

Chapter 14

WESLEY AND I START talking about where we hope we'll be a year from now (the lady will be presiding over party games in the billiard room with a full house of guests; the gentleman will be avoiding aforementioned party games and guests, exercising a horse he rescued from negligent owners), getting so lost in the discussion that we get physically lost, too. It takes us longer than anticipated to find the fourth treasure: a dollar-store gramophone music box whose horn is camouflaged by the surrounding moonflowers, which plays the first few notes of "Somewhere over the Rainbow" before sputtering out.

A bridge we were supposed to cross to reach the fifth and final X is too crumbled to trust, so we lose an hour figuring out an alternate course. Dinner is a feast for champions: premade Mediterranean salads in mason jars, tomato and cheese sandwiches, and blueberry bars that have gotten so gooey that we have to wash our hands in a stream afterward.

"Nearly there," Wesley reports, adjusting his pack. It's cooling off, sky deepening to ocean blue with a dusting of red over the tree line. I spot the first star, which turns out to be an airplane. By the time I tear my eyes away from Wesley's grin, three real stars have appeared.

"Shoot." The metal detector, which I've wedged into the center of my rolled-up sleeping bag, falls out. We're up to our knees in a wide-open field of Indian grass, and the metal detector vanishes the moment it tumbles out. "Hang on."

Golden stalks ripple as Wesley twists at the waist to look me over. "What's wrong?"

"Dropped the metal detector."

He gets out his phone, tapping it a couple times to wake up the white-blue light. I do the same, but before I can drop down to select the flashlight my screen changes and my finger lands on a different button instead. "What the . . ."

Gemma Peterson is waving at me.

I've accepted a video call.

"Oh my god, you answered!" she exclaims. "Where are you? Are you outside?"

Wesley swings a confused glance toward my phone. "What's that?"

"Maybell," Gemma gasps. "I have a TON of stuff to catch you up on, oh my god oh my god oh my god. Where've you been? How *are* you? It's been forever!" She doesn't leave room for me to answer. "You won't believe it when you hear about—" Her eyes grow enormous, jaw hitting the floor. "Holy shit. You actually went and *found* him?"

"What—I—"

Wesley's behind me, he and Gemma staring at each other over my shoulder. Gemma bounces up and down, squealing at a sonic pitch. "Holy shit! Holy shiiiiiiit! Did I actually connect you two? Did I make this happen?"

Wesley's face wrinkles in confusion. "What's she talking about?" he asks me.

My throat closes up. I can't breathe, can't think. My face is a furnace, so I know it's turned red and I know it's obvious. Adrenaline surges while my limbs weaken. *Have to get out of here.*

"You're the picture!" she cries. "You're the picture I used for Jack! This is just too much."

He moves closer, eyes sharpening. "My picture?"

I need to say something, but I dropped my voice in the grass and can't find it. It's gone. This is it. My worst fear realizing itself out of nowhere, no warning.

"The picture I showed Maybell! When I was sending emails from the boyfriend I made up for her, which I was actually talking about with this guy I'm seeing earlier today, because good lord, wasn't that a missed opportunity if you think about it? If I'd called Nev and Max from the *Catfish* show, we could have gotten on TV. And they probably would've paid us. But it looks like you went investigating on your own."

My pulse accelerates to a dangerous speed, face hot, ears on fire. I try to regulate my breathing but I'm broken, a vast panic of white, wordless alarm, and I'm paralyzed. Even with my mouth open, I draw in too little oxygen and the world begins to fuzz and fray at the edges.

Something wrong is happening to my body.

"Wait," Wesley says.

She steamrolls right over him. "I still feel terrible about that, but if you—like, are you *dating* now? 'Cause if you are, it was kinda worth it I guess." Her nose is an inch from her screen, trying to see. "It's getting hard to see you. Can you turn a light on or something?"

It's getting hard to see her, too; I've got tunnel vision and Gemma's a brushstroke of blurring colors. My chest is cold, a solid block of ice, even as unbearable heat radiates from my cheeks. I try to pin my focus on something—*Look normal, look normal*—but my mind blanks. I can't focus because I'm panicking. I'm focusing on panicking. It makes the panicking worse.

"Maybell?" It's Wesley, moving closer. I feel his presence at my back, towering over me, and yet I'm not here at all. I'm drifting and loose, sky expanding until it's wider than reality, bending the earth beneath me into a ninety-degree curve.

"Um. Um." I pick up syllables here and there, struggling to piece them together. "Hold on." I hand him my phone, tuning out Gemma's loud chattering. I don't know why I hand him my phone. *Got to get out of here.*

I am walking away, to anywhere, it doesn't matter. One foot in front of the other, breathing shaky, this unsteady new life I've been slowly building shattered. I can't tell if I'm walking slowly or if I'm running, because I can't feel my legs and I'm spinning outside of my body, up and away into the sky. My legs are too wobbly for the task of carrying me, so I sit down and work on putting my soul back inside my body. *Come on, come down from there, get back in here.*

I'm a bog body now. They'll find me in a thousand years and someone will look down at my shriveled remains and say, "Maybe she was somebody important." The name and personality they cultivate for me will be my immortal contribution to this world.

I close my eyes, focusing on my breathing. It's just me and the wildflowers and the wind, and if I am very, very careful about my movements, I might not be flung into outer space.

The wildflowers around me stir and sigh. The wind says,

Maybell?

Says,

Are you all right?

Just once, I wish the universe would give me something nice without throwing in unwelcome side effects. Wesley *just* started opening up to me. He's being caring instead of broody, talking and listening. A friend. Now that he knows my secret, he's going to slam a door on whatever this friendship might have elevated to, shifting back into the taciturn man I met at the beginning of April. He isn't going to want anything to do with me. I've blown it.

And before you answer, it continues, *just know that you don't have to say yes.*

I tilt my head back to see that the wind is moving closer. It has such gentleness for its size, soft as down, still waters running deeper than you'd think. It hides in trees to be alone and yet prolongs treasure hunts so as not to be alone. It gave its bedroom to a stranger and lets her wear its pendant, doodling her make-believe café with a few inaccuracies that have since grown to be canon.

"Hey." He lowers to the ground, curving over my sprawled form. Haloed by the stars. "You going somewhere without me, Parrish?"

I watch him, heart ticking pitifully, the white, fizzling buzz settling as I come back to myself in increments. "I don't know."

He lies down beside me. "Have I ever told you about why I want an animal sanctuary?"

He hasn't.

Now I'm wondering why I haven't asked.

Wesley tells me a story about his preteen self, about his slew of brothers and parents, an apple-pie family on a farm. He says that even in a picture-perfect family like his, where the parents did everything right, he still didn't feel like he belonged. He tells me he butted heads with them about his "vegetarian phase," which "wasn't realistic for farm life." They raised cows, and the first calf he helped deliver was one he named Ruby when he was seven years old. He got attached to Ruby, raising her himself, feeding her colostrum out of a bottle. She had to join the dairy herd when she was two, but she loved Wesley and came to him when called, like a dog. He was her human.

When he was twelve, his parents told him it was time for Ruby to leave. She wasn't producing as much milk anymore, so they wanted to cull her. He loved Ruby to bits and pieces; she was *his* cow. He cried hard, begging them to let him keep her, so upset that he got a nosebleed. His mom gave in and said he could keep Ruby. But then a week later, Ruby was gone.

"I kind of lost it," he tells me, "but Mom explained that they'd found a better home for Ruby on a farm upstate."

I wince.

"Yeah. She felt bad, but farming is a business and dairy cows that don't produce milk are money pits. Anyway, I found out later what 'a farm upstate' really meant, and . . . now I want to be that farm upstate."

My heart has been torn out of my chest.

"Wesley," I say calmly. It requires all of my restraint not to wrap him in a bear hug, even though enough time has passed since this happened to him that he can speak on it unemotionally.

"Yes?"

"I am going to get you a thousand elderly roosters. I'm going to raid farms and steal their Rubys." I spread my arms. "All of this will be cows."

Wesley bursts out laughing. "That might be the sweetest thing you've ever said to me?" He returns my phone. "I take it you're feeling better. I told your friend you'd call her back tomorrow."

That's not happening. "Thanks. She isn't my friend, though."

I sense he wants to ask questions but is too polite to. "No more running off, okay? There's no escaping me anyway."

"Sorry." A new kind of embarrassment is creeping in. Fantastic. "I don't know what happened."

"I do." He sits up, studying me closely. "I think you had a panic attack."

A *panic attack*. I blink. Wow. "Is that what that was? I've never had one before. I don't think I like them."

The corner of his mouth hitches somewhat. "I get panic attacks all the time."

"Really? I've never seen you have one."

"Oh, you definitely have. Some are invisible. Some, I try to mask by . . ." He throws his head back, thinking. "By being argumentative, I guess you'd say. One of the reasons I've liked passing notes back and forth is because it's easier to say what I mean to say without defaulting to arguing. Because of nerves."

"You're grouchy to hide panic attacks and nerves?"

"Don't give me too much credit. Sometimes I'm grouchy because I'm part cactus." His eyes are warm. "You handled it really well."

I'd laugh if I had the energy. "Liar."

The other corner of his mouth joins in, a full smile taking

shape. He reaches slowly, looking a little nervous, to brush the hair out of my eyes. Then he leaves his palm on my forehead. I close my eyes again, shuddering an exhale. "That's nice."

"Yeah?"

"It's like a weight, so that I don't fall into the sky."

"We can't be having that. The hand stays."

I smile. Just a tiny bit. When I steal a peek at last, all of Wesley's amusement is gone, worry clear in his eyes.

Listening to him talk in his low, rhythmic tenor has calmed me. "Thank you," I say. "I feel normal again. Or almost normal." I'll never take almost-normal for granted again. I'm *exhausted*.

"Now I'm going to ask you something difficult," he ventures.

I brace myself.

"I would like for you to tell me about Jack."

My focus strays past him to the Little Dipper. "All right. I can maybe do that." But only because he shared first. Only because to look at him now, I can't imagine him responding with unkindness.

So I tell Wesley about Gemma, and Caleb, and Jack. Who, interestingly enough, I haven't given a second thought to in what feels like ages. And whom I'd regarded as the ideal boyfriend even though in retrospect it was a laughably superficial connection. If he'd been real, we wouldn't have been a good match. "I liked the *idea* of a spontaneous, world-traveling, loud, social-butterfly boyfriend," I admit, blushing, "but in reality I think I'm better suited to . . ."

"Yeah?" Wesley prompts. His voice is strange, like he's borrowed somebody else's.

"I think someone a little more serious, a little more grounded," I make myself finish, "to balance me out. Someone understanding. Dependable."

He's quiet for a spell. And then:

"Hm."

"Hm," I agree, painfully aware of, well, *everything*. The grass flattened beneath me, the cool air whispering against my cheek, the smattering of stars in a vast, velvet sky. The warm body beside mine, with a big, ballooning thought bubble I want to pop with a pin to see which words fall out.

"I still don't understand *why*," he says out of nowhere, puzzled. "I mean, you told me *why* she did it, but it still doesn't make sense. Even if she had the best of intentions, who treats people this way? She could have just told you she had feelings for Caleb, and knowing you, I'm sure you would have reassured her she had nothing to worry about."

"I think it's because a guy she once dated came into the hotel and hit on me. I wasn't interested, but I guess she didn't fully trust me after that. The most frustrating part, though, is that during all that time she was distracting me with Jack, she never even asked out Caleb! She got over him pretty quickly, so it seems so pointless in hindsight. All that energy, and for what? Gemma picked the most drastic option for plan A. I think she likes the drama."

"Maybe it's a good thing we can't understand the type of person who'd act like that," he says darkly. "I'm glad you're going to have a hotel of your own and don't need to be around that parasite and her father anymore. You know that saying about success being the best revenge? With your work experience, Falling Stars is bound to be successful."

Oh, boy.

It's coming out.

I can't keep it in. "I have another confession."

He listens, not interrupting.

"I'm not a real event coordinator." I clap my hands over my face. "I was a housekeeper. They gave me the promotion so that I'd sweep what Gemma did under the rug and not raise any complaints to corporate, but I never got the go-ahead on any of the events I planned. None of the activities I pitched were accepted."

"Hm," he says again. "Well . . . a history of housekeeping is just as handy as event-coordinating experience, when you think about it. You'll know better than most how to clean everything that needs cleaning, keeping every room looking nice. That's important. On top of that, you have all these ideas for how guests can have fun during their stay. Having lofty goals and something to prove is a combination that'll get results."

I can't believe he isn't mad. "I lied, though."

"I lied about the cabin being a two-bedroom," he points out. "I didn't tell you right away that the jewelry was fake."

"Those are *nice* lies." I should stop pushing, but I can't stop. It's incredible: messing up and not having the other person automatically go away, leaving me for dead. "My lie was self-serving."

"But you were right," he argues. "Falling Stars would make a great hotel."

"Maybe the only reason I wanted a hotel is because my subconscious internalized that postcard long ago."

"Maybe you saw the soul of Falling Stars and knew what it wanted to be, even before you found that old newspaper."

Stress makes me theatrical. I fling an arm across my face, resolved never to get up again. "Stop being nice, I can't handle it. Take the whole thing for your animal sanctuary," I declare. "Even the ballroom. We'll put pigs in it."

He grabs my arm. Pulls me up. "C'mon, drama queen. There's treasure out there for us."

"Aren't you weirded out?" I can't help asking. "I mean, I thought I dated your *picture*."

"Weirded out?" He releases a long-suffering sigh. "How do I say this?" He tips his head back, searching the dark sky for answers. "How do I say this."

I slide him a questioning look.

A hand hovering at the small of my back makes direct contact, urging me forward. "You have nothing to be embarrassed about. Absolutely nothing. I'm deeply, *terribly* flattered that you would have swiped right on me." Turbulent eyes cut to mine, then into the grass. "Makes me wish I'd had a real Tinder profile that day."

"WONDER WHERE THE TREASURE could possibly be," I say wryly as we approach the mailbox erected on a post in the middle of nowhere. Its red flag is up, parcel ready for collection.

He gestures for me to do the honors. I'm inexplicably nervous as I open it, revealing spiderwebs and a brown waxed-paper envelope.

"Are you going to take it?" Wesley asks when I hesitate.

I pull it out; it's light, containing a sheet of paper at the most. There's a saddening finality to this—I'll open the envelope and then . . . it's all over. These one-sided interactions with Uncle Victor that Violet should have experienced instead, and this mutual adventure Wesley and I are on. I'm not ready for it to be over.

"Can we wait until tomorrow to open it?"

"Sure." Wesley doesn't press with questions. He simply clamps his flashlight between his teeth and unzips my bag to tuck this treasure among the others.

Then he hits me with the question that makes my stomach drop. "Ready to set up camp?"

The long answer to this is an internal shriek that lasts approximately ten minutes. The short answer is a deceptively (I hope) casual "Yep."

This is fine. I am fine.

I am totally fine, never better, as I hold the flashlight for Wesley while he sets up the tent for us, clutching the hunk of metal in both hands so the stream of light doesn't wobble and give me away. I'm freaking out and he's focused on his task, infuriatingly calm. Unless he's freaking out, too, but hiding it better than I am. I remember what he said about masking his panic attacks and narrow my eyes at him. He could be having one right now for all I know.

Or maybe it's no big deal to Wesley that we're going to be lying next to each other all night. Or two nights, if we happen to get a freak snowstorm that strands us here in this field. I mean, it's seventy-ish degrees and a snowstorm is unlikely, but stranger things have happened. We could be stuck here for days together—a rogue porcupine could shred my sleeping bag, forcing us against our wills to share a single sleeping bag. What a shame that would be. I can't even entertain the thought.

I entertain the thought in vivid detail with half of my concentration, the other half funneled into maintaining my cool and collected composure, an *I don't even care* expression. I've known all week that this was coming, but imagining and experiencing are as far from each other as the North and South Poles. Nothing could have prepared me for this panic, this flustered, thrilling, scary spiral. Nothing is going to happen tonight, I know.

I realize I haven't shaved my legs in four days and respond to Wesley's chitchat with a smile, I am sure, that makes me look like I'm in pain. Maybe I'm underestimating myself. I'm fully capable of ignoring him while lying next to him. I can pretend he's a wall.

"I brought one with a plastic see-through ceiling," he says, tapping the tent's dome. "Good for stargazing."

"Mm-hmm," I say tightly. My pitch is the last key on a piano.

Wesley shovels our bags into the tent. "Gimme a minute? Just gonna change my clothes. Then we'll trade."

I bob my head. "Yep, yep, yep."

He quirks an eyebrow at me, then disappears into the tent. I nearly buckle. I have absolutely no business letting myself visualize what he's doing in there, but I do. I squeeze my eyes shut, consider bolting into the trees, and command myself sternly to not hear that rustling noise that is unmistakably a pair of pants being removed. I simply do not possess the strength this situation requires of me.

He emerges in his KOEHLER LANDSCAPING shirt and gray sweatpants that steam up my glasses. Hair mussed. His rain-and-earth-and-bonfire scent wafting stronger, refreshed, reaching out to punch me in the stomach. A chyron of explicit language rolls across the bottom of my field of vision. "Your turn."

"Cool, thanks," I squeak, sliding past him. Our gazes clash and can't get unlocked for a moment, the function jammed. I drag mine away, the weight of oceans, limbs clumsy, and it's fine, I think, that I know how I'm going to die now. Not everybody knows.

The volume in this tent as I unzip my bag is obscene. Either my legs have swollen or my jeans have shrunk, because wrestling them off is an embarrassment. Wesley absolutely, 100 percent hears the racket of my shirt going up over my head. I scrub on my deodorant, smooth my hair, scrub on more deodorant for good measure, and fight my way outside to brush my teeth. I do so a good twelve feet from the tent, in the dark, so that Wesley can't see toothpaste foam dribbling down my chin. I am losing it, perhaps.

Then there's nothing left to do but climb into the mouth of the beast. I crawl in first, feeling Wesley's warmth, his size, at my back as he follows suit. With both of us in here, the space is impossibly small. Loft-of-a-cabin small. I hold my breath as he reaches over my prone body. Our eyes meet in the near-blackness, and I follow the silver arc of a shooting star in his irises as Wesley zips us up inside.

Nowhere to run now.

Chapter 15

I AM BURIED ALIVE UP to my neck in a sleeping bag, every breath a thunderclap, cold puffs of fog curling in and out of my mouth.

"Wow, I'm so tired," I lie, unprovoked.

Silence. And then:

". . . Yeah."

"Time to count sheep, I guess." I roll in the opposite direction of Wesley, features twisting into *Kill me now*. I will never be cool.

"Does that ever work for you?"

"Sure." I'm lying again. Being nervous is turning me into a liar. "I mean, no. Have you never tried it? What do you think about before you go to sleep?"

He falls quiet. I think he's trying to figure out what I'm really asking. "It's like sheep, but Maybells. A whole bunch of you, one after the other, skipping through a field."

I'm too keyed up for my sarcasm sensors to work, so I have no clue if he's joking. Before I can blurt out any questionable nonsense, he thankfully keeps talking. "What about you? Do you go to your happy place?"

It takes me a second to remember that my happy place isn't this tent, smelling of nylon, bug spray, and old garage. He's referring to the coffee shop.

"Yeah, usually." With the exception of this past week.

For years, shutting the door on the real world and dropping out of a hole in the clouds into my make-believe café has been an automatic transition. It requires full cooperation with abandoning the here and now, vacating my body. Here and now, I'm so aware of my body that there's no way I'm going to be able to leave it. I'm powerfully aware of Wesley's, too, how the back of his hand grazes my thigh through our sleeping bags. "Sorry," he murmurs.

"It's fine." Boy, is it. I wish he'd do it again.

The reminder of my café flips a Pavlovian switch: pink shafts of light slant through the plastic skylight, then vanish as they rotate like a lighthouse beacon. I can already smell sugar and flour, hear the notes, lighter than air, twinkling out of a retro jukebox that harbors all my favorite music. I know where my invented customers with their blurred faces will be waiting in stasis, a magic wax museum where everyone comes to life when my hand turns the doorknob to enter. Inner peace is only a heartbeat away, an irresistible invitation.

Resist I do, pink neon shrinking from Wesley's profile, receding into the night like banished spirits. "Do you really think about a whole bunch of skipping Maybell sheep?" I ask.

"Are you sure you want to know?" His voice is low and dangerous.

Yes.

No.

This is a feast of terrible ideas. *Don't start anything you can't finish,* I tell myself. We live together, a fact that will be true no matter how many regrets I wake up with tomorrow in the glaring light of day. I will *not* jeopardize my peace, my dream career, for a man. No matter how surprisingly sweet he may have turned out to be under his crispy shell.

"No," I decide, uncertainly.

Wesley's silences are even more frustrating in the dark. I can't read his face to know if he's disappointed or relieved.

Damn my aversion to thick silences. "Your bedroom is right above mine."

"I've noticed."

I respond too quickly, almost sitting up. Almost pouncing on him. "How?"

"You close your window at about three in the morning, whenever the temperature starts to drop."

"I'm sorry. I didn't know it was that loud." I like fresh air, but he's absolutely right—I get too cold in the middle of the night and have to shut my window.

"It isn't. I have trouble sleeping, so I'm usually awake at three anyway. That's why I can hear it." He adjusts his position, sleeping bag rustling. "It's nice, in a way. I don't feel so . . . by myself."

"I know what you mean. I'm not sure I'd even want to live in that house by myself, anymore." I wet my lips. "I mean that I *wouldn't* have minded, but having had company, and knowing that having company is better—" I twist the knob on that sentence until it shuts off. I'm rambling nonsensically.

"No, I know what you mean." We're repeating ourselves now, and can't help but laugh. It breaks the tension.

"I stayed in a tent like this when I went to camp as a kid," he tells me. "I refused to participate in the trust fall and the counselors told my parents I was combative."

I giggle. "Of course you did."

"Are you calling me combative?" he says, mock stern.

"You? Noooooo, never. You've been a prince from the jump. Trying to get me to sell my half of the estate, eating breakfast at seven because I wake up at eight—and don't even try to tell me that's not on purpose—"

"All right, all right," he cuts in before I can pick up steam. "I'm sorry. It takes me a while to get used to new people. And I didn't see you coming, so it was even harder. Didn't get a chance to prepare myself."

"I think I'm growing on you, though." I know I sound smug. It's because I am. I poke his ribs and he convulses. My laugh kicks up an evil notch.

He pokes me back. "It's like if you throw a frog into a pot of boiling water, it'll jump out. But if you heat the water slowly, it gets used to it and stays put. You were already boiling when I was thrown into you."

"My apologies. I can't help being this hot."

He doesn't laugh at my joke. "It's getting easier to handle. I'm not minding being boiled, nowadays."

Our next period of silence descends naturally, but if I shone a flashlight over all the dark space that surrounds us, it would illuminate a hundred lingering words. My lips part, trying to summon the right ones. Most of the time, I feel like I live all the way down inside of myself, deep, deep down, so far away from my voice that I hardly hear it and certainly nobody else ever does. I've been told before that I blend in, difficult to notice, easy to talk over. But ever since I realized Wesley notices me, it's like I've gone to the surface of myself and stayed there. I'm not used to feeling the world at such close range, having an effect on my environment, present in my own life. I'm run ragged by it. I don't have the wherewithal to project a more flattering version of myself, stumbling when I aim to be charming and likable. I'm bare-bones Maybell.

"You over there counting sheep?" he asks.

"It's a parade of Wesleys now, one after the other, skipping through a field. In tuxedos."

"I don't mind that at all." The smile in his voice makes me smile, too.

"You still counting Maybells?"

"Oh, definitely not. I'd never be able to fall asleep that way."

If I go digging into that I will end up taking a shovel to the face. "Look, that's Orion's Belt." I raise my arm.

"Ursa Minor." He raises his arm, too, letting it lean ever so slightly against mine. I press a little; he presses back.

"They didn't have this many stars in Pigeon Forge."

"Restricted viewing up there," he agrees. I think Wesley's prejudiced against large towns.

"This is the HBO of skies." At once, we both say, *"Starz,"* and laugh at our corny joke.

My hand tilts, fingers curling back. His fingers claim the spaces between mine, just resting like that. I wonder if he's looking at our hands, too. Listening to the telltale thud of my pulse.

"I see the letter W," he tells me.

I bend my neck, and if the movement brings me closer to him, that's entirely accidental. "Pretty sure what you're looking at is an M from the wrong angle." Our arms fall, side by side between our sleeping bags. Neither of us moves to withdraw.

His face shifts toward mine, breath stirring my hair. "I'll let you have it."

My jaw hurts, refusing to unclench. My face, exposed to chilly air, is hot, while my covered body is ice cold, muscles coiled tight. Walking home tomorrow is going to be a punishment.

Bats flap overhead, and even in my sleeping bag I can feel the cold seeping up out of the soil, through the tent's fabric. My stiff back is beginning to think that getting closer to nature is over-rated. I remind myself it would be inappropriate to ask Wesley to be my blanket.

The silence deepens. Our long day is catching up to me, my eyelids shuttering, when he whispers, "Are you awake?"

Here's my chance to leave tonight at a wise stopping point. I will simply say nothing, feigning sleep. He'll fall asleep, too. Danger averted.

I waste no time answering, "Yes."

"I found out something that embarrassed you today," he replies after a moment's hesitation. "I'll tell you an embarrassing thing, too. The *most* embarrassing thing. To make us even."

"You don't have—"

"Neither did you, when you saw my drawings in the loft. But you did. And it's easier right now, in the dark, to be braver. So I'm going to tell you." He exhales a soft breath, turning on his side toward me once more, closer than ever. All I'd have to do is give an inch and I'd have his lips to my forehead. I shiver, fingers curling around my shirt to restrain myself.

"I've never been with anyone."

Time goes liquid, pooling between us. The temperature goes up like a Roman candle. "You mean . . ."

"Yes."

My heartbeat thumps in my ears. My arm is positioned crookedly under my head, tingling with pins and needles as it falls asleep, but I can't move.

He's so soft, unbearably, when he prompts, "Say something?"

My throat is packed with sand. "I'm trying to come up with a response that doesn't sound like a proposition," I confess hoarsely. "Wesley, that isn't embarrassing at all."

He shifts onto his back again, arm across his stomach. "It bothers me. There's a stigma, especially for guys. *Especially* for guys who are about to hit thirty. It's not that I *want* to be a . . . you know . . ." He can't bring himself to verbalize it. "But it's hard to meet people when you have social anxiety as bad as I do. I panic. Or I want to say one thing, be a certain way, but it gets all tangled up on its way out of my mouth. A pumpkin trying to be flowers and coming off like a cactus. It's frustrating."

"You're much more flowers than you are cactus," I tell him, meaning every word. I hope he believes it. "But for what it's worth, pumpkins are the best."

"Anyway." I think he's rubbing his eyes. "Maybe I've overshared. I'm sorry. It's late, and I'm tired."

Of course. He's tired—he's not hinting anything. Not suggesting. He definitely does not want me to roll on top of him and have my wicked way. The only Wesley who will let me thread my fingers through his hair and crush my mouth to his is the imaginary one. Which I feel guilty thinking about, but I can't help it.

"I'm honored you trust me enough to tell me something like that." I bite down hard on my tongue, reaching for his hand. He acknowledges it with a mellow squeeze, rubbing his thumb across the back of my hand.

"The only reason I was able to admit it is because you're so easy to talk to. It feels like you . . ." He inhales sharply. "Like you pay attention."

My body is rigid with tension, collecting in my temples. I could be imagining it but I think his muscles have tightened, as well. I am burning alive.

"I don't know what I'm saying," he mumbles.

Before he's finished with his sentence, I jump in: "You're right. I see you."

"Oh." His voice is light as a feather. Winded. "Good."

This is the part where he adds, *I'm paying attention to you, too*, and descends on me with a fiery passion, but that never happens. He only says, "Anyway."

"Anyway," I echo.

"Good night, Maybell."

Disappointment crushes every bone in my body. "Good night, Wesley."

I don't close my eyes. We lie there with our arms still touching, his golden curls brushing my ear, a million microscopic points of contact. Maybe he falls asleep immediately, maybe he lies awake for as long as I do, staring unseeingly at the stars.

I'VE SPENT THE BETTER part of the night debating whether I'm in heaven or hell, but this morning has clinched it. I am for sure in hell.

Deservedly so. There's a pair of warm arms around me, a

sleeping man's chest rising and falling against my back, and the sinful thoughts won't stop coming. Morning breath is the only factor keeping me from rolling over onto my other side to stare at him. Also, manners. But mostly morning breath.

"You awake?" he asks.

I stretch and yawn, pretending I've been out of it. "What? Oh! Mm-hmm." I could lie here forever. Maybe he'll bury his mouth in my neck and tell me how badly he's wanted me, and we'll roll around in this field all day—

"Good. I want to get an early start." He unzips his sleeping bag and climbs over me, grabbing his bag on his way out of the tent. His hand pats my head like I'm a golden retriever. I fall back onto my elbows, shooting a cross expression at his back.

Apparently I've misread last night's signals.

By the time I've changed my clothes and joined him, he's wearing a fresh change of jeans and plain white T-shirt (Did he change behind a tree? Or out in the open? None of my business!), munching on granola.

When he glances at me, I automatically flush and stumble. "Uneven . . . this grass is all uneven," I mutter. "Gopher holes or something."

He raises his eyebrows at the ground, still munching. Nods. "Mm."

I should have packed a mirror. I could have dried patches of drool on my cheek for all I know. I'm sure my hair's on its worst behavior. My hair always has such an attitude problem whenever I especially need it to look good. But on days I'm not going anywhere, with no human witnesses? That's when I could be a Pantene Pro-V model.

After I zip off into the trees for a few minutes (nature calls), I help Wesley roll up our sleeping bags, tent, and supplies. The metal detector is still nowhere to be found.

"Maybe Sasquatch took it," I suggest, enjoying myself. "You said he lives in Appalachia, right?"

Wesley shakes his head. "Not even going to respond to that."

"You just did." I try to sprint away before he can get the last word in. "Last one home has to clean out the gutters!" This is a terrible threat. The gutters have saplings and who knows what else growing in them.

"Have fun with that. I'll just be over here, then." He juts a thumb. "Going the right way. See you in a week."

I veer left. Check his expression. I veer right. He laughs, dispelling some of my unease about waking up to business as usual. This isn't anything like last night, but it also isn't anything like any other morning. We're off the map.

"Ready to see what the fifth treasure is?" he inquires when I circle back.

The brown envelope weighs heavily in my pack, waiting to be opened, but I'm still not ready for this to end. "When we get back. It'll be our reward for not getting eaten by bears."

"Bears are solitary creatures. If we meet one, we'll outnumber it. Meaning no bears will be running after me when I outstrip you."

"Hey!"

"You snooze, you lose."

"I can see why they didn't like you at camp."

Wesley laughs again—I've got to start counting them, comparing numbers to yesterday's best score. "No, they didn't like me at camp because I wouldn't do *this*." He stops short in front of me and leans backward.

"No!" I cry, but it's too late, he's already tipping back. My arms reflexively snake around his middle as if I have a prayer of holding this enormous specimen up, but he's stopped tipping. Wesley locks his arms over mine, holding me to him. He turns so that I can see his grinning profile.

"Gotcha."

"Thank goodness," I sigh. "You're too much man for me."

"Where there's a will, there's a way," he replies, releasing his hold after another beat. I can't tell if he's wistful or joking.

This is the trouble with crushes. You begin to doubt whether they're reciprocated, even if on paper the signs are all there. If I ever get married, I think I'll be wondering all the way down the aisle if the wedding's an elaborate prank and the groom will say *Gotcha!* at the end. I can't trust my own judgment here.

The hike home flies by much faster than the hike out, since we're not stopping to hunt for treasure, and we're making good enough time that I don't think the lunch I packed for today will be necessary. We stop mostly for my benefit, my poor legs and back aching. Wesley makes me reapply that minty green goop every two hours.

I can't resist. "You missed a spot," I say, dabbing more on his nose.

Wesley smiles, eyes crinkling. "So did you. Here, I'll help you out." He presses my forehead, leaving a green handprint.

"Thank you so much."

He winks. "No problem."

Tree canopies blocking the sunlight throw off our sense of

time, and when we saunter into a clearing the sky looks more like late evening than noon. Dark clouds gather ahead, rolling our way.

"That doesn't bode well," I mutter.

Wesley grabs my pack from me, leaving our shovel behind. "We've gotta hurry."

"I am physically incapable of going any faster. My shoulders are still angry that they didn't get a mattress last night."

"I'm kind of used to the sleeping bag by now," he replies, calling to mind the image of his sleeping bag in the loft, and the colored-pencil Maybell I discovered there. "You need me to carry you?"

Is he serious?

He is. Of course he is.

Wesley's offering a fantasy and doesn't know it. If I say yes, forcing this poor man to carry a fully grown adult on top of everything else he's already carrying, I truly will go to hell.

I spend a handful of seconds considering it anyway. "You're strong," I sigh, relinquishing this opportunity, "but not invincible. That'd kill you."

"I'm not that strong at all," he replies modestly, head ducking, "but for you, I can be strong enough."

He quickens, shooting forward so that I can't see his face. I'm so glad he can't see mine, either. It's of paramount importance that we get back as fast as possible so we can get away from each other. If I'm in Wesley's company for another hour, I'm going to irreparably embarrass myself.

I have feelings for you, I hear myself hypothetically gushing. *I'm so sorry, I didn't mean to. They snuck up on me.* Wesley's hypothetical shock, followed by mortification, is bad enough to hasten my pace. The detail that my muscles are melting marshmallows is irrelevant—self-preservation demands sacrifice sometimes. It's growing increasingly clear that I need a week of no contact to salvage my wits. I can't be trusted anymore.

Wesley doesn't get the memo. He does horribly destructive things like passing me his canteen to make sure I get the last drink and pointing out which animals the angry clouds resemble. He touches my wrist gingerly between two fingers; I grind to a halt at once, and my soul twirls up out of my body when he kneels to retie one of my shoelaces.

I can't watch. I clench my teeth, staring resolutely at the approaching rain clouds, but he's ruined clouds for me, too. I'll never be able to look at one again without thinking, *Hey, it's a floppy-eared bunny*, in his deep, pleasant rumble.

Head bowed at my waist, one of his knees digging in the mud without so much as a flinch, a second thought, Wesley's long, callused fingers that paint sea monsters on ballroom walls and make things grow from the earth are delicately handling my dirty shoestrings. He murmurs, "Over, under, cross the bridge, make a loop and right on through." A mnemonic device about tying shoes cannot be what sends me over the edge. I forbid it.

"We're getting pretty close, right?" I ask when we take off again, more than a little desperate.

Wesley throws me a sidelong glance. "You getting sick of me?" His tone is playful, but I detect apprehension.

"Listen, I'm just trying to protect you from the rain." I return his smile with a wobbly one of my own. "Lest you forget, you're wearing a white T-shirt."

He barks a laugh. "So?"

"*So*, people in wet white T-shirts are distracting. Don't look at me like that, this is a *thing*. Everybody knows."

His brown eyes glint, then glide down my tank top and jeans. "*Your* shirt is white."

I have to do a double take. So it is.

His eyes are darker when they meet mine again. I'm hanging from this cliff by one finger. A cold raindrop taps one shoulder, then the opposite one when I turn to look. Wesley squints at the sky. "Here we go."

We crest a hill, Wesley's truck materializing in a field a hundred yards off like a mirage.

Tap, tap, tap becomes a downpour, slicking my hair to my face and neck, clothes sealing to skin. Wesley's hair darkens, curling, dripping over his cheeks, spiking his eyelashes.

"It's cold it's cold it's cold it's cold!" I squeal, running as fast as I can. Wesley flies alongside, and even with the burden he's carrying all by himself, I think he's putting a damper on his endurance. He'd be at the truck already if he weren't matching my speed.

The heel of his palm meets the base of my spine, jolting me forward even faster. We're fifty yards down. "Should have stayed in the tent," I sputter. "For another night. We'd be dry right now." Relatively, anyway.

"I didn't know that was an option," he responds, fingers curling into my waist and gripping harder. I'm not sure he's aware of it.

"I guess"—I'm out of breath, panting—"that we couldn't, after all. Not enough food."

"I'd find some berries."

"You can't subsist on berries. I've seen how much you eat. You'd need bushels."

"I don't need anything."

It's a strange thing to say. I turn to study him, but we've made it to the truck at last and he's yanking my door open for me. Small lakes are collecting around all four tires, but before I can try to hop over one to get inside Wesley picks me up handily by the waist and deposits me on the seat. He then flings our equipment into the back and darts around to the other side. When Wesley slams his door shut behind him, safe and soaked, we take a moment to slide down in our seats. Eyes closed, breathing heavily. Rain pummels metal and windows, so much louder in here than outside.

When I open my eyes again, he's watching me. Sure enough, his shirt's so wet that it's nearly see-through, molding to every contour. My focus drops to his chest, which is rising and falling deeply—I try to correct the impulse, quickly raking my eyes upward, but it's too late. My thoughts are too obvious to need words. Wesley's eyes flash moments before the lightning strikes. A frisson of heat shoots through me as I peer into their depths, and if you were to look on at us from above I think you'd spy smoke undulating against the windows, two people inside a crystal ball with their fate sealed.

He reaches for me with both hands and slowly, carefully slides my glasses off my face. I stare as he peels up the hem of his shirt, exposing an inch of golden skin, and uses it to wipe the spots of rain off my lenses. He hands them back, skin warm against my freezing fingers.

I don't know what compels me to do it, but I reach out, too. I touch a thumb to a raindrop sliding over the arc of his cheek, following it with my finger all the way down to his lower lip. He watches me from beneath lashes at half-mast, beautiful wide eyes going liquid black. There are dark shadows beneath them, easier to discern in the dimness of the car.

A crack of thunder splits the air; we swivel to face the windshield. Wesley swallows hard as he puts the truck in gear.

We drive.

I can feel every particle of air moving against my skin. The heavens are swirling purple and green, lifted from an illustration in a storybook, all the colors so impossibly and exaggeratedly saturated. Long grasses are blown flat by rain, a forever stretch from here to Falling Stars. Here in the enclosed cab of Wesley's truck, dry heat gusting out of the vents, it could be the end of the world.

Wesley nudges the brakes, slowing down even though we're nowhere near the house yet. Then we stop entirely. The look on his face drowns out all sound, din pushed beyond our bubble by magic. "That's a lie," he says quietly.

Blood drains from my extremities, rushing to my brain. "What's a lie?"

He stares straight ahead, deathly pale save the bright red blooms on his cheekbones, ruddy blotches under a stubbly beard. I follow his line of sight, trying to see whatever it is that he's seeing. Wesley's elbow bends, white-knuckled fist easing the gearshift into park.

"Is something—?" I begin to ask, when Wesley unbuckles his seat belt without warning and gets out of the car. He's going to run.

Oh *no*, he's going to run.

But he doesn't. He rounds the hood of the car, stride powerful, coming right for me. All of my attention telescopes down to that minute flex in his arm as he throws open the passenger door.

My jaw drops, another question forming.

He cradles my face in his hands, ever so gentle. I slacken in the fierce hold of his stare, his pupils hungry stains drinking up the iris. He is himself, endearing and unsure, but he's also under siege by something new: steely determination. Wesley's mentioned he often has trouble expressing himself, but mouths can speak in more ways than one. For this, all he needs is a kiss.

He answers my question with shuttering eyelids, no room to wonder anymore because this isn't an *I like you, maybe* or an *I'm into you, a little* kiss. It's a force that cuts me off at the knees, stealing the breath from my throat like pulling rope, both of us tangled and tethered to each other as we pitch over the cliff's edge.

He jams the button on my seat belt to release me, bringing me to him. I snatch him closer, too, greedy. My arms slide around his neck as though they belong there, slick with rain. I smile dreamily against his mouth, face upturned, mist in my hair.

"I'm sorry," he pants when we break. "I had to . . . I *had* to—"

I don't let him finish, not done falling yet.

I drag him back for more. Wesley goes rigid, then every part of him loosens, a small sigh escaping like a candle blown out. He wants and I want, no chance of miscommunication. Kissing him, I feel powerful. In command, even as I fumble and paw. There's no such thing as a missed mark, only shifting ones.

At long last, I get to do what I've so badly wanted for weeks, plunging my fingers into his hair. Thanks to rain, the strands are more slippery than supple, fresh water lifting the strong scent of his shampoo. His mouth is pure satin everywhere except a crescent of tougher skin where his top teeth have dug into his bottom lip for years. Anxiety. Nerves. Self-punishing, but so painfully sweet with me.

We break to readjust, trying out new rhythms. While I sense his self-consciousness, perhaps comparing this kiss to what he thinks it should be, I wish he could know how much I love what it *is*. It doesn't matter how much pressure he applies, what angles we meet each other at, or his level of confidence. It matters that he gives himself at all.

I want everything, I want all of him, I want to familiarize myself down to every freckle and fine line.

His kiss is the Fourth of July, a Southern summer night. Cicadas and the tongues of smoke off a burning firework—*hiss, pop. Hot.* A bead of sweat rolls down his temple and *oh*, he's good with his hands. Firm, reverent hands, one sliding along my scalp to cup the back of my head, the other undecided between jaw, waist, hip. He feels better than I ever dreamed, and I've done quite a lot of dreaming.

He leans back slightly, brows drawn together in mingled desire and trepidation, still not quite sure if he's doing the right thing. "More," I murmur into his ear. Wesley shivers, but that crease between his eyes disappears and he switches our positions, him on the seat, pulling me onto his lap. I have to tilt my head so that I don't bump the roof of the car. There isn't enough room for us to sit like this comfortably with the door shut, so we leave it hanging open, cold rain streaming in.

My hand lingers at his throat, and the close touch seems to steal something from him. He lets his head fall back, Adam's apple bobbing up the arched column. I kiss that, too. His breathing comes shallower, shallower. The red blooms on his cheeks are roses, his eyes hooded and glassy.

I like it here, his hand decides, spanning broad fingers across my hip, pressing into a sensitive divot where muscles join. I make a soft sound in his mouth, involuntary; his palm flattens, pressing more, more. I move against him just right, feeling a hard ridge in his jeans. My skin sears even as goose bumps radiate, awareness never this heightened, and I feel the full vibrancy of it as I burn and burn and burn.

"I'm rusty," he admits, clearing his throat. "I've never slept with anyone, but I've kissed. It's been a long time, though."

"You're perfect," I tell him. He doesn't kiss like an expert, like a Casanova who's smooth and sure of his every practiced move. He kisses like Wesley. That's the new standard.

We kiss and touch and taste, until the rain abates, until my mouth feels bruised and my body is dying for more. But we taper to a natural close, both somehow knowing that this is a kiss, only a kiss. Whether he wants a dynamic with me in which we'll ever go further than this, I can only guess. As for me, I'm still trying to remember why this was a bad idea. Right now, it feels like there are no bad ideas.

Eventually, I slide off his lap and we emerge in a different world from the one we last stood in, both a little disoriented. When he's back in the driver's seat, he sits up straighter than usual. His gaze flicks to the upper-right corner of the windshield, to something in the sky that's caught his attention, but I can't remove mine from his face. He looks utterly wrecked in the most wonderful way.

I am under Wesley Koehler's skin. I don't know how deep, but I'm there, and I am not imagining it.

Chapter 16

MY FLIMSY, DESPERATE PLAN to hide out from Wesley until my feelings for him have ceased to exist has a toolbox full of wrenches in it. For one, it's hard to do what's best for you when what you *want* isn't what's best for you. And what I want is to make out with Wesley again. If we're going to coexist as platonic pals for the foreseeable ever, putting our tongues in each other's mouths is not the way to achieve that. I need distance. I need space. I need to eat oversized bowls of tasteless, hearty moral fiber for breakfast.

Once we're inside the house, I croak that I need a shower, to which he responds that he does as well, leading my mind down a sordid path. A path with cozy alcoves where lovers can rip each other's clothes off. Falling Stars has such alcoves in abundance. I start dreaming of Wesley under a waterfall resembling the one in our mural; I don't know what he looks like in the nude, so I conjure up Michelangelo's *David* for a baseline, southern region hidden by a grape cluster of bath bubbles popping one by one. I smack face-first into a closed door before the last bubble pops, smarting my nose.

It's all on him now. I'm counting on Wesley to shut down and be all brooding and tight-lipped again. It wouldn't hurt for him to be a little bit awful, too. Maybe he'll insult something I dearly love, like the plastic flowers I've stuck into every crack and crevice, and I'll stop spending my unconscious hours from midnight through eight a.m. in the red-light district of my brain, lying on a chaise longue as he paints me like one of his French girls. We've got to vaporize our attraction. It's the only way to save this relationship.

Wesley has no regard for crafting a professional relationship or successfully living together in harmony. He's ruthless sabotage, strolling into the living room just as I'm stretching out with hot chocolate and the remote, *The Great British Bake Off* queued up to be my date for the evening. He's designed to test my restraint in a cream cable-knit cardigan and charcoal wool trousers that I doubt he's worn more than once. Freshly shaven. Faint traces of cologne, which he never wears, waft toward me. He's taken special care to smooth his hair, too. I'm dressed in a hot-pink romper and a sparkly wrap like the fun nanny who's going to entertain his two children while he goes on a sophisticated date with the governor of Vermont.

"Hi. Hello," he says to me without any guile whatsoever, raking a hand through his smooth hair to undo all that hard work. Goddamn it, it's even sexier disheveled.

This isn't fair.

Wesley saunters closer, clueless to the danger we're both in. I gaze back at him from the red velvet couch with narrowed eyes. "Hello."

"How's it going? Are you, uh . . ." He pivots to glance at the

TV, picking at a stack of Violet's books on the shelf. "Watching Netflix?" He straightens the books' spines. *Let Love Find You. How to Forget a Duke. The Incurable Matchmaker.*

"Yes," I reply guardedly.

He nods, distracted, and toys with a fake sunflower I've jammed into a crack in the wall. Fake flowers are a personal affront to him. "I'll grow you some real ones, if you like."

This is where I must ruin myself. Whatever it was that Wesley saw in me this afternoon that provoked him to put the car in park and ravish my mouth cannot be permitted to stay here between us. Goodbye, deepest connection I've ever had. Goodbye, adorable bear who cleans off my glasses with his shirt and ties my shoelaces. I'll never forget you. "I like plastic flowers better than real ones."

He should hiss and make the sign of the cross, but he doesn't. "Monster," Wesley replies affectionately, twirling the stiff petals. Then he puts it back. "There are a few silk flowers upstairs. I'll bring them down for you."

Oh, for the *love*. I can't even scare a man off correctly! Maybe it's the romper. It shows too much cleavage.

He's close enough that I'm now breathing through my mouth so that I can't be broken down further by his delicious fragrance, but it's no use. The buttons on his cardigan are miniature wooden elephants. We are approaching fatal levels of dreamy. *Mayday! Mayday!* In a small corner of my mind, I jump out of a moving vehicle.

"That's . . ." My mouth is dry. I don't trust myself beyond an "Mm."

"You want some company? We've still got that last wish left to honor, if you're game."

Damn, he's right. We're three down on Violet's dying wishes, with one more to go. *Wish 4. Movie night with a friend is sacred law, don't forget. Wesley, I'd love for you to make my favorite cinnamon-sugar donuts for the occasion.*

"You want to watch a movie and make donuts? With me?" *Please say yes*, I mentally beg. *But also you have to say no.*

He shrugs. "Pretty much have to, don't we? The thousand-year curse and all that."

An interesting development from the man who, only last month, told me that Great-Aunt Violet's wishes weren't serious and behaved as though he was intent on ignoring them all.

I'm contemplating how to phrase that I need a rain check on this activity when Wesley sighs. "It was the kiss, wasn't it," he says defeatedly.

"What?" I know exactly *what*, but I'm stalling for time.

"The kiss. You didn't like it. Or you don't like it anymore. You've given it some thought and wish you hadn't."

"Are you kidding? I've thought about nothing else and wish we were kissing *still*." It's out of my mouth before I can swallow it and boil the truth in acid.

Wesley's expression transforms, glowing brighter, sharper. He steps forward. Dangerous, dangerous.

And I am weak. My spine was manufactured by Charmin. I want to be commanding, stern, intimidating, but I am raindrops on roses and whiskers on kittens. My resolve is dandelion fluff. When he looks at me *like that*, my inner vocabulary bursts apart like a piñata of candy conversation hearts. What was all that I was saying before about Maybell Parrishes being the last bulwark against zombies in the apocalypse? What a bald-faced lie. I'd be the first to bow submissively and declare my zombie allegiance.

"Is that so?" he asks with lethal softness.

I stare at him with *Oh no* eyes, hoping he'll become grotesque if I stare long enough, but the worst thing possible has happened: he's wandered into a pool of golden light under a wall sconce and looks more like an archangel than ever.

"Yes," I admit, swallowing. "That is so, but it would be a bad idea. I think . . . I think spending time together right now is a bad idea."

He stops inches away, hands in pockets. His chin lowers, dark gaze boring holes through mine. He drops a quiet but severe word like a pin, echoing in the stillness.

"Why."

I fight the impulse to cover my face. If I can't see him, maybe I'll be strong. Well, if I can't see him and can't smell him. Or hear him. I need a sensory-deprivation helmet.

Finally, I admit, "Because I'm attracted to you." It comes out in a whoosh.

"That's—ah—well." He revolves in a circle, examining the ceiling. "That's good? Yes. That's very good." Oh *heavens*, he is blushing fiercely. "Because I am also." He clears his throat. "I am also . . . I am attracted to *you*." He takes his hands out of his pockets, blinks at his palms, and slides them back into his pockets again. He still cannot look at me.

It is the most painfully articulated "Same" ever uttered by a human being. I am seized by the mad desire to get down on my knee and propose.

He deflates. "I don't know how to be smooth."

"Wesley, you don't need to be smooth. It's a good thing you aren't, actually. I wouldn't survive it. You're already too wonderful for your own good."

He looks like he doesn't know whether to be happy or suspicious. Suspicious wins. "I'm trying to figure out the problem here."

"It's complicated."

His forehead wrinkles. "Is it the Jack thing?"

"No." I couldn't give two tosses about the Jack thing. Jack was a cardboard cutout of a person, and Wesley is—well, Wesley is *Wesley*. There's no comparison. That part of my life has quite rightfully faded into hazy irrelevance.

He looks down at himself, appraising his lower half uncertainly. "It's the pants. They're too much."

"I promise you, the pants are excellent. I have the highest respect for your pants."

He quirks a brow. It is the deadliest eyebrow I have ever seen. I scan his person for the invisible scissors he must be using to snip at my moral fibers. I only have one or two of them still intact.

"During an argument that we had," he tells me, pitch low, "you called me beautiful. And an insufferable ass. But *beautiful*. I haven't gotten over it."

His stare is unwavering in the golden light, cutthroat and holy, compassionate yet demanding. Even though he is tall and straight as a statue, there is still movement in him somehow. An undercurrent of unease he's fighting off with every shred of will he possesses. "I should have told you. I wanted to." His eyes are molten, transparent with feeling. "I think you are beautiful, too, Maybell. I think that you walked into my life and absolutely ruined it with how beautiful you are. I haven't gotten a single decent night's rest since we met."

My traitorous thoughts try to flee but he shuts the windows on them all, locking every door. I collapse.

Into the couch, a complete goner. My bones have simply stopped working. "You're killing me," I rasp.

Wesley bends over my deceased frame, brows knitted in their everlasting concern, but his mouth—his *mouth*, oh, it's the eighth deadly sin—twitching with gentle amusement. "I'm sorry."

He is not.

"Fmmphhhhff."

"Hm?" He cups a hand behind his ear.

"I said that I take back what I said about you not being smooth. You've been holding back."

He helps me upright, then ruffles my hair with a serene smile. "Do you really not want to do the last wish together, then?"

I hear my doom and gloom when I reply, "I see no way around it."

"Don't sound so eager."

I use his arm to pull myself up off the couch. He makes himself immovable, a boulder in tossing seas, to support me. "Sir, I will happily make donuts with you. I will even watch a movie with you. But I refuse to be glad about it. And I refuse to do any more kissing, even though kissing you was the most magical, time-stopping phenomenon I've ever experienced and I will perish before I let another man's lips near me."

A choking sound escapes him.

"I'll take that as a compliment, I think? I'd rather you told me why you don't want to kiss again if it was so phenomenal, but for as long as you feel that way, I won't dare try." There is no woe-is-me in his voice, no bitterness.

"Is it too much to ask that you be less nice?" I bemoan.

He gives me a once-over. "I don't understand that thing you're wearing. Your top is attached to your shorts. How do you go to the bathroom?"

"Yes. More comments like that. And it's called a romper, by the way."

"The color of it washes you out."

My jaw drops. *"Hey."*

Wesley grins and grabs my hand, pulling me along after him into the kitchen. "Just kidding. Pink is perfect on you, of course. Every color is—but pink? Pink is a Maybell color."

My eyes are slits, and Wesley just laughs.

"SUGAR, BUTTER, NUTMEG, SALT," I order, pointing at the ingredients I measured out. "You're going to mix that together in the larger bowl. Once it's thoroughly mixed, add an egg, then mix some more."

Wesley nods once. "Yes, ma'am."

I won't lie, it's nice to be the one who knows what they're doing. It's also nice to watch Wesley doing my bidding.

He pulls an electric mixer out of an upper cabinet with ease, and I'm right back to being jealous. I would've needed a chair to get that out.

While Wesley mixes, I dump flour and baking powder into a different bowl. He interrupts, delicately brushing my nose with one knuckle.

"Flour?" I guess, rubbing at it.

"A bruise. You hurt yourself?"

On the door, while imagining him naked. It's what I deserve. "No," I reply quickly. "That's probably just a shadow."

He looks skeptical as I duck my head and squirm away.

"Add this stuff a little at a time to your bowl," I instruct, pointing at the flour/baking powder mixture. He's marginally sloppy for my standards, pouring in too much at a time. I bite my tongue but ultimately can't help taking over. Technically, Wesley *is* fulfilling the terms of the wish; he's making Violet's favorite cinnamon-sugar donuts. I'm merely assisting.

"If I can just squeeze in here . . ." I step in front of him, my back to his chest, commandeering his carton of milk. Wesley frowns, empty hand still raised in the air.

"Shhh." I pat a fingertip over his lips, feeling them twist up into a smile.

Then I happily return to showing off, stirring the batter like a pro, pouring it into a piping bag. "Like this." I demonstrate, piping batter into one of the cavities of my donut pan. "You fill it up about halfway."

"May I?" He reaches.

I quickly pipe a second one (I *love* piping, it's so satisfying), then hand it over. Wesley raises the metal nozzle to my cheek and squirts cold batter directly onto my skin. One dollop. Two dollops. One long, curving dollop.

"It's a smiley face," he says, gleeful.

I grab his piping bag. "That's how you lose your privileges."

"Aw." He towels off my cheek as I make quick work of the rest of the pan. "Turn that frown upside down."

I try to glare at him, unsuccessfully.

He's all innocence. "Now what?"

"Oven. We'll set a timer for eight minutes, but it might only need seven. And then . . ." I drift off. He's using leftover batter to doodle a *W* on top of the pan. I put him to work preparing the topping: one bowl of melted butter, another of cinnamon and sugar.

"Now what?" he asks again once the pan's in the oven and the timer's been set.

"Trust fall!" I cry, and fall back. His sturdy arm encircles my waist well before I hit the ground, of course.

"Don't do that! I was all the way over there!"

I cackle. "I'm pretty sure that one was on Violet's list. *Wish number five: Do a trust fall.*"

"You could have actually fallen!"

"Could I have, though?"

He scowls. "No." Then he leans in, lips at my ear. I instantly erupt in flames. "You say being close is a bad idea, but then you go and fall onto me."

"Hm?" I spring away, busying myself filling the dishwasher.

"You heard me." He begins to leave the room.

"Where're you going?"

"To set up the movie. It's sacred law, don't forget."

While he's doing that, I take a much-needed breather to slap myself. *Get it together!* This is a critical period. If I can refrain from swooning all over him, then I don't see why we both can't have what we want long-term: a hotel and an animal sanctuary, without stepping on each other's toes. We'll likely bicker at times, but a little bickering between equal inheritors is much less damaging than bickering between salty exes forced to live in close proximity to each other for the rest of their lives. This is the mature decision. For once in my life, I am going to look before I leap, and save myself from pain.

I know I'm right in this, but knowing I'm right doesn't make me any happier about it.

The timer dings while I'm preoccupied with an internal speech that is half pep talk, half threat. "They're ready!" I shout.

When he doesn't pop back in, I assume he must be busy choosing a movie and pounce on the opportunity to roll the donuts in the topping myself, which I confess I wanted to do anyway. Once I'm finished, I lay them aside, wash my hands, and set off to scold Wesley for not doing the thing that I'm glad he didn't do.

He isn't in the living room. I walk by the television, which I left paused on *The Great British Bake Off*, but instead of the charming Noel Fielding gracing my screen I get a horrifying eyeful of Pennywise the clown. "Jesus *Christ*."

I wheel around, panning the room. "Wesley!"

No response.

I plant my hands on my hips. "I am not watching *It*." I punch the exit button on my remote as fast as I can, then click on *Legally Blonde*. Much better.

Wesley jumps out at me from out of nowhere, hands in claws. I scream.

He laughs and laughs and laughs. I hate him. I really, really want to hate him. I am not even close to hating him. "The look on your face!" he howls, doubling over.

"You about finished?" I level him with the most hateful look I can muster. "Where the *hell* did you come from?"

He flashes a lopsided grin. "Wouldn't you like to know."

"Yes."

"You're cute when you're mad. Like that movie with the duck who says the sky is falling? Have you seen that one? That's what you remind me of, and when you're mad it's hilarious."

How very flattering.

"It's a *chicken*," I snap.

Whatever my face is doing is really cracking him up. I am on the fence about finding a stepstool to stand on so that I can climb up there and give him a good dressing-down when he relents. Wesley crosses the room, flattens a palm to the wallpaper, and digs his fingers into it. The edge of a camouflaged doorway gives, swinging out to reveal a black corridor.

I gape. "Where did *that* come from?"

"Secret passageway."

I'm already hurrying inside. Far behind me, Wesley's complaining that I changed the movie: "What'd you do that for? I've been busy setting up a joke. Now the red balloon won't make any sense."

"If I see a red balloon in this house, Wesley Koehler, you're going to be in big trouble. I *hate* clowns."

"Balloon?" I hear a loud noise that is inarguably the pop of a balloon. "Never seen a balloon in my life."

The secret passageway leads to the library. I decide to teach Wesley a lesson in karma by shutting the light off and squeezing myself inside a large, deep bookshelf. When he walks by, I reach out and grab his ankle. He shouts, releasing a string of curses he then spends five minutes apologizing for.

I lie on the floor laughing.

"Oh, you'll be sorry you did that," he says darkly, offering me a helping hand. "I know all sorts of secret passageways in this house."

"So do I."

"You didn't know about the one in the living room."

My eyes narrow with challenge. "Close your eyes and count to twenty."

Chapter 17

H E ISN'T THE ONLY one who knows a thing or two about this old house. There's a large framed painting in the hallway upstairs that conceals a storage area. Not very big—Violet used it for ice skates and tennis rackets, if memory serves—but big enough for someone to curl up inside of if they wanted.

"I can hear you running up the stairs!" he yells after me.

"Stop listening!"

"You're bad at this game."

"You'll eat your words."

I clamber inside the hole in the wall, close the picture behind me, and sit as still as possible. I'm a lot bigger now than I was the last time I sat in here. I have to squish my head between my knees to fit.

Wesley finds me in under a minute. "Hey there."

"You cheated!"

"I *bested* you." He bites into a cinnamon-sugar donut. "Are these my words? They're delicious. I'm so good at making donuts."

"I tell you to stop being nice, so you subject me to killer clowns and bad sportsmanship."

"Your turn." He shuts the picture frame on me again. I hear his muffled shout down the hall: "Count to twenty! And use Mississippis!"

Twenty Mississippi seconds later, I'm diverted in a number of dizzying directions thanks to Wesley's switching on every television set in the house. *Jumanji* is playing on FX, stampedes of animals throwing out red herrings every time I think I've heard him. The surround sound he's set up in his art studio to amplify a spooky playlist is particularly evil.

"Gotcha!" I cry a dozen times, using a broomstick to poke flickering curtains and lumps under his bedspread. No Wesley to be found.

I shoot him a text. I see you.

It's a bad bluff, and he knows it. Actually, I see YOU.

All the hairs on the back of my neck stand on end.

He adds: Ha. Bet I made you look.

Come out, I demand.

Can't. Hide and seek is on Violet's list.
Wish number 6.

And to think I've been comparing him to angels.

But texting gives me an idea. I call his phone as I creep along, smiling wickedly when I peek around the corner of a hallway and spot a tiny white-blue light floating. I follow it, and footsteps, into

yet another secret passage I had no idea existed. Not simply a secret passage, but a secret stairway, leading into the ballroom
downstairs. It was hidden behind a heavy floral curtain that I'd
assumed was just another window. I'll never trust a curtain again.

I was right on his tail all the way down the stairs, so there's
only one place he could have hidden so quickly. "Hmm, wonder
who's behind that Christmas tree," I muse into the phone when
he answers.

He walks out in a huff, hanging up the phone. "You cheated."

"I *bested* you, you mean."

His mouth curves.

"I can't believe there are all these hidden passageways," I say.
And if I sound jealous, I can't be faulted for it.

"The trick," he tells me, "is listening for hollows." He raps the
wall. *Thud.* Raps it farther along. *Thud.* Raps it again, right over
our mural. The sound he produces there is different, more of a
drumbeat. I gasp as he magics another camouflaged door out of
the ether. This one isn't terribly impressive; I wouldn't even call
it a closet. A deck of cards and a Gatorade from the nineties sit
inside.

"Did you know this was here all along?" I demand.

Wesley's insufferable smugness is answer enough.

I'm indignant. "Why didn't you show me?"

"Maybell," he replies seriously, "one doesn't become the un-
beatable hide-and-seek champion by sharing all one's secrets."

I'm going to kick him.

I think he can tell, because he spins around and begins counting loudly. I fly off, determined to stun him into oblivion with my
next hiding place. Let *him* wander aimlessly forever.

And then the perfect spot hits me: the white wardrobe in the living room. It's one of those fixtures your eyes become so accustomed to skating past that it's practically invisible. As I make my way into the living room, my phone vibrates with a text from Wesley. He's snapped a picture of the donut pan, missing half its occupants. Love these, he says. I try not to preen.

The wardrobe doors are stuck, which they always have been, given their age. Then again, I've never had reason to try very hard to open them. I grit my teeth and yank. "Are you painted shut?"

From the other room, Wesley bellows: "Fourteen . . . fifteen . . . sixteen!"

No! Fear boosts my adrenaline, and my next yank nets results. I pull the left door bodily from its hinge. And gape.

"Wesley!" I shout.

He comes running. "What?"

"You'll never guess what's inside this wardrobe."

"Is there snow? A lamppost? Weird little goat man on his hind legs?"

I seize the front of his shirt, dragging him over. He doesn't look at all displeased about it. Then he stands next to me and gapes, too.

"It's . . ."

"Yes."

"All along!"

"It would seem so."

"And!" He snaps his fingers, wild-eyed. "Upstairs! The other white wardrobe! I never thought about it before. That one is directly on top of this one. It makes so much sense."

The wardrobes are hiding an elevator.

Since the antique furnishings have been sealed to the wall, Wesley fetches an axe, asks me politely to stand back, and sends white chips of wood airborne. Once it's all been cleared away, we stand back in disbelief.

It's a touch smaller than I'm used to elevators being, but still nice looking after all these years of disuse. Burgundy carpet. A gold control panel. A brass grille in elaborate art deco style. The air emanating from it is dank and cooler than the rest of the house's temperature, a bit like a cave.

"This has just been hanging out inside the walls," I sputter.

Wesley opens the grille, stepping inside. "God, I love this house."

We're not stupid enough to press any buttons or try to operate it, since there's no way it isn't in dire need of a mechanic, but it's fascinating to stand in the elevator even when we're not going anywhere.

"You know what this means," Wesley says, marveling over the floor indicator, a gilt half-moon.

I poke at the grille, all the holes in its pattern. "It means I have a hundred more spots to stick plastic flowers."

A gleam of white teeth in the semidarkness. "I found you, so I win the game."

"You've got me there." I lounge against one wall.

His smile is rueful. "Almost." Wesley leans against the wall opposite. "Secret for a secret?"

His tone instantly has me on guard, but I can't turn down the chance to uncover one of Wesley's secrets. "All right."

"You first. Go ahead and ask me something."

I'm not prepared for this, so the question that tumbles out isn't one I'd pose if I were employing any sense. "What do you really think about when you lie down to sleep?"

The glow of the living room television flickers at the mouth of the elevator, painting the left half of his face an eerie, otherworldly blue. The rest of Wesley falls to darkness. "I think about you," he says, each word deliberate. Forced to admit. "I think about you, and it doesn't help my insomnia at all."

My breathing grows labored. "One more."

He smiles, letting it slide. "All right."

"What's inside all those boxes in the shed?"

I can tell this question takes him by surprise. "Artwork. The boxes used to be in my old bedroom at the cabin, but when you moved in I had to hide them somewhere." I digest this, speculating whether he'll let me take a look at his other drawings. I like being able to see the world how he sees it, discover what interests him enough that he feels compelled to capture it on paper.

Then his tone drops. "My turn."

Damn. "Go ahead."

"Do I even have to ask?"

My first thought is to deflect, or distract. But then it dawns on me that none of this is easy for Wesley. *Of course* it isn't. Wesley is standing in front of me in trousers he wears only on very special occasions and cologne he never wears at all, trying to impress a woman. He has opened up to me even though it's hard. Facing his fears. Terribly shy, but putting himself out there anyway.

And I think: Maybe I'm not making the mature decision after all in deciding we shouldn't go a little further, seeing what might bloom between us.

Maybe I'm making the safe decision. The coward's one.

He shifts his weight, jarring me from my self-reflection. Right. He has anxiety, and taking my time coming up with answers to questions that required valor to ask is essentially torture.

"It doesn't matter," I say slowly, "because I think I might be wrong." Anyone can hurt me, but at this point choosing to miss out on what *could* be is going to hurt me, too. What if it ends badly?

What if it doesn't?

Hoping for the best isn't necessarily reckless, and nothing—not the good nor the bad—is guaranteed in life.

"Maybell," he presses. "You have to tell me what that means."

I step forward, summoning all my courage. My heart is racing a hundred miles an hour.

Wesley just might be the most anxious, most relationship-shy person I've ever met, but here he is putting himself out there anyway. Maybe it's my turn to be brave.

I raise my hands into his hair, watching his pleased surprise register. "I'm not the type of person who takes risks," I say, letting the silky strands ripple through my fingertips.

His eyes are solemn. "Neither am I."

"I stayed at a job I hated, that didn't appreciate me, for too many years because I was scared of giving it up for the unknown. All the men I've been involved with in the past were bad for me, and I think a part of me knew that deep down, but I picked them anyway because I knew subconsciously there wouldn't be a future with any of them. I knew none of them would last very long, and my life wouldn't be changed. I'd go on being the same, with the same life." I draw a bracing breath. "The devil you know."

His hand slides up my arm to cover my wrist, a small, melancholy smile on his lips. "I understand."

"But I quit my old job, and my life got better. I moved here, and my life got better. Such big changes. I met you."

His smile widens, just a fraction.

"And my life got better. So what I'm saying is I would very

much like to kiss you again, if you wouldn't mind. I have nowhere to go from here but up."

He watches me for a moment, calculating whether I'm sure about this, then lets his forehead tilt against mine. "Close your eyes and count to twenty," he murmurs against my lips.

I don't even make it to one before his mouth covers mine.

My fingers slip into the diamond cablework of his clothing, pushing through to the soft, worn shirt beneath; he bands his arms around me, hauling me close. I am new to his kisses, his touch, after getting briefly acquainted with them for the first time mere hours ago, and it's distressing, how badly I've already missed it. I think I have been waiting all my life for a man who says *I understand* and genuinely does. Who is just as unsteady on his feet as I am when it comes to trying something new and scary.

We back out of the elevator still locked in an embrace, me pressing myself as close as I can get. His skin is searing, tongue twisting around mine with fierce enthusiasm. We keep finding ourselves holding our breath for too long and have to break for gulps of air, then dive right back to it.

"You're so tall," I grumble, stretching up on tiptoe.

Wesley's arms clamp around me more securely as he lifts me off the ground, my feet dangling. "Better?"

I give him a peck on the nose. "I could get used to it."

"I'd imagine so. I don't know how you go about life, all the way down there. Seems awfully rough."

"It was." I wrap my arms around his neck and get to know him some more. "C'mere."

Now that I've given in, I can't stop. I'm on a steep downhill slide, rolling as fast as I can. Maybe I'll crash at the bottom, or maybe I'll never find the bottom at all. Maybe we'll roll like this forever.

Only one way to find out.

Wesley kisses me all the way into the kitchen so that he can grab another donut, showing me the *W* he doodled out of batter. It baked up puffy and deformed. "Look, I made you."

He turns it upside down.

I take a bite. "We forgot to watch the movie."

"Whoops. Guess this means we'll have to have a do-over." He pretends to be sad.

"*Nooo*, anything but that."

I grin. Wesley grins back. Tonight is sweeter than frosting on a cupcake and anybody watching us would probably get a second-hand toothache, but I'm not minding one bit. Nothing about life at Falling Stars is turning out the way I expected it to.

Thank goodness for that.

"What are you doing Friday night?" he asks, clasping my hand and twirling me like we're dancing. "I wanna take you out on a date."

My heart leaps. "Friday is so far away."

He's gratified by my impatience. "Got a busy week ahead. Plus, I have very specific plans for where we should go on our date. I'll warn you, the location is somewhere difficult to access, so it might take a while to get there. But it'll be worth the wait, I promise."

"What sort of plans?" I ask curiously. "Where are we going?"

"Can't tell you any more than that." I'm twirled again, which might not be the best idea, given how lightheaded I already am. He's an ungainly dancer, all thumbs and left feet. "Be ready to go at eight?"

"You can pick me up at my door."

We bid each other good night, parting ways—he up the grand staircase, and I to my bedroom one floor below his, where I know I'll be feeling him through the walls all night. To my credit, I wait until I'm safely in my room before I tip back onto the bed and swoon.

WESLEY WAS RIGHT ABOUT having a busy week ahead. I don't know if I'm grateful for how little time I have over the next few days to obsess over our looming date now that I'm a sentient storm in a teapot.

Falling Stars is coming together. It felt at first like a slow transformation, but now the final touches are happening all at once. The dose of reality is all the more overwhelming since I don't have a team to collaborate with. The hotel is *my* pride and joy, *my* responsibility, not Wesley's or anybody else's. How did I not appreciate the scope of this massive undertaking? Hotels are easy to run in the abstract, when you're daydreaming about them but still have plenty of time before the real work begins.

I've registered my business and am scheduling inspections, checking in on the status of applications for various permits and licenses. I'm conducting outreach to magazines and newspapers all over Tennessee, hoping they'll want to write about the hotel, offering journalists free stays for opening week (which I'm tentatively slating for the first week of September, depending on how long it takes to receive all the proper certifications). I've got to go *hard* on press with targeted Internet ads, but ads are expensive. On top of everything else, I've got to master the art form of being my own social media manager. If only Wesley would let me post pictures of him mending fences and pruning shrubs, we'd book up all the way through next year.

On Tuesday, I contact my local landmark preservation commission to begin the process of nominating Falling Stars to be declared a historical landmark, which would not only be fantastic for publicity but would also grant me tax breaks and leeway on building code. I respond to a message from a site acquisition agent with a cell phone company about a potential cell tower lease. They want to install a tower on the property, which means I get to negotiate fees and generate some extra income.

I like the problem-solving that comes with heading my own projects, anticipating kinks in the plan and conquering them. I like the spreadsheets, the rigorous search for good deals on hand towels, flour, lightbulbs, cleaning supplies. Coupon hunting and menu drafting: dinners will be served in the dining room unless guests request room service; if they put in an order for lunch, the meal will be dropped off at their door in a picnic basket along with a laminated list of picnicking spots on the grounds. Guests can grab their breakfast in the kitchen and enjoy it wherever they like.

I can do this. I'm going to prove to the world that I can do this.

Chapter 18

ON WEDNESDAY, I DRIVE to the farmers market in Maryville to chat with local vendors in hopes of establishing partnerships. Everyone is warm and small-town friendly, asking all kinds of questions about the hotel. Even though I probably waste too much time chatting, I walk away from the market feeling like an absolute god: I landed discounts on bulk orders in exchange for using and advertising their products exclusively. Falling Stars is officially in business with Kiana's Stationery Shop, an artisan soap and lotion maker called Lather Up, and Huckleberry Homestead, who in August will start delivering homemade butter, cheese, and sourdough. Their cows are free-range, they say, and there's a live feed of them playing with toys on the farm.

I come home to a leak in the washing machine hose, an inch of water covering the laundry room floor, and the painters that I caved and decided to hire are busy spraying the front of the house maroon. "Excuse me," I call politely, waving to get their attention. My voice is too timid—nobody hears. I stretch, nearly on tiptoe, and speak louder. "I'm sorry, but that's not the right color. It's supposed to be pink."

One of the guys, Phillip, screws up one eye as he scans the big splotch of new paint. "It's sorta pink."

In what universe? I raise my arm and point. "That is maroon."

The guys split dubious looks among one another, shrugging. "Maybe maroon is what you ordered," Phillip suggests.

"No. I know what I ordered, and it isn't even close to this."

One of them, the youngest, is barely seventeen. He scratches his chin worriedly, mumbling to them in an undertone that he thinks I might be right.

They ignore him. "It'll look different once it's dry," says Phillip with the highest confidence. "The clouds are casting a shadow over us right now, which makes it seem darker. Trust me, once we're done you're gonna love it."

"I don't want maroon." I'm beginning to panic. When they turn around to get back to work, I lose it. A much braver person than I am possesses my body and uses it to bellow, "I! Don't! Want! Maroon!"

Dumbfounded, they stop what they're doing.

"Calm down, now, sweetheart," the oldest one entreats.

No, he did *not*. "You can call me Miss Parrish," I snap.

Phillip snickers.

I'm about to do something that'll get me arrested when Wesley's truck pulls up the driveway, bed stacked with lumber that will become a shelter for his animals in short order. He climbs out, frowns at the house, and says in a quieter tone than the one I initially tried out myself and nobody heard, "That's not the color we ordered."

"Oh?" Phillip plasters on a baffled smile. "You sure? Here, let's look it up." He looks up the information while my spinal fluid simmers to a froth. "What do you know! You're right."

And then he apologizes. To Wesley.

We eventually get it ironed out. I continue my part of the conversation through clamped teeth, but fortunately no one tells me to calm down again. The new paint won't be in for another two weeks, however, and their next availability to come back isn't until mid-July. Leaving Falling Stars gray with a patch of maroon.

I am a professional. It is the only reason I do not scream.

"You know what? You're fired." I don't have time for this. I have a washing machine hose to deal with, a bank to call, and security cameras to set up. Not to mention, I might have chatted with a young woman I met at a gas station on my way home from the farmers market and spontaneously offered her free board at Falling Stars when I found out her landlord is going to be kicking her and her little boy out of their apartment at the end of the month. I need to bake a dozen of Wesley's favorite bear claws before I break the news.

Phillip grimaces. "You paid us already. Come on, now, I know a small mistake was made—"

"Everybody makes mistakes," I shoot back. "Your real mistake here was being condescending to me. I will not tolerate that disrespect and I demand a full refund." I gesture flippantly at the house. "Plus damages."

Phillip gapes. Appeals to Wesley, the rational and unemotional male.

"Condescending?" Wesley echoes. There is no trace of the generous, sensitive man I have come to know. He is made of stone. "You heard her. You're fired. Full refund, plus damages."

I march inside, resisting the urge to slam the door. I'm putting together a selection of banks when Wesley finds me to report that the painters left. He reads over my shoulder. "What's that for?"

"I'm thinking about applying for a small-business loan. Want to go in on it with me? We can split it between the hotel and sanctuary." I know he's hoping his savings will cover the cost of a new barn, but there are plenty of other expenses to contend with. Animal food, medical supplies . . .

Wesley makes a face. "Depends. Could we do it online?"

"I think it's better to do it in person. Make an appointment, go talk to a—"

"Hold that thought." He squeezes my hand and walks out of the room.

"—loan officer," I finish flatly.

He doesn't come back for forty-five minutes. When he does, he's flushed and appears mildly irritated but smiles at me. "Counteroffer."

I raise a hand imperiously. *Well?*

"My brother Blake would love to come on board as an investor."

"Is that so?"

His smile tightens. "I'll warn you, Blake is ruthless. And very clever. I've given serious consideration to the possibility that he might be Lucifer. But he's the best businessman and investor there is, and rich as sin. I asked him to help us out, but Blake doesn't give away money. He enjoys putting stakes in businesses. Which means he'll want to come down here to see for himself what we're doing with the property. A hands-on approach."

So this must be the fourth brother. There's Casey, happily married, designer of websites. Then Michael, with a cattle ranch, who swings a fist if you call him by his real name, which is Humphrey. He told me yesterday about Tyler, a violinist so extroverted that Wesley gets hives simply by standing next to him.

"You asked him for a loan and he agreed just like that?"

"I asked him and he said no. So I called our mother." He leaves it at that.

"So . . . what now? How much is he willing to give us? What are his interest rates?"

"He's coming to visit in three weeks to negotiate that." He doesn't sound thrilled about it, which I can't resist pointing out.

"I don't like Blake," he deadpans, "but I'd rather make deals with the devil than go talk to a loan officer I don't know. Besides, if he becomes too much of a pain I'll just call Mom again. I think she's the only person on earth he's afraid of."

After we've finished mopping up the laundry room, I come clean about the woman I ran into at the gas station.

"I hope you don't mind," I say in a rush. "She might not even come. I gave her our address and told her that if her luck hasn't changed by the end of the month, she has a place to stay. I know I should have asked you first, since this affects you, too, but—"

"Maybell." He sweeps me up in a reassuring hug. "Your big heart is one of the things I like best about you. I can't be mad when you use it."

I tip my head up. "Yeah?"

"As long as you keep some room for me in there," he says with a shrug, a transparent stab at being casual when I know he's feeling anything but, "what're a few neighbors?"

. . . .

THIS WEEK HAS BEEN up and down, but Thursday night finds me in the kitchen, smack-dab in the middle of my slide into hysteria. "How difficult would it be to start canning preserves?" I'm wondering aloud to Wesley, who's reserving tickets for upcoming livestock auctions on his laptop. "You've got all those bee boxes. We could do honey. And our own branding. Falling Stars Honey. Falling Stars Pumpkin Patch." I gasp. "Falling Stars Petting Zoo."

"No," he says firmly.

"We'll see," I mutter, adding it to the *Maybe* list.

"Strawberry patch," I continue. "We'll grow all our own produce and be the thriftiest sons of bitches who ever lived." I get swear-y when I'm on a roll. "We could plant an orchard, right?" I'm scribbling the name of every fruit and vegetable I can think of. "Blueberries, peaches, zucchini. We can be self-sustainable. Salads and casseroles. Huckleberry pies. We'll recycle our own toilet paper."

"We will not."

"In the fall we'll do apple picking and pumpkin carving. A corn maze."

"Hope you enjoy planting corn mazes, because I'm not doing it," he vows. "I will *never*."

"We'll harvest the corn and use it to feed your animals."

"Fine, then." Wesley sags in his chair. "Ugh. Somebody needs to stop you."

I'm unstoppable. I envision myself reading press validation that my hotel is a hit. Positive reviews on my website. This can be a place where newlyweds and families and best friends on a road trip build happy memories. And maybe they come back year after year, making it a tradition. It's all I could ever want, to be a part of that, for the journeys of strangers to bring them here, where they'll make new friends with each other (and, I can't help hoping, with me). Falling Stars will always be the happy-memories place for me—a warm and loving home. I want to share that with the world.

The first year is going to be a hurricane. Endless organizing, cooking, cleaning. And shopping. For meal prep alone, so much shopping. The draw of Falling Stars is its solitude, where you can see the stars and hear yourself think. Hiking. Exploring. Isolation. I'm selling Zen here. Guests won't want to make a thirty-minute trip to buy dinner or pick up a toothbrush they forgot at home, so it's imperative that I have every essential and comfort item a person could ever need in stock. If I survive the first year, and turn a profit, I might be able to hire more help.

Hours pass with me bent over my laptop and disorganized papers. Wesley ensures I don't starve to death by tentatively poking a bowl of Cheerios in front of me. I scarf it down so quickly that I don't taste anything. "Charades," I mutter, scribbling. My hand is sore and sweaty. "A murder mystery dinner theater. A live band! With accordions!"

Wesley leans across me and scribbles out that last idea as soon as I jot it down.

"I am *not* biting off more than I can chew," I tell him fervently.

"Never said you were."

"Anyone who says that is severely underestimating my jaws."

"I have no doubt," he replies calmly, clicking a pen as he glances over my proposal for the biggest lettuce garden known to man.

I'm running numbers on ketchup now. Why is ketchup so

expensive? Two dollars and fifty-two cents is highway robbery. Do I have the energy to pursue homemade-ketchup making? I smack myself. No! I'm already in too deep with crocheted coasters.

"It's because I'm a born multitasker," I rave. "I was born under a Libra moon, probably. Strong as an ox. We Maybells see your *You can't do this* and we raise you an *It may take me longer, but just watch me.*" I raise my glass of lemonade in a toast to myself. "We're weeds growing out of the cracks in concrete: even when we should have been defeated long ago, you can't keep us down."

Wesley is wordlessly collecting my things and shuffling them into a neat pile.

"I will make my own potpourri even if it kills me," I declare.

Wesley pulls out my chair. "All right. Time for bed."

"What?" I clutch the edge of the table. "No! I'm not ready to go!"

"It'll be here for you in the morning. Fresh eyes."

"No! I can't go to bed, this is too important." He steals me away as I reach for my spreadsheets and color-coded life planner. "I'm a Maybell Parrish! I'm the survivor who writes it all down in history books!"

"Of course you are," he says tenderly.

As he begins to drag me off, my emotions ping-pong in the opposite direction. I've bitten off *way* more than I can chew and now I'm choking on it. "Who do I think I am?" I moan in despair. "Why did I think I could do all this? I couldn't even give myself the quitting story I deserved."

He looks down at me with a quizzical brow, asking without asking.

"I snuck out like a coward. No fanfare at all. I gave them my youth, Wesley, and there were days when the only thing getting me through was the fantasy about how I would quit someday. How I'd go off on my boss. Never did." I give up, going slack. He catches my melting form and drags me down the hall with my socked heels gliding.

"Well, go back and quit."

"You are not serious."

"Am so."

"I already quit, though. Back in April. My boss left me nasty voicemails about it. If I show up now, they'll march me out with security."

"Sounds like an amazing quitting story. Who cares if you don't work there anymore? If you regret not going down in flames, go back there and go down in flames."

I cock my head, considering it. "Huh."

"Better late than never," he prompts.

I let my head loll back as I admire him. "You have such a beautiful point."

He snorts.

"I'll go back to Around the Mountain and get the quitting story of my dreams if you'll do something you've always wanted to do, too," I tell him.

"Like a pact?"

"Yes. Perfect." I revel in the sound of that, imagining the all-seeing Fates at their loom, weaving our tapestry. "An unbreakable pact."

"I've always wanted to go to Loch Ness," he remarks. I can't tell if he's merely indulging me right now. From his tone, he sounds greatly amused.

"Someday I'll quit that job I don't even have anymore, and you'll go find your Loch Ness Monster and keep it a secret from everybody. I'll even come with you."

Wesley laughs. "Deal. But my one condition is no pictures. We *never* photograph the supernatural."

"I'm being serious."

"So am I."

"Let's shake on it."

He squeezes his arms tighter around me and shakes my whole body. I tell him he isn't funny, which is a lie. Then I tell him that was a lie, because I say whatever I'm thinking when I'm sleep-deprived. "What if this is all just a simulation," I mutter.

He tucks me into bed, taking care to fluff my pillows and refill my water. I bet if I ever get sick, he'll bring me heating pads and chicken noodle soup.

"Wesley, if I don't finish my to-do list right now, I'll never have peace. You don't understand. My brain literally won't be able to turn off."

He turns on my white-noise machine and shuts off the light.

"I've got so much to do. I can't sleep. *Physically*, I can't sleep. Not even if I try."

"Mm-hmm."

"Just one more email. I'll make it a quick one. I am really good at . . ." My eyes close against their will. "I am so good at emailing. Not everybody is, you know."

"You're the best at emailing." His voice is warm with affection, and my little balloon heart swells beyond capacity.

"I love your smile," I prattle. I can't see his smile right now, but I can hear it. "You smile so much more now than you did when I met you."

He wavers at the door for so long that I think he's left.

"When I'm around people I don't know, I rarely smile," Wesley confesses at length. "When you smile, people look at you more. I prefer to blend in. For nobody to notice me."

Snip, and away it flies. Goodbye, heart.

"It's impossible not to notice you. I would know a Wesley in a room full of imitations. I'd know a Wesley anywhere. Go out into the woods right now and I'll find you in thirty seconds flat."

"I don't mind *you* noticing me," he admits, door creaking as he begins to close it behind him. "At least, not anymore. But you're the only one allowed to, okay?"

"I'll add it as a clause to our pact." I shake hands with the air.

I am going to get out of bed. No one can stop me. My last intelligible words that I announce to the empty room are: "I'm allergic to cayenne pepper. Don't tell anybody."

Next thing I know, it's one in the afternoon the following day.

Chapter 19

I AM FACING MY CLOSED bedroom door at 7:59 p.m. on Friday, already sweating through my dress, waiting for that knock that just might mark the beginning of everything.

This is the sixth outfit I've tried on—if I had the time, I'd probably change again—light pink with cherries all over. It's supposed to be a knockoff of a strawberry-print dress I love that's way out of my budget, and although it doesn't look anything like the Amazon picture, it fits nicely and twirls whenever I turn. I stressed myself out trying to land on a decent hairstyle, unable to commit to a high pony when I know I'll end up with a headache, unable to do a fishtail braid like the one in the tutorial. I messed with it until my previously gleaming locks got frizzy, ended up having to wash and style it again, and now it's damp, hanging loose, because I don't trust myself to experiment with it anymore.

I have never been this nervous.

There's no reason to be nervous. This is *Wesley*. Gawky, shy, uncomfortable, unintentionally charming Wesley.

Knock, knock, knock.

My heart springs into overdrive. This is it. I haven't been on a first date in . . . it's best not to count. A long time. What will we be doing? Where are we going? Will he kiss me again? I clutch my purse like it's a life preserver and rethink my choice of shoes. If we're doing anything outdoorsy I'm going to regret these heels.

I open the door and all of my intelligent thoughts fall right off the shelf.

The man on the other side is tall, broad shouldered, strong jawed, in a suit of blackest black. Dark blond hair falls in waves that make me think of ivy tendrils. He's the god of spring, powerful but sweet, burying things to make them come alive. The god of spring carries earth and rain on his skin wherever he goes. His brown eyes are topaz—a glass of root beer held up to the light, widening as he slackens against the door frame like he's just been wounded.

"Oh . . ." His gaze rakes me. His eyes go wider still, and he rubs his chin. *"Wow."*

I resist a million electrical impulses: to look away, bite my lip, cross my ankles, fiddle with my purse, fidget with my hair. To say apologetically, *The dress doesn't look like the one I ordered*, or minimize myself with a grimace and a *My hair's misbehaving*. When he looks at me that way, I feel like a goddess.

I feel . . .

"Yes," I agree, drawing myself up strong and tall. "You are a lucky boy tonight, Mr. Koehler."

He nods, not a whisper of humor in it. "I am."

In heels, I don't have to jump to kiss him, but I do have to yank his lapel to get him to dip his head. One hand slides up his smooth cheek, and I leave a kiss on the other. When I pull away, his eyes follow me in such an intimate way that I get tingles all down my spine. "You look incredible, as always. Where are we going?"

Wesley inhales a bracing breath. Puts on a practiced smile that quivers just the slightest bit, trying very hard to cover up his nerves. His hands are clenched at his sides. "I'm taking you to heaven."

I must be hearing things. "Wesley *Koehler*. Is that a pickup line?"

He holds out a stick of chewing gum. "You might need this."

I frown, but he doesn't move until I accept it. "Is this a commentary on my breath?" I brushed my teeth *twice* before this. And flossed. And swished mouthwash until my eyes watered.

"You'll see." He swallows, smile widening as I side-eye him irritably, popping the gum in my mouth. Then he takes my hand and leads me toward the front door. Just as I reach for the knob, however, he loops an arm around my waist to haul me close to him and turns in a different direction.

"What are you—"

He shakes his head, striding down the hall with me in bewildered tow.

This half of the house is dark. I try again: "What are we—"

"Ah-ah-ah," he admonishes me, clucking his tongue. Then he abruptly spins so that he's walking backward in front of me, face-to-face. He takes my hands in his, turning again down a different corridor. In my peripheral vision, I see his brilliant smile transform his whole body, but I can't look directly at him because I've been swept away into another world.

There are clouds in the corridor.

A whole night sky: great big puffs of cotton threaded with twinkly lights hanging down like raindrops. I think he made them himself, affixing the cotton to paper lanterns and suspending them from the ceiling. We walk under and around cloud after cloud, the only illumination in this long, dark hallway.

"You're probably experiencing a change in atmospheric pressure," he tells me, raising our hands together and flattening our palms before his left laces tightly with my right and his other hand finds the small of my back. He brings me close to him, then reverses our positions in one fluid motion. Then again.

I realize we're dancing.

He waltzes me down the hallway, eyes sparkling, wholly riveted on my face. Neither of us is getting the steps right, but I'm not even the tiniest bit self-conscious about it and he—oh, he's a dream, just marvelous, mesmerizing, painfully *luminous* in the glow of a sky he made all for me. "That's because we're up in the clouds now, going higher and higher," he says.

"I see that," I reply, hardly able to get the words out because I'm beaming so hugely.

"You see that bird that just went by?" he teases. "Caw, caw!"

I fall sideways just a bit, giggling. He catches me, holding me closer. Our graceless stumbling makes me throw my head back and laugh harder.

"*Whooooosh,*" he says at my ear, a smile in his voice, "there goes an airplane."

I shake my head, but my heart leaps out of my body with a parachute. I feel wildly out of control, like I'm standing in the surf and the water's pulling at me, trying to knock me off my feet. I've gotten close to this feeling before, manufactured in the superficial relationships of my fantasies, but that feeling falls flat on its face in comparison to this.

I am bubbles and butterflies. I am fizz floating into the night sky. I don't know what's happening or what *will* happen because for once, I am not orchestrating any of this. The lines are all unscripted, every second a thrilling surprise. I'm spinning out, carried away in a current. I want to fight it and I want to surrender.

My knees go wobbly as the identity of this feeling rips its mask off and declares itself to me, but Wesley thinks my heels are the culprit.

"All that effort, and you're still all the way down there," he tells me with a crooked grin. I blow a bubble with my gum, letting it pop in his face.

We've reached the end of the hall. Wesley reaches behind him, fumbling for a doorknob without turning. I think he wants to continue monitoring my reaction.

I arch a brow. "The conservatory?"

His expression is sly. "Is it?"

My forehead scrunches, but then the door is open, and the huge bags of soil I've seen him drag in here are nowhere to be found. "A bell chimes," he says lowly, "when we open the door."

"I didn't hear a . . ."

My brain blinks out. I'm stationary as I wait for backup generators to kick on, letting pieces fall together slowly.

The sunroom, which I handed over to Wesley in exchange for the cabin in our negotiations, is not the conservatory he's been talking about. There *are* plants, big floppy ferns in pots, but my attention flits past them to the red vinyl booth sidled up against the glass wall. The opposite wall is painted pale purple, lower half adorned with aqua tiles that spread over the floor. It smells like plaster and new construction, drilled wood and fresh paint. There are succulents in hanging baskets and a travel poster on the wall that says, in vintage style, WELCOME TO FALLING STARS. On closer inspection, it isn't a poster at all. He's painted the design directly onto the wall, then hung a frame around it.

"Over here is the display case," he tells me, motioning at a bank of empty space, "filled with donuts. Up here is the old-fashioned register." He raps the register-less countertop, which I realize was taken from the bar in the lounge upstairs. A coffeepot that's probably as old as I am, carafe stained amber, awaits.

Part of me has gone away from Falling Stars, from Top of the World. I'm in Lexington, Kentucky, fourteen years old. In the car with Mom, world black, snow pushing against the windshield. We're bundled in coats, hats, mittens, still-warm leftover pie from the diner between us in a Styrofoam container. We're listening to syndicated radio host Delilah on the radio, and while we didn't scratch millions from the lottery ticket, for the present moment we're a peaceful family unit. The happy spark of memory infuses me with warmth.

My throat closes up. "It's perfect."

The rotary phone is blue rather than beige, nonfunctional, cord cut off. It automatically becomes canon. There's only one red vinyl booth; the rest of the seating is thrifty substitutes, red-painted card tables with mismatched patio chairs. The bar stools don't spin, and they're yellow, but I wouldn't trade them for anything. He's lit a candle called Blueberry Pie, the scent too weak to over-power the rest of the room. I picture Wesley picking out candles at Casey's General, hunting for ones that smell like baked goods.

The cloud lights are in here, too—on the floor around us, hanging from the ceiling, reflecting off the glass wall to imitate a café in the night sky. Rain begins to fall outside, pelting the panes.

It's a miracle I can stand upright when I am, in fact, melting.

"Do you hear the jukebox?" He's behind me, hands at my waist, lips at my ear. He points at an old red Zenith radio sitting atop a pile of extra tiles.

"It's playing my favorite song," I reply, voice quivering in spite of my best efforts. I glance sideways at the glass wall to see his reflection. We stand in a room that is half shadow, half heaven, with softly glowing clouds, their number doubled in the glass wall. He is the most radiant thing in here, smile dazzling.

"You haven't seen the best part yet." Wesley moves my hands up from my mouth to my eyes. "Don't look."

I shut my eyes tight. "I can't believe you did this. How long have you been working on it? How did you— I can't even— You are . . ." I can't drum up any coherent speech, babbling. "You are . . ."

"Yes," he replies from several feet away, a touch smug. "I am, aren't I?"

My cheeks hurt from smiling. "You truly are."

Click.

"What was that?" I ask. "Please let it not be my morning alarm. Am I asleep? I hope this doesn't all disappear when I open my eyes."

"Don't worry, it's here to stay." Wesley's voice is closer than I anticipated. "And . . . *open.*"

I do.

Ohhh!

It's my sign! *Maybell's Coffee Shop.* The words are painted on an oval piece of wood. Below them, he's shaped a donut out of two hot-pink neon wires that plug into the wall, feeding through the back of the wood.

My vision glitters and the image appears in my mind's eye like a premonition: I see myself adding books to this room, stacking them wherever they'll fit. Whole rows of romance and science fiction. A cappuccino machine. Menus that double as bookmarks . . . *pairing the perfect book with the pastry of your choice.* The thought lands with a fateful *BOOM* that rattles the floor and ceiling.

"I hope you don't mind Subway sandwiches for dinner," he's saying, scratching the back of his head self-consciously. "I wanted to cook something nice for you, but the clouds took longer than expected and—"

I leap at him, throwing my arms around his neck. I kiss his cheek, his chin, his forehead. "Wesley! How dare you be this amazing! Who gave you the right?" I don't stop to let him respond. "What about your conservatory? This was supposed to be yours. We made a deal. You can have the cabin, then. It's yours." My name is on a sign. My name is on a sign on the *wall*. With a neon donut. I cannot believe this. "Thank you so much."

"You're welcome so much." Wesley is trying to be modest, but I can tell he's exceedingly pleased with himself. Good. He should be. "I wanted to bring your happy place to life."

"And all along, you were just *out here*." I am off the rails now. "Being you. And I was over *there*, not even knowing."

"Now you're here," he replies cheerfully, leaning back so he can view me better.

"Now I'm here," I echo. I am so giddy that I'm making myself ill. If this feeling is what I think it is, I'm going to die. This cannot be sustainable. How do couples spend whole years feeling like this about each other? How do they not combust?

"Ready for five-star cuisine?" To my surprise, he sidesteps the red booth and takes us to the counter, pulling out a stool for me like a gentleman.

Subway is one of the only takeout places in Top of the World, the other being Benigno's, a little pizzeria. They sit side by side in a building that used to be a sawmill and sabotage each other's advertising signs. Thunder cracks over the house as he pushes me in, foul weather interfering with the static that seems to be the only sound Wesley could coax out of the old radio.

"So this is what you've been doing all day." I can't get over it.

"Just the clouds. The rest I've been doing whenever you're out of the house, or asleep." He pulls two hot chocolates from behind the counter, setting them before us. You wouldn't think that hot chocolate and veggie sandwiches would pair well, but he's noticed my favorite drink is hot chocolate, and *that* means everything. "What have *you* been doing all day?"

Other than crying over my hair, my day's actually been rather productive. "I had a chat with Ruth's daughter Sasha over the phone."

"Really? Why?"

"The last time I talked to Ruth, she mentioned her daughter had quit culinary school to get away from an ex-boyfriend. I'm going to have my hands full around here—preparing three meals a day would take up too much of my time. Plus, I'm good at baking but I don't have the range for lunches and dinners day in and day out. I wanted to know if she'd consider being my chef."

"What'd she say?"

My adrenaline is surging so high that I can't taste any of my food, which I eat anyway, feeling that rise of excitement and stress flood me all over again. Excitement and stress is the line I've been straddling for a while now. "She's going to come over and discuss the possibility in a couple of weeks. She wants to see the kitchen first—I'm gonna have to get a second fridge, and maybe other appliances, if she needs them. She wants freedom to plan her own menus." I add in a rush, "All vegetarian meals, of course."

Wesley puts his sandwich down. Stares at me. "You don't have to do that."

I wave him off, inexplicably blushing. Maybe it's because I'm showing my hand here, betraying that what is important to him is important to me. "No big deal."

He's turning pink, too. "I would never pressure you to only serve vegetarian food. It's a personal decision. I don't expect—"

"I know." I cut him off with a pat on the hand. "Do you honestly think, though, that after hearing about your childhood pet cow, I'm ever going to bring meat into your house? Nope." I take a sip of my drink in a *Case closed* gesture. "Not happening."

We stare down at our plates. We are both flustered, both unable to take a compliment, both wanting to give compliments rather than receive them and both being bad at verbalizing our feelings. I'd laugh out loud at how disastrously awkward we are if I weren't channeling every drop of energy into staying put on this stool when all I really want to do is maul him.

He reaches for a Subway napkin. Takes a pen from inside his jacket and unclicks it, hand poised in midair for three seconds.

That is very wonderful of you, he writes, and slides the napkin over to me.

My face heats even more. I take much too long settling on a reply. *You make it easy.*

He rereads that line over and over. "You make it easier," he says finally. "So we're really doing this, then." He pushes his plate away. "A hotel and an animal sanctuary. An interesting combination." He clinks his mug of hot chocolate against mine. "To Violet."

"To Violet." I finish my drink, then add, "Thank you, by the way, for taking care of her. I'm sad that I never met her as an adult, and built a relationship with her as two adults rather than caregiver and child. I think we each thought we'd failed the other."

He listens. Nods slowly, writing on the napkin some more. "She would have liked adult Maybell, I can tell you that. She would have liked who you've grown up to become."

I lean into him, more for the excuse to be close than any other reason, and smile to see that he's sketching me.

"Your pendant," I muse, tapping the miniature version in ink.

"*Your* pendant," he says, briefly touching the one that rests against my chest. My skin responds with goose bumps. "Looks better on you."

I prop my elbow on the counter, chin in hand, posing for him. His eyes flicker from me to the drawing, me to the drawing, the edge of an amused smile flirting at his lips. "You can move a bit, you know."

"Hm?"

"You're being so still."

"I don't want to mess you up."

He tips his head back, searching the ceiling. The sound that escapes his chest is a cross between sigh and laugh. "Maybell, I can draw you from memory. With my eyes closed."

"Is that so?"

"Hands behind my back."

"Now you're just bragging." I steal the napkin from him, help-less not to admire it. "That's it. We need an art gallery down here for the guests to look at. I'm your number one fan, of course, but there's room for more in the fan club."

He sits forward over the counter, fingers in his hair, tousling it and trying to cover his face. The strands are too short to do the job, so he suffers in the open. "The drawing is pretty because the *subject* is pretty. I like drawing you."

I'm not finished inflating his head. The man needs more ego. "The flowers you've put in the background are the best combination ever designed."

"I was inspired by the flowers I see you gravitate toward whenever you're in the garden."

The storm outside rages and Wesley brings the lightning, radiating all around his magnificent frame like a halo. His eyes lock on my mouth, darkening.

I think he's going to kiss me, but then he eases off his seat. As I turn, he takes my hand and pulls me along with him. We move to the center of the room, pressed close.

"Um." My heart is the ocean slamming against a rocky shore. "Hi. Hello."

For once—*once*—that anticipation, that tingling on the nape of my neck, that intoxicating awareness injected straight into my veins, isn't vicarious. It doesn't belong to an imaginary Maybell in a fantasy, a guess at what she might feel. It's mine. And I think: At what point did my happy place stop being a dream and start being the person in front of me?

"Hello," he returns, palms cradling either side of my face. "I'm trying something."

"Try anything you want," I reply, and he gifts me a half smile, then a kiss on my temple.

My pulse pounds, vision tunneling. The lights in the clouds begin to slide, converging together.

"A lot of times there's a disconnect between what I want to do and what I can get up the nerve to do," he confesses. "But with you, I'm anxious in a *good* way. Let's see if I'm any good at this."

"At what?"

I think I know *what*, but I can't hold still. Suspense is eating me alive.

He retreats. I watch his reflection in the glass panes shift closer until he's behind me, hands roving up either side to grasp my upper arms. The room tips onto its side, everything in it rolling except for us and each golden filament of light. The air is weighted, dropping lower, lower.

In the glass, his mouth hovers at my throat, just below my ear. Every molecule in my body sings. "I would like to touch you," he says faintly. "If that's okay."

The air is so heavy now that it's a drum pound.

"That would be perfect." My voice sounds foreign to my ear, husky and strange.

He drops a kiss to my neck, eliciting a shiver. Then he blows softly along the hollow, migrating over to my shoulder. "This," he says, toying fondly with my hair. "This is what I've wanted."

Tension thickens as his hands gain confidence, no longer hesitating. He circles me, eyes going dark. Swipes a thumb beneath my chin and raises it so that I'm meeting his inscrutable stare.

"I've wanted it, too." I want to swallow the rest, but the truth escapes. "Badly."

I think he likes the truth. It makes him hold me closer.

I explore the planes of his chest, stomach. Then he can't hold himself back any longer and wraps his arms around me, face descending with palpable intent. There's a bright moment in time as we look at each other, and we *know*, like we've shared the thought with telepathy, what tonight means. Then there's a brush of lips to initiate. And another. There's warm breath, me tilting his jaw in my caged hand to see how malleable he is. He bends to my will easily.

His tongue slips into my mouth and it's two things at once: quick pulse, hot blood turning in my ears. It's languorous, long fingers of molten gold in a slow spill across the floor, burning the room away. With every thumping beat of my heart I am being ruined. I never want anyone to hold me again if they don't hold me like this.

"What are you thinking?" he asks, our reflections watching each other.

My heart is too large to fit inside my chest. "Honestly?"

"If you're willing."

"I'm thinking that I've had dreams about getting our hands on each other and none of them live up to this."

He bites his cheek, eyes downcast. "You dream about me?"

"I can't help it."

"No, I . . ." He wets his lips, picking words carefully. "I love that you do."

"There's the literal dreaming," I venture. "And then, you know." How do I say this without saying it? Oh, well. Caution to the wind. "Fantasizing. Everybody fantasizes."

I'm starting to worry that I've overshared when he stares at me with a keen intensity and he says, "Can you tell me?"

"I could show you, if you'd like."

He takes one step backward, which seems counterproductive, but I think he's signaling that he is paying attention. "Tell me how it starts."

"It starts with us standing in the sunroom that was going to be a conservatory but is now a café. You've just done an amazingly romantic thing with some clouds and it's got me feeling all swoony."

"Oooh, I like this so far."

"You pick me up."

He obliges with zeal, scooping me to his chest like a knight rescuing his princess. I think about where we are, where we could go next.

"You carry me out of the room."

So he does.

"And we go . . ." My bedroom is too far. I'm in practical mode, hunting for the nearest soft landing pad. "Into the living room."

So we do.

He lets his forehead fall to mine. "And then?"

"You notice a plaid couch," I say, "that looks big enough for two people even if one of them is the size of Thor."

He laughs. "All right. I'm noticing it."

"And you say, '*My*, it's been such a long day. I think I have to lie down immediately in this room where there is only one couch to lie on.'"

Wesley tries to keep a straight face. "My, it's been such a long day. I think I have to lie down immediately in this room where there is only one couch to lie on."

I grin. "You lay me onto the couch first, delicately, and admire me for two full minutes. You've never seen such beauty."

He sets me down. A flash of lightning slants across his chest like a jagged blade and the emotion in his eyes steals my air. "I haven't," he murmurs.

"Two minutes is a long time," I amend. "You admire me for a few seconds, then turn in a slow circle."

Raising a brow, he complies.

"You tear your shirt up over your head." Wesley snorts, but my expression is stern. "And you do it ferociously, with animal magnetism."

He gamely peels his shirt off, tossing it aside.

My attention takes a leisurely stroll across all the bare skin he has on display. It's *decadent*. "You flex your arms."

He gives me a dry look.

"You have to," I insist. "That's how the fantasy goes."

He flexes, and I fall back snickering. Wesley sighs melodramatically.

I want to see how much I can get away with. "You say, 'Is it hot in here or is it just me?'"

He makes a face. Grumbles. "Is it hot in here? Orisitjustme."

"It's you," I assure him, enjoying myself. "Then you—"

"Start to get impatient," Wesley finishes darkly.

"No, you do not. You start doing a striptease."

His eyes flash. "*Or*, I walk over to you."

"*Or*, you shuck your pants and helicopter them over your head."

Wesley leans over me, fisted hands pressing into the couch. His voice drops low, scraping my skin. "I kiss you."

I loop my arms around his neck, only too happy to give in. "Yes. That's exactly what you do."

So he does. Softly, softly. Again and again.

I'm starting to feel warm, a bit delirious, and lean back slightly. "Just real quick."

"Yeah?" He withdraws.

"Not to be down on myself or anything, but this is your first time. And, uh, I don't know what you've been imagining, but . . ." I scramble for phrasing that won't kill the mood. "I'm not a Victoria's Secret model. You might have idealized what the woman in this experience would be like. I've done this, but not a lot. Also, I just ate, so I'm going to be a little bloated—"

"You're beautiful. I'm going to love whatever's under here," he says, sliding a hand up my torso. A bolt of heat zings through me.

"Okay, but—"

"Maybell." He stops me with two fingers pressed to my lips. "Don't be giving me disclaimers, you don't deserve that. I'm going. To love it."

I let go.

The kisses change tempo, get deeper, needier, and there are long fingers gliding up my wrist, palms, lacing through mine. He settles over me, asks, *Is it okay if I touch you*, and I say, *Yes*. I'm giving him tremendous power over me by wanting him the way that I do, so much that it sticks in my throat, making it difficult to breathe. He's giving tremendous power to me by trusting me enough to be intimate like this.

"What happens next?" I ask.

Wesley reaches behind me and bunches up a fistful of my dress, tugging it to mold tightly against my curves in the front. "I think you know what happens next." His mouth slants over mine, the pressure of his kiss desperate, before he draws away to drink me in, eyes tracking down my body.

"What if we . . . ?" He exhales raggedly, playing with the zipper up my back.

"Yes."

"And then we . . . ?"

"*Yes.*"

He fishes into the back pocket of his trousers and withdraws a foil square. "I bought these a couple days ago, just in case. I didn't want to assume anything. But I kind of hoped."

I press two fingers to his lips. "I'm glad you did."

Wesley smiles against my fingers, relieved.

He unzips me, then I have to do a bit of wiggling before the dress is a puddle of fabric on the floor. My temperature is so high that the air is an icy bite. I would have thought I'd feel terribly vulnerable on display like this, but his gaze traverses my body with such longing, with such naked, blazing lust, and I feel like the most gorgeous creature that ever walked the earth.

Wesley drags his fingers over his face, eyes large.

"*Fuck,*" he utters weakly.

It is a heady, gratifying thing, to watch this man unravel.

He explores with his hands, glancing at my expression every so often to make sure I haven't changed my mind, that I'm enjoying it. "I can't get over how soft you feel." He plants a kiss on my stomach, traveling up between my breasts, each touch reverent. He takes it in turns to be sweet, dirty, sweet, dirty, switching on me without warning. The sensations he's . . .

My mind empties of words.

His *tongue.* His *hands.* I'm. It's. *Oh.* I have to bite down.

When my hands explore him, too, he hisses through his teeth and pulls back somewhat, knee digging into the couch to hold his weight. His stomach muscles contract as my hand slides down them. "I know how this goes, but I've never done it before, so I might need some help."

I am on fire. Anticipation is to blame for why I nervously babble, "Teamwork makes the dream work."

Wesley's chin falls onto his chest, body shaking with silent laughter. "Oh my god."

"I'm sorry."

But it dispels some of the tension, relaxing me enough to smile.

I claim his mouth again and he surrenders the self-doubt and insecurities building up inside him, letting instincts take over. The rest of our clothes come off. I smooth a hand over his chest and push so that his back hits the couch, and his eyes widen. Taking charge takes the pressure off of him. I straddle his hard, muscular body and introduce him to the finer things in life.

"Jesus," he rasps again and again. "Jesus. God."

"I had no idea you were so devout."

A rumbling laugh swiftly ebbs into a groan, and he draws in a deep breath until his ribs protrude. His eyes pierce mine, brows pulling together ever so slightly. Before I can ask *what*, he moves.

A quick study, he rolls us and seamlessly assumes control. Pupils blown. Lips swollen. Pleased half smiles as he learns what I like; soft laughs and grated curses as we both learn what *he* likes.

He feels wonderful,

wonderful,

wonderful

and it isn't because of any particular move he's making, or because he's some kind of god in bed, but because it's him, and I think he just might feel the same way about me.

A dozen manifestations of Wesley have tried to imitate this. Wesleys on windy hilltops, soaked in rain, chests heaving, hair dripping. Wesleys leaving footprints in the sand on a warm beach. Princes and baristas.

He doesn't kiss like a dream, doesn't touch like a fantasy. He is Wesley, real. My imagination will spend the next thousand years chasing the memory of this: Wesley. Real. It will never get it right because he is beyond imagining. Nothing beats real.

HOURS LATER, WE'RE IN my bed. When we collapsed on my mattress we both announced that we were going to sleep like the dead tonight, but reality has made liars of us because we're not used to having company when we sleep and each of us keeps jolting awake whenever the other one moves. It's a lovely gift that keeps giving to see him next to me. I kind of like that I keep forgetting his presence every time I'm about to drift off to sleep and then abruptly startle; this means the truth of his being here sinks in over, and over, and over again.

Wesley reaches up to stroke my hair, smiling only with his eyes. I feel more than accepted when he touches me, when he holds me and smiles at me. I feel *wanted*.

I feel like I've finally found home.

Suspended in a state that isn't quite dreamland, not quite wakefulness, I scroll through my mental calendar. We've got so much coming up in the next few weeks: his brother will be visiting before we know it to discuss investing in us, I'll be meeting Sasha Campos in hopes that she's going to join me in my new adventure, and I could possibly have that young woman and her son from the gas station staying here soon. I've got to get the last of my legal ducks put in a row. The house painted up into everlasting sunset.

Wesley's got sections of wild overgrowth to clear in preparation for four-legged friends (and a few with wings). Once the hotel opens, Wesley will still leave from time to time for landscaping jobs. I, on the other hand, am going to be homebound for the foreseeable future.

Which means that if there are any last hurrahs in order, the time for them is now.

"Hey," I whisper, prodding him. "Are you awake?"

"I don't know."

My mouth twitches. "You don't know if you're awake?"

"I don't know anything right now," he replies hoarsely. "What's my name? Never heard of it. My brain's as smooth as a scoop of ice cream and I'm not mad about it." He folds his arms beneath his head, staring at the ceiling. "So I'm going to lie here and just be absolutely stupid for a while."

"I think we should make good on our pact," I tell him, effectively shattering his afterglow. "Quitting at the resort. Going to Loch Ness."

"We will."

I sit up, laying a palm to his chest where his heart pounds rhythmically. "I mean now," I elaborate gently. "I think we should go *now*."

"*Right* now?" He's still half-asleep.

"I found a buyer for Victor's coin collection. I was going to put the money toward a pool, but I think we should do this with it instead. Before it gets so hectic around here that we miss our chance. When I feel like I really need to do something, I don't want to put it off." I swallow. "From here on out."

Wesley pulls himself up onto his elbow, a fathomless silhouette save for the twin gleams of his eyes. He stares and stares at me, and then finally says, "All right. Let's do it."

Chapter 20

WHEN MORNING DAWNS, WE'VE got our plane tickets, set to take off at eleven forty-five a.m. We're bleary-eyed and groggy but there's a thrum of exhilaration in the air and we're already packed, in the car, on our way to Around the Mountain Resort & Spa. I'm going to quit a job I don't have anymore in legendary style, and then Wesley's going to find proof of the Loch Ness Monster but never tell a soul about it. We are a *pair*.

"Car music?" he suggests, fiddling with the dial.

"I'm too amped up for music." Which sounds absurd, but I think the extra stimulation would feed my anxiety and then I wouldn't be able to go through with my half of the pact.

We play I Spy instead, which consists of the same three colors (red stop signs, green trees, and yellow DRIVE CAREFULLY signs indicating twists and turns). There aren't too many cars on the road until we reach Pigeon Forge at a quarter to nine.

"Wild Bear Tavern," he observes, lifting an index finger off the steering wheel. "They have takeout. Really good German toast."

"I'm too amped up to eat."

I'm wearing a red power suit with shoulder pads, hair in a messy topknot. I look like a high school secretary from an eighties teen comedy, which is to say, I look extremely excellent and like a person who makes firm decisions.

Wesley pulls through the McDonald's drive-thru anyway, ordering us both pancakes from the breakfast menu. My stomach's sloshing something fierce, but he made the right call—I feel better once I've eaten.

"You ready for this?" he asks, nudging me to polish off my orange juice because he thinks I could use more Vitamin C.

I half-laugh. "Ahh . . . no." Then I shake my head, smiling wanly. "Kidding. Ready as I'll ever be! Let's go."

I still don't know what I'm going to say when I get inside Around the Mountain. I've decided to wing it.

"This is nuts," I can't stop saying.

Wesley doesn't argue.

"They've probably forgotten who I am." I'm sort of but not really joking. "I'll tell them off and then somebody will go, 'Who was that?'" I'm chewing my nails, leaning forward as far as the seat belt will allow. I crank the air conditioner to full blast. "Jeez, it's hot in here. Do you think it's hot in here?"

"It's just you," he jokes.

My knee bounces at warp speed. "This is nuts."

"Oh, definitely. But here we are."

I jerk around, panicking. The giant statue of the bear strumming a banjo rears up overhead. The lodge is directly behind us. We are in the parking lot. The *parking lot*.

Where Wesley puts the truck in park.

"What?" I cry. "How are we here already?"

"You've got this, Parrish." He tries to fist-bump me. I would laugh if I didn't think I'd throw up immediately afterward. "Do you need me to come in with you?"

"Nah, I'll be fine. Keep the engine running in case we need a quick getaway."

For his sake as much as my own, I plaster on a confident smile and slide out of the car with watery joints. I'm going to hate doing this, maybe more than I've hated doing anything I've ever not wanted to do, but I can't wait to be the version of myself who is on the other side of having done it. The Maybell who stands up for herself. Who cares if I'm about two months too late and this mission probably looks batty from the outside? It's never too late to make waves.

I am, right this very moment, becoming the kind of Maybell who walks calmly across the parking lot, and the kind of May-bell who pushes through the front doors. The kind of Maybell who stands in the lobby of the building where she spent her entire adult life.

Nothing has changed. The rocking chair that seats eight fully grown humans is currently occupied, camera light flashing, and the lobby smells strongly of chlorine that launches a dozen memories. I can hear splashing and yelling from the indoor water park. What was I expecting? Of course it looks the same. It hasn't been that long since I was here, even if it feels like a year has passed.

I square my shoulders. On behalf of the miserable Maybell who spent Christmas day handling stiff sheets from the honeymoon suites and having ten minutes shorted from her already pathetic lunch break, I am going to walk up to Paul.

I am going to say, *You were a bad boss. You spent all day on Russian dating websites instead of doing your job. You promoted me to event coordinator and then wouldn't let me coordinate events, and for that, you suck* profusely. *I want you to know that I quit because of you.*

After that, I imagine Christine will happen by, scowling like always. I'll tell her to go to hell and it will be *everything.* I'll astral-project into orbit, lighter than air. A feather on the breeze, whipped cream on a cupcake. A living sunbeam.

That's the high note I'll leave on. And I won't, no matter how tempting, glance back at their stricken faces. It's like heroes in an action movie ignoring explosions going off behind them.

And that will be that. A proper quitting story.

"I'm so happy to see you! Oh my god!" I blink rapidly as someone crushes me in a hug. "You're back!"

Gemma.

"You look *so* cute," she squeals. "Are those shoulder pads?" She pokes my shoulders. I'm so thrown by her presence, which has blown up my vision of how this would go, that I simply stand there and gawk. The only thing about Gemma that's changed is the new card attached to her lanyard that reads: EVENT COORDINATOR. "What have you been up to? Tell me everything."

I meet her wide, expressive eyes, holding my breath. And then I realize.

I'm not here to quit after all.

"I am here to tell you," I say, voice quavering. My hands curl, nails biting into the plump flesh of my palms; the sensation is an anchor, keeping my feet flat on the carpet so that I can't vacate my body. Then, with a steadiness I do not feel, I start over. "I am here to tell you that you hurt me. And that it wasn't okay."

Gemma's eyebrows jump up her forehead. "What? How did I hurt you?"

"You were supposed to be my friend. But you tricked me, playing with my feelings, and after the truth came out, my hurt feelings still came second to yours. I am a *person*, Gemma. You treat other people badly. So I think somebody ought to tell you."

Her smile slips, lips parting in surprise. I watch her vibrant inner light go out.

"I trusted you," I go on, trying not to cry. It can't be helped. I'm not sad about what she did anymore, but baring my emotions like this has me on the edge of myself, and I am so intensely exposed that the tears arrive without permission. "You lied. You embarrassed me. Used me. Took advantage of me. I don't know how it ever got from you confessing you'd tricked me to us just pretending it never happened and you acting like everything was okay. Everything hasn't been okay for me."

"I'm—" She's sputtering. "I've already apologized—"

If I let her interrupt, she'll take control of this conversation and I'll never get it back. Somehow, I'll end up comforting her. "You wanted me to forgive you because you didn't want to have to feel guilty anymore," I say in a rush. It drops like an anvil, and she snatches her hands back from where she's been wringing them in front of her, waiting to be held. Coddled. "Wanting to be forgiven isn't the same as being remorseful.

"I know you could be incredibly nice," I go on. "You bought me a birthday cake. We went to the movies together. We went shopping. And that was fun! But I think the reason you went out of your way to be extra, extra nice was so that you could then get away with occasional cruelty. I never called you on it. I should have confronted you, but I didn't, because even as the protagonist in my own life, my feelings came second to yours."

Her face is changing color, but the impossible has happened: Gemma Peterson is speechless.

"I let you think that your apologies were enough, even though they were empty, and I could tell you didn't appreciate the full extent of what you'd done, how awful you made me feel. I should have stood up for myself. The quick forgive-and-forget wasn't fair to me." My chest is unbearably tight. I do not feel lighter than air or that all has been made right with the world. Just the opposite: I'm tasting my breakfast all over again. The room spins.

But this has weighed heavily upon my heart, and I persevere. "So here I am," I finish quietly, "better late than never, to tell you that your forgiveness is not the point. You need to learn how to be a better friend. If you keep treating people like their emotions don't matter as much as yours, like they're just background roles in your life, you will end up all alone."

A pregnant pause follows, in which I expect Gemma to land on habits and gush apologies like she used to. Meaningless ones, because she wasn't sorry at all—she only wanted sympathy.

She does not apologize. Instead, she is angry.

"Well, I am sorry you feel that way—" she spits, complexion going red and blotchy.

I give her shoulder a mild squeeze. "You don't have to say anything. Just sit with it, okay?"

When I walk away, I look back once. She's already walking away, too, in the opposite direction. She is going to go find the nearest person and complain about me, and garner their sympathy. There will be crocodile tears. I'll be the villain in her story for a while, but then hopefully, as time passes, what I've said will sink in. Maybe not consciously. But maybe she'll start to do better by others. That is going to have to be enough for me.

Out in the parking lot, I find Wesley pinning my hotel brochures under somebody's windshield wipers. Little pink rectangles wave in the breeze on every car in the first two rows. He revolves to take me in, squinting against the sunlight. "Well?"

I sigh.

"Didn't talk to my old boss. Didn't give the middle finger to Christine." I hang my head, still nauseated. My skin is overheated yet clammy, my arms and legs weak. Not at all how I thought victory would feel. "So. Didn't exactly go down in spectacular flames like I set out to."

Wesley tips my chin up with one finger. One corner of his mouth lifts. "Of *course* you didn't."

"You didn't believe in me?" I return, half in jest.

"Just the opposite. My Maybell is not a vengeful person. Her head is in the clouds because she can see the beauty in the world from up there. Going down in flames doesn't suit."

I don't know how to respond to that, choosing to lean my cheek into his palm. At thirty years old, I am finally accepting that I am simply nobody else but myself. I will always only be me. A little bit naïve, a lot idealistic. In the regard of many, understated to the point of forgettable, and easy prey, because my heart is so large a target. But those who deserve to be in my circle will like me just as I am, and will treat me the way I deserve to be treated.

"On to the next," I announce, linking my arm in his. "It's your turn now."

At that, Wesley's tender expression falters. "I feel like your part of the deal was easier."

"Yeah, but yours is gonna be way more fun."

....

IT'S A FIFTY-MINUTE DRIVE to the airport in Knoxville, in which we dream about what we hope Scotland will be like. We hope the weather will be sunny and the Loch Ness Monsters in the mood to be glimpsed by humans. We hope we won't get stuck behind people who like to recline their seats on the plane. I am doing most of the hoping. Wesley is mostly nodding along to all my chattering and growing progressively more pale. When we park the truck and get our luggage out of the back, his face is alabaster.

"Hey." I rub up and down his arm. "Okay?"

My brain zings in a billion directions. *He's mad at you*, it suggests. *You did something wrong.* Did I? I scan for anything I talked about on the drive over that might've offended him.

A darker thought creeps in: maybe he's thinking about last night and regrets it.

I study his figure, which hunches over slightly, and feel my forehead crease with worry. He was in such a great mood last night, or at least I thought so. Now I'm second-guessing. It's possible that I was so preoccupied with how fantastic I felt that I projected my good mood onto him and didn't notice he didn't feel the same . . . except, that can't be right. He was happy. He expressly told me so.

After spending the night with someone, you don't see them exactly the same way come morning. Sleepovers are a level unlocked in intimacy. I've been thinking we're closer now, but what if he's reconsidering me? Us? Going on a trip with someone you're reconsidering being in a relationship with would certainly render a person pale and quiet.

I overcompensate for his quietness by being extra chatty. "Little disappointed that the connecting flight in Chicago only leaves us an hour of wiggle room. We could've gone sightseeing. What are some good sights in Chicago? I think they've got an important baseball field there, if you like baseball. Probably some museums. Deep-dish pizza. Maybe we'll find somewhere in the airport that serves deep-dish." We wend our way through clusters of people in the busy airport.

"This place is packed," he grates, pressing himself into the side of the escalator we're ascending as far as he can manage. A man bumps him with his bag anyway.

"Sorry," the man says.

Wesley grants him a wincing smile and then faces straight ahead like he's on his way to a guillotine.

"Do you want to get some snacks for the plane? I think there's a Cinnabon past the gates."

He responds with a curt shake of the head. A string of people pass us on the other side of the escalator and he guards me with his arm.

"What about reading material?"

He shakes his head again.

"Wesley." We step off the escalator, heading for security. "Are you sure you're all right?"

"I think the pancakes are giving me an upset stomach."

"Oh, no." I smooth a hand down his back. "I can go buy you some Rolaids."

"No, I'll be all right."

"You sure?"

He nods jerkily.

"But are you *totally* sure? You look a little green."

He pats me on the top of the head, a little messily. "Shhh. Don't worry yourself."

I am an *idiot*. I smack my forehead. "It's the people, not the pancakes. You're bothered by all the people!"

If Wesley slopes his shoulders any farther inward, he'll topple over. "Shhh!" he repeats, glancing erratically around. "The people will hear you." We're at the security checkpoint now, tugging off our shoes.

"I won't let anyone talk to you," I vow. "Not that anybody would. I think most people just want to go about their business."

A woman in line smiles at us. "Good morning. Or afternoon, I guess. Just about!" She checks her watch. "I'm on my way to Miami. What about you folks? You flying together?"

Wesley's face becomes a mask. I've forgotten *this* Wesley: the one who clams up around strangers, whose default setting in these situations is to glare. I see this behavior now for the defense mechanism that it is, wanting others to perceive him as rude so that they won't come any closer. He shows everybody else a lie, which is a real shame. They don't know what they're missing out on.

"We're flying to Scotland!" I exclaim.

"Oh, that's fun! What's the occasion?"

Wesley bristles. *Don't worry, I'm not giving away anything private of yours*, I think, willing him to hear it. "Just want to see if it's really as green as it looks in the pictures," I reply breezily. He relaxes somewhat, but not all the way.

The woman and I go back and forth a few times until it's her turn to deal with TSA.

"Okay, well, I'm sure the people in Chicago won't be as friendly as the people in Knoxville," I mutter in Wesley's ear.

He forgets to remove his belt when passing through the metal detector and fumbles nervously with the buckle while trying to get it off.

"You all right, buddy?" a TSA agent jokes. The comment is lighthearted, but I notice the shell of Wesley's ear turning pink and it makes my heart hurt.

"Soon enough, we'll be in Loch Ness and we can avoid everybody," I promise him once we're both in the clear. "Just you and me and the monsters."

We make our way to the plane, only one bag for carry-on. We've got his sketch pad inside, and for me, a ton of Mad Libs. I hate to keep asking if he's okay, since I think it just makes things worse, but I can't help saying, "You still want to do this?"

"I'm fine." He laces his hand in mine.

Once we're inside the plane, however, he freezes up. Right there in the middle of the aisle.

"What's wrong?" I peer around his shoulder from behind.

He doesn't respond, staring at the tiny seats. "There's not enough room."

Right. He's not a small person, and legroom is going to be a distant memory soon enough. "You can use up my space for legroom," I assure him. "I don't mind. Take my armrest, too."

We sit down. He closes his eyes, breathing deeply in and out.

I don't know what to do, how to make him feel better. All I can think is to hug his arm and rest my head on his shoulder. Other people are packing in, fitting their bags into the luggage compartment. Elbows and jackets brushing. Loud voices of parents instructing their kids. I dig in my bag for chewing gum.

"Atmospheric pressure," I say, offering Wesley a stick. I think he'll smile, like we did yesterday when he offered me gum for our pretend trip into the clouds. But he looks miserable.

"I'm going to throw up."

I stare, fighting panic. Wesley is miserable and I need to make him feel better but I don't know how. "I think they have bags for that." I rummage around for one, but he rises unsteadily to his feet.

"Bathroom."

"Okay."

I watch him go, then turn back around in my seat. I'll have to distract him during takeoff. Tic-tac-toe, maybe. I page through his sketchbook for a blank sheet and stumble upon a cartoon of two people in an old-fashioned elevator. The man is standing over the woman, body curving almost protectively, but he is smaller than I know him to be in real life. His profile is angled, hiding most of his front. The focal point is clearly the woman, gazing up at him, the only one privy to his beautiful face. He's drawn a thought bubble over his head connected by three white puffs, and inside it, an explosion of hearts.

I'm so absorbed in the illustrated Wesley and Maybell that I don't immediately tune in to the *This is your captain speaking*. I don't start really paying attention until it becomes clear that we're about to take off. Right now.

I've buckled myself in but unbuckle to get up. The flight attendant points at the lit SEAT BELTS ON sign, and I say, "I've got to go get my—" I've never thought about him in these terms before, but: "Boyfriend. He's in the bathroom."

The flight attendant frowns and bustles past. Opens the door. "He's not in here."

"Then where—?" I break into a cold sweat, but she's hailed by someone who needs help, so I'm on my own. "Wesley?"

The plane isn't that big. If he were here, he'd be able to hear me. If he heard me, he would respond. Which means Wesley is not here.

I need to get up. I need to find him.

But lucidity has fled, my legs have locked up, and I'm lost. How can I go find my Wesley when my legs won't work and I can't think straight? Where did I go wrong? I have to fix this. I have to move.

Except I can't, because the plane already is.

Chapter 21

LAND IN CHICAGO AT 1:36 p.m. Alone.

I don't have the faintest memory of what I did on the plane. I don't think I opened my bag to utilize any of the prepared activities. If I stared out the window the whole time, I don't remember it. The next thing I know I'm in a vast, busy terminal standing outside of a duty-free store. Which is not where I need to be.

I go through the motions of finding my gate, sidetracked by every man of tall proportion. I know that Wesley isn't here, but I can't help trying to find him, anyway.

I wonder, as I'm boarding another plane without him, if he's still in the airport in Knoxville or if he's at home right now. I hope his stomach has calmed down, and that he feels better. I don't stop to ask myself why I'm still here until I'm already in my next seat. I should have booked a flight home. What's the point of going to Scotland now? This is Wesley's dream, not mine. I'm just supposed to be along for the ride.

When I turn my phone back on, a new text message pops up and relief surges over me until I see that the message isn't from Wesley. It's from my mother.

Thinking about you! Come visit soon.

I stare blankly at the screen. This is ordinarily the part where I respond with *Thinking about you, too! Yes, we need to make some plans.*

And then we never make plans.

I've spent a long time feeling like I torpedoed my mom's dreams, her future, by existing. But if I've learned anything from living with Violet Hannobar's ghost, it is that life is short, and the single most important thing I will ever do on this earth is showing the people I love that I love them.

You're invited to come to my house this summer. Second week of August. Please know that you always have a safe place to stay if you need one.

After sending the text, I pull a brown paper envelope out of my bag and lay it across my lap. My intention was to open it together with Wesley, but he's not here and I desperately need to busy myself with something, anything, to avoid dwelling on what he may be thinking about right now.

The fifth treasure.

I slit the envelope open, a sheet of familiar lilac stationery tipping out.

To my Mighty & Majestic Violet, Most Wonderful Wife,
Everlasting Star, 1989 Blount County Fair Blue Ribbon
Winner of Best Rhubarb Pie,

And so you've reached the end of another treasure hunt! I don't
know how long it's taken you to get here, or how many hunts
you've completed so far. There are nine other maps hidden within
the house and grounds. I hope you draw them out for years, and
that each treasure makes you smile and remember me.

I love you so very much. You are indomitable. An inspiration.
I'll be watching and cheering you on from beyond.

Yours,
V

I lay the paper back down. I fold it in half, tears welling in my
eyes, but then I see—

There's more. Different handwriting scrawls across the back of
the paper.

I love you and I miss you so much, you cannot imagine. I'll wait
to go on my next adventure until you and I can be together again.

Violet knew where the treasure was.
She'd found them after all.

I HAVE A LOT of time to think while I cross the Atlantic. I fall
asleep, dreaming of treasure and mythical creatures, a helping
hand reaching out to me in a dark, moonlit wood. A hand-painted

sign with my name on it and a tinfoil star. Anxious brown eyes. Blue ones in colored pencil.

When I gather our bags at Heathrow in London, it is half past four in the morning. But in Tennessee, it's ten thirty at night. My flight to Inverness isn't for another three hours. I am so exhausted that I should find a chair and pass out.

He has not texted, has not called. But he answers on the first ring.

He waits for me to speak first. And what I say, after dwelling for so long on what I would say, is: "Are you all right? And before you answer, just know that you don't have to say yes."

Wesley doesn't sound like he's a whole ocean away. He sounds like he's right next to me. "No. I am not. I am so sorry. I am so, *so* goddamn sorry."

I curl inward toward a wall, hair falling across my face to shield him from inside the phone. "I wish you had told me you wanted to get off the plane."

"I don't even remember getting off it. I panicked. I went into the bathroom because I thought I was going to throw up, but it was so small in there, and . . . I'm very, very claustrophobic. I thought I'd be able to power through it, but then *bam*, there I am in the airport again, and there goes your plane, taking off into the sky."

"But you . . . you lived in the loft. In that tiny space. It's practically a coffin up there. And you slept in the tent."

"It was different in those situations because I could have run, if I'd wanted. I could have gotten out anytime. But in an airplane, I'm a captive. There's nowhere to run." He hesitates. "That, and the alternative was unacceptable. If I didn't sleep in the loft and pretend it was a second bedroom, you wouldn't have taken the other bedroom. If I hadn't slept in the tent with you when I had an opportunity to, I wouldn't have been able to live with myself."

I sink down against the cold wall to the floor, folding my knees to my chin. "Why didn't you tell me?"

I can hear his fear, his self-loathing. "Because it was one more thing wrong with me, on top of everything else. I wanted to be fine. I wanted you to believe I was fine. If I told you everything that was wrong with me, Maybell, you wouldn't want to be with me anymore."

"I accept that challenge. Right now. Lay it out."

His speech stumbles. "What?"

"Tell me everything that's wrong with you. Give me your worst."

He does.

"My brother got married in Rome. The flight was so bad that I seriously considered never coming back to the States—I went as far as looking into how to stay there on a work visa. I hate restaurants, because when I sit at tables I feel trapped. Something about sitting down across from someone and it being socially unacceptable to leave at any moment makes me panic. It's one of the reasons why I can't date. Dates like to go to restaurants. Forcing myself to ask someone out when I have social anxiety is hard enough, but adding to that, how am I supposed to explain to a woman that I get anxious at public tables? I don't even like sitting at a table for holiday meals with my family. I stand up along the wall with my plate.

"I've sat at a table with you before, so you might not have noticed this. But with *you*, I know I can get up and leave at any time without having to explain. Knowing that makes all the difference.

It's the same panic whenever I've had to go to the doctor or the dentist, or when I bought my truck and had to sit in a tiny room on the other side of a desk from the car salesman. I start thinking about how I wouldn't be able to just get up and leave if I wanted, for whatever reason, without grabbing people's attention. Without being asked questions, and having to explain something I myself don't entirely understand, and . . . I don't know. It's hard to explain. Whenever I meet with clients, I always have them take a walk with me outside while we go over plans, rather than using an office. I don't know if this is ever going to change. It's just the way I am. I think that you are going to give up on me. That you are going to want someone easier.

"Until I've gotten comfortable around someone," he continues, "I get nervous about communicating with them because they don't know me yet, and they don't know the issues I have. I'm putting all my energy into trying to present myself as normal, which I get into my head about. Whether it's real or not, I can't stop imagining that they're judging me. Which makes it worse. My mind goes blank, and I just . . . I can't find the words. I freeze up. It's mortifying when the words won't come. It's so much easier to pretend I have a personality where I don't *have* any words for anyone, that I don't *care* to, rather than not being able to find them."

I think about this intensely claustrophobic man up in that hot, airless attic closet, night after night, while I sprawled out in his big comfortable bed below. He did it for me, before he even liked me.

I think about how I crash-landed in his insular life—how difficult that must have been for him. But even on his gruffest day, he couldn't help but slip up and be caring. The real Wesley was always shining through, rosy shafts of light, like a treasure chest with its lid ajar.

"Listen very closely: I've listened to everything you just said and I love you. Do you hear me? I've heard all of it, and it's the easiest thing in the world to love you. You don't have to hide anything from me, because I love all of it, every little bit. You have to let me love it all, okay? I love you. Say it."

I think—although I cannot be sure—that he might be crying.

"I love you."

The airport blurs into another realm, lights, sounds, and people fading out. My heart is back in Falling Stars. "No, you goofball. Say *that you are loved.*"

"You love me."

"Yes. I knew who you were when I fell in love with you, Wesley Koehler. I fell in love with you just the way you are. Now say it again."

"You love me."

"You bet I do. What parts of you do I love? Which ones?"

"You love all of them."

"Good. Write it down so that you don't forget. Carry it in your pocket. I loved you yesterday, I love you now, and I'll love you in the morning. When I come home in five days, I'll love you then, too, and I'll tell you so to your face."

"I . . ." His voice is raspy. "I cannot *wait* for that. Maybell, I love you so much, you have no idea. Every part of you. Everything."

"I know you do."

"Write it down," he tells me.

We are both emotionally collapsed, so we hang up with the promise to talk again in a few hours after I land in Inverness, and then do another check-in after I make it safely to Beinn Dhearg, a B & B in Loch Ness.

Disconnected from his voice, I slowly inch back into my environment and reckon with the reality that not so long ago, we were on our first date. Now I am in the UK alone.

But.

And this is a *but* that Means Everything:

Somebody out there cares. Somebody out there loves me, every part of me. Everything.

sleighbellparrish@gmail.com
YOU RECEIVED AN ECARD!

Wesley (koehlerwlandscaping@gmail.com) has sent you an ecard from American Greetings:

You are a whaley special person!

VIEW ECARD

---

sleighbellparrish@gmail.com
American Greetings: Here's a copy of your ecard

Recipient: Wesley

Bzz bzz! You're the bees' knees!

VIEW ECARD

———

Maybell: Good morning! Still a little jet-lagged but first night at the b&b was pretty good. It is BEAUTIFUL here

Wesley: Well that's because you're there

Maybell: Awww 😍 Heading to the Dores Inn for a late lunch, then off to do some exploring. Will send you lots of pics! Prepare for your phone to be buzzing all day

Wesley: It feels weird to be here alone

Maybell: You're never alone. I'm right there in your pocket.

Wesley: 😌

———

Wesley: Very early here but I can't sleep because I know you're touring the highlands and isle of skye today. I looked up the weather and it's supposed to be cold so please bring a jacket and plenty of water

Maybell: I'm going to need to buy another
suitcase for the souvenirs I'm getting you.
Don't get your hopes up though because
it's mostly rocks and dirt

Wesley: My favorite

Maybell: Literally just glass jars with
pebbles from Dores Beach, some
interesting moss I found, and the
tiniest wild yellow primrose with its
roots intact

Maybell: I'm also taking notes. Copious
notes. With terrible illustrations of local
plants. I am a botanist now, basically

Wesley: No more, please, I can't handle
it. I am already a wreck of a person.
What have you done

Maybell: Sorry

Wesley: No, you're not

Maybell: Not at all, no

Wesley: Me neither. There's still a little bit
of me left if you want to destroy that too

Maybell: For your birthday I've
decided to get you a sheep

Wesley: That's it

Wesley: There's nothing left

Maybell: 😒

You ever think you were single for no reason and then you meet someone and realize you've been waiting for them without knowing it? I know I'm not the first to have this thought or to write it out. I'm sorry these words probably aren't my own, because I want to give you original genius, but they're the words that I feel and I wanted to share them with you.

Another evening in Loch Ness, and Wesley's latest text is a heartbeat in my hand. I look down at his message, trying and failing yet again to come up with the deep, nuanced response it deserves. He thinks he's alone in not being able to find the right words when he needs them, but he isn't. Not even a little bit.

He makes me lose mine all the time, and all he has to do to accomplish that is be himself. His serious, darling, perfect self, whom I would not change a single thing about.

I am on a rocky shore overlooking a loch in the Scottish Highlands, yet another impossible-sounding statement I've made within the past couple of months. Life is starting to look less like going with the flow and more like steering the boat. Who knows where I might be a year from now? The possibilities are infinite.

I snap pictures: a boulder, clouds reflecting off the water, a tree. It's been a long day of Loch Ness Monster searching, so I'm running low on new finds to capture on film and resort to artistic shots of my sneakers. Shadow puppets. An apple core that remains from my lunch.

I raise my camera phone to frame the dramatic panorama of mountain summits and valleys, swathed in mist. It's a gray, gloomy day, with robust winds and a chill that leaches through my clothes, but perhaps this is the type of weather that will entice Nessie to pop her head above water. You never know.

"I won't even take a picture of you," I tell the water seriously. "I promise I'll keep the secret. All I'm asking for is a look. One quick little glimpse."

In my mind's eye, the ballroom mural paints itself into the scene: the *Felled Star* pirate ship breaks through the water's surface, crumpling in the iron grip of the kraken; the little trees with their soft brushstrokes appear one by one. Out of nothing arises the *My May Belle*.

The historic paddlewheel riverboat lazes by, my mother leaning on the balcony, calling hello with a white handkerchief. The water is deep green, sky a hot summer haze. Someone dressed in a red-striped suit from the Mark Twain days strums a banjo. A calliope plays. And a monstrous head rises out of the water, scales gleaming in waning daylight.

I take a picture of it all, the painted people, ships, and monsters, but my phone's not advanced enough to pull them properly out of the nonphysical plane and they come out looking like water, like rocks and trees and sky.

My phone vibrates, the word that matters most to me lighting up my screen.

I'm already smiling when I answer. "Hey, you."

"Hello there."

His friendly rumble warms me all over, sparking instant happiness. It's the closest thing we get to real magic in this universe.

"Tell me all about your day," he says, instantly making me feel at ease, at home. He might as well be next to me in the flesh. "I want to know everything."

"A red squirrel took a chip right out of my hand. I honestly don't think I'll ever be the same—he ate the chip *right out* of it. *Right* out of my hand. It's the highlight of my life."

"I'm incredibly jealous. What are you doing now?"

"Walking. I'm at Dores Beach, not far from the inn."

A smile lifts his voice. "Take me there?"

I canvass the trees, the emerald mountains smeared with drizzling rain. The shoreline, cut up into jutting angles. "You are walking along a stripe of pale rocks that the tide can't reach. The water is a pretty navy blue, little waves crashing onto shore with white froth. We're holding hands. It's all quite peaceful."

"I'm happy to be here with you," he says.

"Watch your step. Driftwood."

"Ahh, good catch. But please do zip up your jacket. It's getting chilly."

"Do you feel that mist on your face? The sky's darkening. We'll have to leave soon, but not yet. Not until the water is full of moonlight, because what if Nessie's nocturnal?"

"Exactly." He pauses. "If I'm quiet from time to time, it's because I'm smiling too big to talk."

I press one hand to my chest, holding very, very still, because if I don't I'm going to go flying away into the clouds. The phone is my only grounding weight, his voice my tether to earth.

"Come on, now, you're falling behind," he tells me, and I pick up the pace again.

"I'm coming, I'm coming."

"Please do remember what I said about zipping up that jacket. Don't want to catch a cold out here—especially since your hair's damp."

I zip my jacket and remove my glasses to wipe off the gathering mist. "You hear that bird? Caw-caw!"

He laughs. Then halts. "Don't *tell* me your shoes are untied again."

"They're not."

"They certainly are." He sighs. "What am I going to do with you?"

I look down, playing along, and what do you know—they certainly are. So I begin to lower and lace them up, but he interrupts.

"Let me."

I slide my glasses back onto my face, and that's when another memory steps out of my head and into my surroundings. It's a remarkably lifelike memory, sparing none of the details: an old jacket with plaid lining; golden hair ruffling in the wind, one eye squinting against an oncoming downpour.

Rain is the perfect weather condition for a love story, so naturally, it must be raining at the conclusion of it. There could be no other way.

The man treading closer, all of his features sharpening into focus, is so clear, so present, so real. He stops a few feet away, hands in pockets, forehead furrowed in thought. My breath circulates in my lungs like a sealed potion, unable to escape. Painful.

When he finally speaks, his tone isn't quite sad but contemplative. "I'm so sorry I'm late."

The world glows bright and wonderful. Not a dream. Not a trick. He's here.

"You're right on time."

He kneels before me, lacing my shoe. Everything falls quiet, quiet, quiet. The rain is soundless, the volume of the breaking waves dialing all the way down until it clicks off. Color fades away, and there is nothing, nobody in the world, but us.

Wesley removes something from his pocket, then hands it to me. A note.

Maybell Parrish loves me.

"I read that note ten thousand times on the flight over," he confesses, standing up. The paper is already worn out, ink smeared sideways with a thumbprint. I am going to fill his pockets with more reminders. I'll put them in his boots and his wallet, all over the house, the grounds. I'm going to bury treasure.

"I'm so proud of you," I whisper, reaching up to capture either side of his face in my hands.

Wesley lines up the edge of his flattened hand against my forehead, shielding my eyes from rain. "I'm a little proud of me, too, to be honest."

"Good. Bask in it. You deserve to."

"I didn't know if I would be able to do it alone. I didn't think I would. And I had a *middle* seat on the plane." He shudders, then begins to smile in an automatic mirroring of mine. "I buckled myself in, held on to this note like a lifeline, and soon enough I was up in the air and everything was out of my control. No chance to escape."

"You are the bravest person I know, Wesley," I tell him solemnly.

"This is what you and I do. We take turns being brave." The glint in his eyes dulls somewhat. "I can say no to a lot of things, but not to special experiences with you. I've decided that's the line I'm drawing for myself."

"When we go home, you won't have to talk to anyone but me for six months straight if you don't want to," I tell him. "When guests start arriving, I'll tell them you're a ghost of a logger who died in the nineteenth century and that's why you don't ever seem to see or hear them when they speak to you. You've been grounds-keeping at Falling Stars since it was first built."

"We'll tell them another powerful ghost named Violet put a spell over the house that matchmakes all of the single guests with each other." His grin turns wry. "Asking *you* to paint a mural, when I'm the one who paints. Asking me to make donuts when, between the two of us, you're the one with the baking skills."

"I think I'm beginning to see her last scheme. What *interesting* dying wishes for a person to leave behind."

He shakes his head, trying to be long-suffering, but without the heart to be. "She told me more times than I can count that I needed a girlfriend."

"Not to pile on, but you really do."

He devours me with a deeply meaningful look that gives rise to goose bumps. Anticipation. "The second wish, though." His tone is light. Considering. But his gaze is anything but. "Do you suppose it's legally binding?"

The second wish . . . "Which one was that?"

"For the intrepid explorer . . ."

Ahh, of course. *"Finders Keepers rules apply."*

"Well, I *did* find you," I point out. "A coincidence for the history books."

"I believe in a lot of unbelievable things. Coincidences might not be one of them anymore, though."

I'd have to agree. It doesn't feel like a coincidence that Gemma used Wesley's picture to catfish me. It doesn't feel like a coincidence led Violet to bring Wesley and me together at Falling Stars.

It feels like fate. The best myth of them all.

"So." He bends down to kiss my nose. I scrunch it, and he smiles like *he's* the winner here. "Finders keepers." Then he dips his head as though to kiss my mouth but only hovers there. "How does that sound?"

"Like heaven," I murmur against his lips. A happy, low little sigh stirs from his chest, and it's a fire ignited, a permanent mark made on the universe. I am seen. I am heard. Understood. Somebody knows that *I am here*, and it matters to them. If I were to look up at the sky right now, I think I'd see our names in the stars, a new constellation twinkling into being just for us. M + W.

The passionate kiss that follows the declaration of love is the essential ingredient to every romance to ensure it bakes properly, so naturally that is the part that comes next. His mouth meets mine at long, longest last—my heart brightens, glowing in the dark—and somewhere, way out on the black water, there is an extraordinary splash.

5 RISING STARS FOR THE MIGHTY & MAJESTIC FALLING STARS HOTEL!
By Clark William
THE DAILY TIMES

A BLOUNT COUNTY PROPERTY with nineteenth-century boardinghouse roots followed by an early-1900s turn as a hotel has been brought back to life by Maybell Parrish, the great-niece of Victor and Violet Hannobar, as well as Wesley Koehler, the resident groundskeeper and founder of animal sanctuary The Farm Upstate.

The latest incarnation of this historical landmark is a mash-up of its origins: a hotel as well as a boardinghouse. Parrish has grand plans for it (which are too numerous for this author to include in one article), such as an upcoming writer's retreat, an artist's workshop weekend, a biannual treasure hunt, a paranormal investigator weekend—the house, rumored to be haunted, is close to 140 years old—and a corn maze with crop circles.

If you're in the market for a respite from the stresses of life, leave them all at the door and step into this fanciful Appalachian Brigadoon. Meals and laundry services are provided, but if you still aren't convinced, there are twenty-seven farm animals (and counting) on the grounds to feed and play with. Enjoy Turner Classic Movies nights in the ballroom and tea parties on Sunday afternoons, and make pen pals out of past guests as well as guests to come. Finish that manuscript you've been meaning to write for years now while enjoying a donut in Maybell's Coffee Shop on the first floor. Don't forget to pick up your own Fraser fir sapling if you want to take a little piece of the Smokies home with you.

Extended board is low-income friendly, forgoing a big up-front deposit. Parrish and Koehler have transformed the property not only into a vacation destination in the scenic Smoky Mountains, perfect for getting away from it all, but also into a temporary home for two families in dire straits after recently losing their houses to wildfires.

Rich with history and all the comforts of the modern age, the Mighty & Majestic Falling Stars Hotel is a world of its own, where life is a little more whimsical (no guest has yet succeeded in finding all six secret doors) and the air just a little easier to breathe. So what are you waiting for? Your best memories are still on the horizon—all they need is you. Come to the Top of the World to discover the magic for yourself.

Acknowledgments

Once upon a time, a young lady who'd dumped her boyfriend was tricked into reconnecting with him thanks to their scheming mothers, who claimed the young man was horribly ill with pneumonia and that writing him a letter would cheer him up. Carol wrote Bill a letter, then received one back from him the next day, before he could have feasibly received hers. She discovered he was perfectly fine, but fate had already been set in motion—sixty-one years later, here I am. Grandma, thank you for telling me that story, which I then mashed up for my own use (Victor and Violet appreciate it), and for putting your hands on my shoulders when I was an emotional fourteen-year-old, saying, "I understand you." You are a pink-haired legend.

Thank you, Jennifer Grimaldi, for being a fantastic agent and brainstorming partner. I don't remember which phone call it was, but you mentioned coffee shop AUs somewhere along the line and I *knew* I had to use it.

Thank you, Margo Lipschultz, my editor, who found promise

in this story buried under a whole lot of junk I didn't need, and for changing my life when you acquired my first book. Thank you also to Tricja Okuniewska for all of your hard work; to my UK editor, Anna Boatman at Piatkus, for wanting another story of mine; and to a whole slew of extraordinarily talented individuals at Putnam who've had a hand in bringing this book to the world: Sally Kim, Ashley McClay, Alexis Welby, Nishtha Patel, Tom Dussel, Alison Cnockaert, Maija Baldauf, Marie Finamore, Elora Weil, Nicole Biton, Ivan Held, Hannah Dragone, Tiffany Estreicher, Christopher Lin, and Anthony Ramondo.

THANK YOU to all you beautiful humans who gave my debut novel, *You Deserve Each Other*, an outpouring of love I will be eternally awed by and grateful for. Romance readers, book bloggers, booktubers, bookstagrammers, librarians, booksellers, book clubs, you make books what they are and this industry would collapse without you: Kini, Kez, Samantha Carle, Samantha Tan, Addie Yoder, Sil, Brie, The Book Hoes (Shruti, Grace, and Sara), Laura, thehireader, Tej, Nick, Yvette, Wendy, Ella, Rumsha, Danielle, Dana, JeevesReads, Nitya, Bonnie, Nikita, Mith, both Madisons (SailorMadison and Princess of Paperback), jennscletus, Hailey, Deanna, Susan Lee, Christina Pishiris, Christina Lauren, Martha Waters, Mary E. Roach, Kili, Allison Reilly, Liz, Melinda, Mary, Lily, Jana, Pri, Beth, Flora, Purabi, Rachel Lynn Solomon, Hazel, Mazey, Bae Crate, Anjeli, Elyssa, Dahlia Adler, Fatema, Yotesgurl, India Holton, Ananya, Ahana, Mar, Amira, Vee, Silvia, Meghan De Maria, Azrah, Dija, Kaitlyn, Colleen, Mandie, Miranda, Falon, Konstantina, and Jessica. It's impossible to list every single one of you, but from the bottom of my overfilled heart, *thank you*. The amazing support you've given me has made not only my year (a year that, henceforth, shall never be spoken of again) but my entire LIFE. Hugs for all of you.

To my husband and children, thank you for your unconditional love, for making my life so joyful, and for being the coolest, funniest people ever. I'm so lucky that I get to hang out with you guys every day. Thank you to my brother and sister-in-law, Mark and Sam, for reading my book and being so nice about it. And even though they're never going to see this, I would like to thank my favorite band, Glass Animals, for existing.

To my fellow anxious people: you are wonderful and you are lovable just the way you are.

Writing the first draft of *Twice Shy* in 2019 was a TRIAL (the second-book curse is real!!!). When it came time to do a rewrite in the fall of 2020, it became a fluffy escape for me, an idyllic little world with warm characters that was a comfort to visit, and which I fell so in love with. My wish for this book is that if *you're* ever in need of a fluffy escape, Falling Stars can be a safe harbor for you as well.

Thank you for visiting; come back again soon!

Discussion Questions

1) Prior to reading the book, what were your perceptions about both anxiety and shyness? Did any of that change after you got to know Wesley and Maybell?

2) The incident with Jack at the beginning of the book pushes Maybell to seek a fresh start at Aunt Violet's estate. What does she want to change about her life, and how does she go about doing it? What are her obstacles?

3) What was unconventional about the way Maybell and Wesley began and developed their relationship? How did they manage to communicate and get to know each other?

4) How do Maybell and Wesley's contrasting desires for the manor put them at odds with each other? Discuss how they manage to compromise by the end of the book.

5) How do Wesley's art and Maybell's rich fantasy life allow them to express themselves? Did you understand their characters better after having glimpsed their creative sides?

6) Over the course of the novel, how does completing Aunt Violet's wishes bring Maybell and Wesley together?

7) What do you think is in store for Wesley, Maybell, and the estate?

Loved *Twice Shy*?

Don't miss Sarah Hogle's hilarious debut romcom . . .

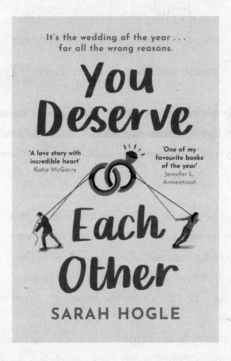

'This book is the perfect dose of sweet, hilarious joy'

Christina Lauren

Available now from

'*You Deserve Each Other* is one of my favorite books of the year'
Jennifer L. Armentrout

Meet Naomi and Nicholas: the Perfect Couple.

Their glorious, lavish wedding is coming up in three short months ... and they are utterly, miserably sick of each other.

Unfortunately, whoever backs out first will end up bearing the brunt of the wedding bill. When Naomi finds out that Nicholas has been feigning contentment too, the two of them go head-to-head in a battle of sabotage, pranks, and all-out emotional warfare to see who can annoy the other into surrendering first.

Now that they have nothing to lose, they're finally being themselves. In fact, they're having so much fun getting on each other's nerves that it starts to feel like something else entirely ...

Perfect for fans of Helen Hoang's *The Love Quotient* and Sally Thorne's *The Hating Game*, *You Deserve Each Other* is laugh-out-loud funny, painfully relatable, and bitingly smart.

Do you love contemporary romance?

Want the chance to hear news about your favourite authors (and the chance to win free books)?

Kristen Ashley
Meg Cabot
Olivia Dade
Rosie Danan
J. Daniels
Farah Heron
Talia Hibbert
Sarah Hogle
Helena Hunting
Abby Jimenez
Elle Kennedy
Christina Lauren
Alisha Rai
Sally Thorne
Denise Williams
Meryl Wilsner
Samantha Young

Then visit the Piatkus website
www.yourswithlove.co.uk

And follow us on Facebook and Instagram
www.facebook.com/yourswithlovex | @yourswithlovex

PIATKUS